Night Over Day Over Night

Night Over Day Over Night

PAUL WATKINS

ALFRED A. KNOPF

NEW YORK

1988

THIS IS A BORZOI BOOK

PUBLISHED BY ALFRED A. KNOPF, INC.

Copyright © 1988 by Paul Watkins

Library of Congress Cataloging-in-Publication Data

Watkins, Paul
  Night over day over night.

  1. World War, 1939–1945—Fiction. I. Title.
PS3573.A844N54 1988   813'.54   87-46102
ISBN 0-394-57047-2

Manufactured in the United States of America
First Edition

"The Old Guard is dead,"
he said to himself.
"We are the last."
ARTHUR KOESTLER,
Darkness at Noon

Night Over Day Over Night

I

"YOU BROKE my heart and now I'm pissed."

"Is that all you came to say?" She stood in the doorway in a nightdress, hugging herself. Her hair was a mess.

"I hate you."

"No, you don't. Look, either go away or come in from the cold, will you?" She turned around and walked off into the kitchen, scratching and yawning.

I SAT at the kitchen table and smoked a cigarette. She took it from my hand, inhaled, gave it back. She toasted some bread in the oven, her knees cracking as she bent down, then skidded a piece to me across the table.

We sat at the opposite ends, chewing the dry bread and looking at each other. When she swallowed, the bread went down
her throat like a piece of slate.

"You are far too young for this. Pretty soon the whole town
is going to find out. And I *do* have a husband. Go find yourself
a sweet little milkmaid down the road."

"I will. That's just what I'll do. I'll do that right now." I stood
up and started to walk out. I got to the kitchen door and a piece
of toast hit me in the back of the head. Then more things started
bouncing off the door and walls. A cream puff splatted on a cal-
endar. I poked my head back into the kitchen and she threw a
bottle of perfume, which missed and smashed somewhere in
the hall.

"Get out. Go and find her then. Just look for someone with
a cow-eyed idiot face and you've found her. And you just see if
she doesn't have some kind of accident. She'll get run over by
a truck. You can't leave me and you know it. You belong to me
now. Besides, she'll smell us. She'll know. Don't worry. Girls
can tell a thing like that. She'll know about you and me the
minute she gets a look in your eyes."

She ran over to the mess of the perfume on the floor and
splashed her hand in it. Then she ran at me and spread it on
my coat. She grabbed me by the neck and wiped the smell of
the perfume through my hair and across my face.

"She'll smell us. She'll smell us and she'll know. You belong
to me." Then she was crying and we were back on the doorstep.
Rain fell through the mist on the fields. "Come back inside.
Come and lie in bed with me. Just for a little while."

I turned around and started walking for the gate at the end
of her garden. She jumped, grabbing me by the throat, and we
both fell into the vegetable patch, which was full of mud and
cabbages.

"I'm not letting you go."

I lay on the ground with the bumps of cabbages underneath
me, and for a second while she caught her breath I looked up

at the egg-white sky and saw the blur of rain coming down.

"I thought you said we were finished."

"I was drunk." She blinked down at me.

"You were not. You were dead sober."

"I was stinking drunk and we're not finished." She grabbed a handful of cabbage leaves and jammed them down my shirt. Then she took some mud and slapped it on my head. "We're not finished."

BUT WE were finished. I left, and she threw cabbages at me until I was out of range.

Benjamin was waiting at the edge of the woods, and I saw the burning end of his cigarette long before the rest of him as I walked through the wet grass, feeling the mud freeze in my hair. When I got close, he wheeled himself in his wheelchair out to the center of the path. He asked if he could come, so I let him. But only as far as the woods.

"What the hell did you do? Kill her and bury her in the back-yard?"

"No. Give me a cigarette."

"So what happened?" He was looking straight ahead as he talked. I pushed the wheelchair over ruts in the hard earth pathway between the pine trees.

"She told me to go away, but when I went she started throwing things at me and told me to stay."

"Is that all? I don't believe that's everything."

"I told her she broke my heart."

"Aha." He put his head back so it was pressing into my stomach, looking up at me from the chair.

"Aha what?"

We stopped on a wooden bridge that ran over a stream, and I parked Benjamin on the hump in the middle. Then I leaned over the stream and spat. Benjamin wheeled up close and handed over a flask of cherry brandy.

"Don't go back. You would only make a fool of yourself if you did."

We stayed on the bridge until it was almost dark, throwing stones into the slow-running stream.

I ALMOST never saw her after that except about a month later when I was coming home from school with some friends near the market. She was rummaging through a crate with tomatoes in it. She had one in her hand and was testing to see if it was ripe. I stopped to look, and my friends stopped, followed my stare to the woman, and for a second we were still, in the constant moving of the crooked-backed people in the market.

She looked up, and when she saw who it was, the tomato seemed suddenly to explode in her hand. She crushed it to juice in her fist, and my friends started laughing. I left before the expression on her face could change.

And I did what she'd told me to before she knocked me into the cabbage patch. I found a girl called Eva Weiden whom she would have called a milkmaid and idiot-faced. We went to dances and wrote notes to each other. We went out to dinner a couple of times to cheap restaurants and we stood holding hands on the walkway by the Rhine. Smiling. We smiled all the time.

But some nights I went home through the woods and felt the blood-shoving motor in my chest turned into a piece of rock.

THE ROCK went away for a while, but when my father died the next year, the rock came back and stayed.

He was really too old to be enlisted, and he had a safe job at the munitions factory. They needed him enough at first not to let him go to the war. It was fine with him.

When Stalingrad fell, they put women to work in his place and the places of half the other people in the factory, including his best friend, Stein.

They both joined up in the Panzer Korps and were put in charge of an armored car.

He came home twice in the two months that his training lasted. He wore baggy black trousers and a wraparound tunic with piping and skulls on the collar. He scraped up the floor with his hobnailed boots, and he was always smoothing his short-cut hair back over his head.

He stayed awake fighting with Mother, and then, when it was past my bedtime, they went out to the woodshed and fought some more. I came downstairs one night to make myself some ersatz coffee and found them dancing in the living room.

Father was wearing a tuxedo and mother was in her wedding dress. No music. There was a bottle of something on the table. The stairs made too much noise for them not to have noticed me creeping back up to bed.

The last anybody at home ever saw of my father, he was leaning out of a train window waving good-bye. My little brother Walther and I stood with our hands in our pockets, up to our knees in steam from the train. Mother ran after my dad, then stood at the far end of the platform until the last carriage was out of sight.

I MET Stein about a month later on my way back from school. At first in the distance I thought he was a Friesian cow which had gotten loose.

He flipped his cigarette into the ditch, and when he hugged me, I could tell he hadn't washed in a long time. His nose was dripping. Eyes red from a cold. He was a very tall man with a stupid Bavarian face, and his black boots were scuffed white.

His hands were in bandages, and the equipment hanging from his belt—water bottle, mess tin, bayonet—was all old. It was worn-out and old like the rest of him.

He stood for a while saying nothing and did not take his eyes from staring at me even when he put his pack down on the side of the road.

"Where's your mother?"

"Still at home. She isn't going to the market until later. What's up? When did you get back?"

"I got in this morning. Aren't you going to ask me where your father is?"

"Yes. Where's my father?"

"He's dead. I came here to tell you myself." He crouched down on the ground and started to draw things out with a stick. "We stopped in a town, and we thought we'd pushed them back. But the fucking Reds came up behind us. I don't know. Maybe they were hiding in the sewers or something. Maybe there weren't even any sewers. I don't know. I went off to take a piss, and I came back, and I'm standing there doing up my fly next to the armored car. Then everything goes up in flames. Some Red snuck up and threw a grenade into the car. Look." He took off his jacket and dropped it on the grass. He pulled off his gray shirt, turned around, and showed me scars that made his back look as if it had been whipped with chains. "I heard your father when the grenade went into the car." He was staring off down the road and talking more slowly now. "He was in the car. He heard the grenade when it hit the floor, and he said, 'What the fuck is this?' That's what he said."

Stein emptied his pack onto the grass beside the road. He was still half-naked, black cap jammed on his head. There were balls of filthy socks and underwear, cans of meat, and loose cigarettes, and, after everything had fallen out, a stream of fine dirt still poured from the side pockets. He unwrapped an undershirt, and in it was a gun, the handle cracked, with Russian writing printed along the side. He pulled out the magazine to show me there were still bullets in it, then handed it over.

"This is for you. It's a Tokarev. From the man who threw the grenade in. It's a good gun. You should keep it." His eyes were very wide. He bent down and put his pack back together.

I aimed the gun at a fence post that separated the road from a pasture, fired and missed, fired again and blew off the top of the fence post. Stein snatched the gun out of my hand and told me to be careful how I used it.

"I got him for you. I didn't let him get far." Stein did up the drawstring on his pack which was olive canvas with leather trim, eventually managed to get his shirt and jacket on, although his fingers were shaky and he couldn't do up the buttons. "These are for you, too." He pulled some buttons out of his pocket, brass with a hammer and sickle on the front and a brass and enamel Russian star. "Did you say your mother was home?"

"Yes."

"Going to school?"

"Yes."

Stein went away up the hill to Pech.

I walked around school feeling dizzy and sick. I sat in the schoolyard and ate my lunch from a paper bag, like a cow chewing grass. When the bell went for afternoon classes, I walked in through the doors of the main building, along the hall, and out the other door, which got me onto the main road leading down the hill into the town.

I sat on a bench outside the Bad Godesberg museum with a drunk who said he knew how I felt when I told him my father had been killed on the Russian front.

During the next few weeks almost everyone I knew said they knew how I felt when they found out my father was dead. And they never left it at that. Always they had to talk about someone they knew who had died, and after a while I would look at them, and it was as if they carried the gray shadows of the dead, like sacks of bones, wherever they went. And, when they could, they unloaded the sacks onto someone else for a while.

MOTHER DUG her claws deep into Stein's shell-shocked head, and he couldn't take it. Told her everything. My father got blown to bits sitting in an armored car, and his last words were, "What the fuck is this?" And to my mother's demand that Stein tell whether or not her husband got a decent burial, Stein had to confess that there had been no burial. The car had burned, and there was nothing to bury. He didn't get a medal. Stein told her that, too.

Mother went out to the sink and began washing her hands. She washed them and scrubbed them until the bones of her knuckles were exposed. Then she took the bus to the clinic in Bad Godesberg, her hands wrapped in dish towels.

I HAD been in the Hitler Jugend two years and the Deutsche Jugend for five years before that. We had meetings three days a week, and there was usually some parade on the weekends. We wore black shorts, tan shirts, and black neck scarves. That was at the beginning. By age sixteen we were wearing all black with red armbands.

It used to be that from there you went straight into the Army, Navy, Air Force, or SS when you were eighteen. At the beginning of 1944 they lowered the age to seventeen.

The day after my seventeenth birthday, I went down the hill from the school to the recruiting office, which was in a small red-brick building next to the post office.

It was eight thirty in the morning, and I was the only one in the waiting room. The place smelled of cigarettes, old magazines, and the rain that fell down the chimney onto the iron log-holders in the fireplace. The ends of the log-holders were shaped like dragon's heads, with rings held in their mouths.

There were posters on the walls:

A flaming background with a bullet-chipped eagle holding a swastika, and, also in chipped stone, the words, "Victory Will Be Ours."

A man, seen from the waist up, Waffen SS uniform, smiling, holding out his hand in greeting: "Your Comrades Wait for You in the Waffen SS."

A ship streaming a Navy flag, cutting through glass-like waves: "Fight with Us on the Sea."

A hand holding a sickle smashed through a wall, and, behind the hole, a sky full of fire: "Europe Has Been Invaded!"

There was no more Navy. No more Air Force either. Only the Army and SS were still recruiting. In Bad Godesberg the SS worked the office half the day, the Army the other half.

An SS man was standing behind the counter at the back of the room, looking into a little mirror fixed on a nail on the wall and cutting the hair out of his nose with a pair of nail scissors. He looked across, watched me shut the door, then slowly set down the scissors.

"Can't come in yet. Not open until eight thirty."

There was a telephone on a table at the back of the room, and a jar full of new, sharp pencils. The SS man was in full uniform: black with silver braid around the collar, shiny belt buckle, the toes of his boots reflecting all the light there was.

"It *is* eight thirty."

He frowned, looked at the watch on his wrist, shook it, then took it off and threw it away over his shoulder. He stood staring at me for a moment, then walked over to where the watch had fallen, picked it up and put it in his pocket.

"Busy in here." I went forward to the desk, down the twelve-pace aisle designed to make a person nervous. I knew these tricks. And the SS man couldn't have been more than five years older than me. I wasn't going to take any of his crap. I got to the desk, set my elbows on the counter, and stared at him. "So tell me why I should join the SS."

He looked down at a shelf set behind the counter that was piled with blank documents and extra pencils tied with rubber bands. He seemed to be searching for a piece of paper that might have the answer written on it.

"It's my first day here." He looked up and shrugged. "I only got out of the hospital yesterday. I'm supposed to be cleaning up until the captain arrives."

"Oh." I backed away from the counter and put my hands in my pockets. "Well, shit."

"He'll be here in a little while." The man took off his black side cap with the skull on the forehead, scratched his head. "I know where the papers are. You can sign up now if you want." He turned to the side and looked to see if the captain might be coming. His movements were slow and careful. His nose was dead straight. I had never seen a nose that straight before. He had eyes that were brown like gravy. "You get a free pencil if you sign up." He held up one of the pencils and laughed. Then he snapped it between his fingers and the two ends spiraled away onto the floor.

"Tell me why *you* joined the SS."

"Me?"

"Sure."

"You piddling with me?"

"No."

He chewed his lip for a while, looking down again at the counter shelf in case the answer might be there someplace. "If you have to go around asking people why you should join, then perhaps you shouldn't. If you don't see the need to join the SS, if you don't have that, then nothing anybody else says should be able to talk you into it. But if you *can* see the need, then nothing anybody says should be able to talk you out of it."

"I may as well join the Army then." I dragged a chair from the corner of the room and sat down on it. You'll have to do better than that, SS man, I was thinking. You can sweat for me before I sweat for you. I smiled at him like a cherub and said nothing.

He walked out from behind the counter and eased himself onto the floor, which was polished like his boots. "But the Army and the SS aren't the same, and you should know that."

"I know it." It was raining so hard on the roof I thought the ceiling would collapse.

"And you shouldn't be thinking you have to have an excuse to join. There may be some reason you don't even know yet. There isn't always an excuse. But there's always a reason. And no one's going to ask you, either. That's between you and your-self." He pressed his hands together as if to pray, then locked his fingers and pushed them out until the knuckles cracked.

"So if you felt all this need, why are you here and not up to your neck in some Bolshevik swamp?" I whipped out a hand-kerchief and honked my nose. I caught you, you fart-talking Nazi, and you blew it.

He shifted himself a little, unbuttoned his tunic, and pulled up his shirt. To the right of the place where his ribs formed an upside-down **V**, there was a spot that looked like an extra belly button that had filled itself in with shiny purple-pink skin. "It's still in there. They say if I move suddenly it will go into my heart or cut some artery that leads into it or something."

He sighed and looked at the filled-in hole. And we both sighed then and looked at the place as if it might move if we concen-trated on it.

"It only happened about five weeks ago. Went through the cigarette case I had in my breast pocket. It's filled in very nicely, don't you think?" Then with his hands gone a little shaky, he fitted a cigarette into his mouth and lit it with a match he struck on the floor, leaving a blue line across the polish. "I want the war to end as much as any Heinrich that comes in here on any given day. I did before, and I do now. No more and no less. I look forward to the calm after the storm. Only the storm is now.

And you're in it." He raised his eyebrows and hid himself in smoke.

After I had left the building, dodged out of the way of the captain as he ran past, doing up his belt, the neat half-moon of his untucked shirt showing from under the back of his tunic, it seemed to me that what I had done was inevitable. No reason or excuse. Sebastian Westland. Waffen SS. Black ink.

The rain had stopped. It was a pretty July morning.

BENJAMIN WANTED to go to Königswinter for the day, so I wheeled him down to the ferryboat, which crossed the Rhine about once every half hour. There were cafés on the ferry landings, either side of the river. We had a beer on one side, then a beer on the other side, and instead of looking around Königswinter, we spent the day going back and forth on the ferryboat, drinking beer each time we made the crossing.

Benjamin wheeled himself across the gridded metal floor of the ferry. It didn't take anything at all to get him soused. There was a warm breeze so we took our shirts off, and people stared at Benjamin, as if a boy in a wheelchair should never let the sun shine on his back.

It was an outdoor café in Königswinter with a lot of people walking up and down the boulevard. Others played chess and Skatcards at the white tables of the café while the waiter dodged between them, wearing his collarless shirt and apron, swinging the full glasses under their noses and lighting their cigarettes. His name was Stock, and he'd left school the year before I did, tried to join the Navy but they wouldn't accept him. Eventually no one would take him because he was blind as a bat. He saw everything through glasses that looked like ice cubes framed in gold.

When Benjamin and I were soused, Stock came and got soused with us. He had been taking slugs of aquavit behind the counter all day, and even his sweat, which he wiped on his starched white apron, smelled of alcohol.

"I shouldn't do this to myself." He took off his glasses, breathed on them, and then wiped them with his shirttail. "I'll be dropping beer all over the place next. Why do you two keep crossing the river? Can't you make up your minds where you want to be?"

"There's a good breeze when you get out there." I smelled flowers from the flower bed beside the café, and a faint breath of tobacco burning at the other tables.

"Is that so?"

"Yes, that's so. Can we have another beer?"

"In a minute. Let me sit for a while. So is there anything new besides school?"

"I signed up today."

Stock put his glasses on, hooking the wire sidepieces around his pink ears, and looked around as if he hadn't heard me. Then he said, "What for?"

"Because they told us in assembly that we had to."

"No, I mean what branch?"

"SS."

Then Benjamin, as if he had known I was going to say it, moving so fast that I barely got the word out of my mouth, tipped his beer glass upside down on the table, so that half the beer stayed in the upside-down glass and a silver crack appeared along the length of it. Then he said very fast and quietly that I had done a stupid thing. A damn stupid thing.

"I wonder if I can do that." Stock turned his glass upside down, spilled beer all over the table, and smashed the glass into five or six pieces.

"Did you hear what he said?" Benjamin was looking at Stock.

"Yes. He joined the SS. The Waffen SS, no?"

"Mm." I nodded and wished I wasn't soused.

"Well, that's a damn stupid thing to do. That's all I can say."

Benjamin took some coins out of his pocket, dropped them in the spilled beer, and wheeled himself off toward the ferry landing.

"What's wrong with him?" Stock tried to put his glass back together. It balanced for a second, then fell apart again. His customers were calling for more beer. He stood up, and his thin body swayed in front of me as I leaned back and pulled the coins from my pocket to pay.

"I'd better go see about him."

"Work hard. Break your neck and legs."

"But of course."

I went over to Benjamin, and a dog had just peed on his wheelchair. The ferry was coming over from the other side. Before I even got to him he turned around and stared.

"You just don't know what you've done, do you, Westland?"

"Calm down, Benjamin, or I'll wheel you through every piece of dog shit in town."

"Let's just go home."

PEOPLE GAVE me shifty eyes in school. They gave me shifty eyes when my father died, too, but that was different.

A boy called Draeger came up to me at lunch break and wanted to know if he'd heard the rumor correctly that I was joining the SS. I was sitting on a newspaper because the bench was wet from rain. Mother had given me chicken and lettuce sandwiches but had forgotten to put in the chicken. She was always doing that. Rye bread. Walther had mashed the plum I had for dessert.

"Yes, I joined the SS. Something wrong?" I forced the bread and flap of lettuce down my throat.

"I just wanted to wish you good-bye, since I know I'll never see you again." He held out his hand and gave me a short, sarcastic bow.

I guess he thought he was pretty funny. That afternoon I took the books out of his locker and threw them down the air-raid shelter steps. The shelter was always ankle-deep in water. Whenever there was an air-raid warning or a practice, half of us would run off into the park rather than go down there in the dark, where we all stood the chance of being electrocuted by wet cables. Sometimes the warnings went on for hours, while the RAF was flying over, bombing Cologne or something. And, of course, during that time everyone had to go to the bathroom. The only thing to go in was an oil drum, so there was a constant tinkling sound of people jangling their keys, trying to be polite and drown the noise, or the rumble of someone trying not to but farting into the drum.

This would be followed by swears or sighs from the person who farted at the thought of never living it down. These people would spend the rest of their lives with names like "Bugle Blower" or "Rolling Thunder."

I didn't get enough pleasure throwing Draeger's books away. When I saw him coming up the main stairway in school, in the slow snake of people returning from the midday lunch break, I drew a pair of fat SS lightning bolts backwards on my palm with my fountain pen. Before the ink was dry, I held out my hand for him to shake, which he did, looked down at me a few seconds later on his way upstairs, then at his palm, slowly pulled out a handkerchief and tried to wipe it off.

For a couple of days I went around with my penknife carving SS lightning bolts on everything, but I didn't get any pleasure out of that either.

"Do you know Mrs. Hammacher at all?" Mother put down her soup spoon and tore a piece of bread off the loaf on the table. Behind her, the face of the clock was shining with the light of the sunset, held in a bar through the window. I could see the strands of gray in her hair.

"No. Why?"

"It's funny. She keeps asking about you when I meet her in the marketplace. She doesn't ask about Walther. Just you."

"Why doesn't she ask about me, then?" Walther lifted his face out of his bowl of soup and blinked at us. His feet didn't touch the floor when he sat on his chair.

" 'Cause you're ugly, Walther." I fired a rubber band at him under the table.

"I'm handsome."

"No. Really, Sebastian. Why does she ask about you?" Mother poured some milk out of the stone pitcher into her bowl and spooned it up.

"No idea."

"I'm handsome," said Walther.

"There must be a reason why she asks."

I kept my mouth shut. I got drunk on punch at the New Year's Eve party at her house, however long ago it was, and she took me upstairs to the attic, and we did it on a reindeer skin which she got when she went on holiday to Finland. Then she told me it was never going to happen again. Since I figured it was my fault and she would tell on me, I said that was fine. But she didn't tell anyone. About a week later she picked me up at school and said she was in the area and thought she'd save me the bus fare. We did it in the car parked in the woods near Remagen. She picked me up at school about once a week, and after every time, when she was pulling her sweater over her head to get dressed again and rummaging on the floor for her shoes, she would say this shouldn't happen anymore. She laughed when she said it. After a while she was picking me up at school every day. Lise Hammacher. Sharp-nosed and violent, her eyes always boring blue trails through my head. Smelling distantly of cologne. Telling me always good-bye forever.

She would cry for her husband while I sat next to her, staring at my shoes. Then she would yell at him that he was never around and he didn't love her, as we drove back to the place where she dropped me off. The times I slammed the door, the car left down the road, and I stood in the rain smelling the exhaust, her perfume vaguely on my clothes, then turned to walk home—I could not count them anymore.

There were rumors. She said so. I never heard any. Her husband came home more often from his business trips. She started telling me to go find someone else. Then there was the morning I wheeled Benjamin to the edge of the woods, walked across the field to her house, and came back with my hair full of mud, and cabbage leaves stuffed down my shirt.

She was thirty-two and I was seventeen.

"So you've no idea what her problem is, asking all the time about you?"

"None at all. Is there any more soup?"

"No, dear."

I set the bowl down in the sink, went upstairs, and locked myself in my room.

"I'm so handsome, handsome, handsome," Walther was singing down below.

Late in the night I put on my clothes and ran through the woods, not feeling the cold, with energy to run for miles churning inside me. I stopped when I got to the middle of the field by her house. The only light was the one by the door. Nothing else. Cold. Wind. My breathing. I walked home, hearing strange sounds far away among the black pillars of pine.

"YOU HAVE made a mistake and the mistake you have made is this." Benjamin and I were drunk again at the Drachenfels Café in Königswinter. Stock wasn't around today because he had a worse hangover than any of his customers. The boy who took his place was called Eschweiler, and we told him that Stock gave us free drinks, which he didn't, so now Eschweiler was giving us every third beer free.

"You are no longer just fighting in the war, Sebastian. You are part of it now. You are part of Total War. You've signed yourself up for a war to the end. You can't surrender. If you did, they would just shoot you anyway. It's like"—he pinched the bridge of his nose—"being on a metronome."

"Metronome."

"One of those things that ticktocks back and forth when you're learning to play the piano. Gives you rhythm or something. It's like that because if Germany was ever to win the war, you would be at the front of it, all the heroes, you a hero. If Germany loses the war, then they will take everything bad that has happened, they will take every human fault they can think of, and they will stick you with it. You will get the blame for the whole war, for all time. They won't give you a grave to lie in, Sebastian."

"Have another beer."

"Listen to me. You listen to what I say."

"You're being very pessimistic." It was bright from the white metal tables, and the Rhine glittered like smashed glass. Barges moved up and down the river, most of them empty.

"Well, you tell me, SS man"—he leaned over and talked quickly—"who you think will win."

"I don't know." We could have been arrested for talking like that. There was a man called Meissner, who used to teach at our school and lecture his class in these things. The Gestapo came for him, dragged him down the hall while he yelled, "Fools, fools!" at everyone he could see. Apparently he grated his teeth down with a metal file in a fit of rage at the station. The report that appeared in the paper said he beat himself up with a rubber hose too, just for the hell of it.

"You do know. It's July now. The Italians have given up. . . ."

"Oh, well, if you're going to talk about the Italians. They put their uniforms on backwards and run away just to confuse the enemy." I figured I'd kill his argument with this.

"And Stalingrad's gone. Africa's gone. They're coming from the east and the west. You know damn well what I'm talking about."

I had thought he was drunk. Perhaps only I was soused. "I don't know about any of this, Benjamin, but I joined up anyway. A lot of my friends did . . ."

"Oh, you mean that old fart Benno Posner. Oh, a good friend. I'm sure he gave it lots of thought."

"It's easy for you to talk because you're not going anywhere in that chair of yours."

"Why did you go and say that?"

"Because it's true. That's what I do know."

We always ended up fighting at the Drachenfels Café, and on the ferry on the way home I swore I would survive. And it seemed right, the water cognac-colored, the sky a mass of honey wheels and clouds.

BENJAMIN WASN'T going anywhere because he couldn't walk. He couldn't walk because he got hit by a truck when he was ten.

He ran across the road in the middle of town with a bag of rock candy in his hands, stopped in the middle of the road, in front of a BMW truck. The truck knocked him across the road into a fruit stand. The people at the bus stop, where I was waiting, were pelted with rock candy.

Everything happened with a disgusting clarity. There were no sounds I could remember.

Clearly he smashed into the fruit stand, and clearly the yellow-green apples rolled out into the road, and a basket of cherries rose clearly into the air and rained dark red balls on the bystanders turning their heads around to stare. The truck stopped, the driver jumped out of the cab, crushing one of the yellow-green apples when he landed, and kneeled next to Benjamin.

Then with this clarity that never left me, the people at the bus stop began to move across the street toward the fruit stand. And I moved too, taking the time to pick a lump of the rock candy off the pavement and stuff it in my mouth.

There was a gathering around him, everyone opening and closing their mouths to shout orders to the person next to them, all trying to take charge, but I don't remember any sound. It was as if they were fish, sucking water in.

Traffic piled up in the street. Men got out of their cars and yelled for the jam to break up, and then when they saw what was going on, they ran to join the others. To add to the confusion. The clear balls of the apples were squashed into nothing under the feet of the crowd.

I got down on my hands and knees, and Benjamin was looking at me. He lay on the upturned cart and on the apples, head on the pavement with an expression that seemed to me quite calm. He blinked a couple of times a minute, slowly, the big lashes flickering on his eyes. He was bleeding from his ears and his nose and his mouth.

A policeman blew on his whistle, trying to make a path for the ambulance men who had arrived, but with the silence that had overtaken me it only looked as if he were trying to bite the whistle in half.

They took Benjamin away on a stretcher, and in ten minutes the street was tidy again, except for the squashed apples and the berries that birds from the rooftops came down and pecked at until there was nothing left.

When the bus dropped me off at home, I ran into the house and saw Mother making bread in the kitchen. The home smelled of baking, and she held up the bowl of flour so she could see the recipe book on the table.

I told her Benjamin was dead, and she dropped the bowl. First, when it hit the floor, it bounced, and the flour jumped in a mass but stayed in the bowl. Then when it hit the floor a second time, it exploded and blew white dust across the kitchen. Weeks later we were finding it under the stove and in corners.

Rumors:

Benjamin is dead.

It wasn't Benjamin who got hit.

Benjamin is dead and his father is out with an ax trying to find the driver so he can kill him.

There was no accident.

Lots of people died in the accident.

Benjamin is dead, and his ghost has contacted Mrs. Faulhaber, who lives up by the dairy.

I WENT to visit him in the hospital a few days after the truck ran over him. He was lying on his back, and the nurse was feeding him applesauce with a wooden spoon. I stayed for five minutes trying to remember all the things my mother had told me not to talk about. Nothing about his legs. Nothing about legs at all or anything you do with legs. LEGS. The word pumped electric red lines across my closed eyelids. I said nothing at all. Benjamin burst into tears. The nurse woofed at me to get out, and I was glad to be gone, hearing Benjamin wailing, "Why did you send him away?" as I shuffled down the rotten-smelling corridors.

THEN THERE was panic for the first few days when he wheeled the bright chair around town. Not really a town, Pech. More of a *Dorf*, a village. He had offers from people to wheel him wherever he wanted to go. He had cakes and some chocolate. He had a crate of bottled cherries from the man at the fruit stand.

It was a panic made of women talking on the vegetable-strewn cobblestones of the market. Of old men rolling on the fat balls of their paunches and chatting in the bars. Then the panic stopped because they became bored with it, gradually at first but gathering speed until there was nothing left.

He started getting in the way. When he realized this, he shut himself up in his room and read books, and sat by himself.

He was able to think so clearly and carefully that whenever I spoke to him I went away afterwards feeling blind or deaf or with some other of my senses clogged and useless.

I wheeled him through the woods like a slave while he talked, staring straight ahead, about whatever occurred to him, and I only nodding and agreeing, whispering, "Yes, that's true. There's truth in that," until I kept quiet from the shame of repetition.

"REGRET TO INFORM . . ." This was the beginning of the telegram, written on something like toilet paper, delivered by the one-armed soldier from the depot in Bad Godesberg a month after Stein had brought home the news.

All that Stein had said about the death of my father did not convince my mother. But the telegram did. Everyone I knew was like that. People could listen to their best friends who had never lied to them before and not believe a word of what was said if they didn't want to. But if they got a toilet-paper telegram with an official stamp on it from someone in a uniform saying, "You are dead," they would probably curl up in a ball and stop breathing on the spot.

She lay on her face on their bed with her head in a pile of my father's old clothes, trying to pick up some trace of his sweat that might bring him back to life for the fragment of a second that she smelled him close by.

At first she wanted to keep the place exactly as it was before she received the telegram.

That all changed overnight. There was a purge, his clothes taken out and burned or given away, his smell scrubbed out of the sheets and the walls and the cupboards. The neighbors obliged, took the clothes away and never wore them, talked about anything, grinding their teeth to avoid the silence in which any of us might have heard an echo of my father's voice, some ghost-muttering of speech shuddering up through the ground, speaking from the fireplace or the woodshed in the garden.

I sat in the attic on a rocking horse that had been my grandfather's, and I listened for the echo. I rocked on the glass-eyed horse and kicked up dust while I waited.

Perhaps it was not even a sound that I waited for. There was no voice I heard. What went through me were the pictures and colors and sounds I remembered. And the way they faded was not with the babbling of the people in the town, but with the piling on of other dead, the obliging and frantic taken away themselves in uniforms and boots and killed, until to cover the echoes rattling down from all the attics, the rest would have had to live in a state of perpetual screaming.

DURING THESE months Mother received visitors in the kitchen and sat at the head of the table, where my father used to sit, and smoked, her legs pulled up onto the chair.

Some days I came home from school and saw the tracks of maybe twenty people on the kitchen floor, and Mother still at the table, puffing smoke rings at the ceiling. After a while there was a yellow stain on the plaster above her.

She used to let the visitors knock until they either went away or came in of their own accord. They set their offerings of jam or vegetables on the side counter. She let them make coffee or tea for themselves, if there was any, showing them the various things to eat or drink with quick flips of her wrist.

She let us do whatever we wanted.

An RAF bomber on a raid over Cologne was shot down and crashed in the woods of the Kottonforst. Soldiers went into the woods, following the great path of black smoke in the trees. They also stopped us from going in to have a look. A couple of hours later they brought out one man and said they'd found him swinging from the branches of a pine by the cords of his parachute. The rest were either dead or had jumped out earlier.

Mother came out of her house, stirring an egg into a big pottery bowl filled with oats.

The soldiers, all of them old reservists, wore civilian clothes with yellow armbands on which was written in black ink, "In the Service of the German Army." They had taken his sheepskin flying jacket and his fur-lined flying boots. The airman was wearing gray-blue trousers and a gray-blue shirt with a pair of wings sewn over the left breast pocket. He was walking in his socks, the ends of his trousers dragging on the ground. The reservists made him keep his hands in the air, and pushed him through the street with the butts of their rifles. The Englishman had dark hair and rosy cheeks, and tried to look bored by the whole business.

The street was crowded, crowded for the town of Pech, anyway. It was quiet, except for the two soldiers at the rear of the procession squabbling over who would get the jacket. It was a beautiful jacket with a big brass zipper down the front, and I wanted it. I sat on the wall of our garden and chewed a piece of licorice root.

Mother swung open the small iron gate at the start of the garden path, walked into the street in front of the pilot, smashed the bowl at his feet.

The procession stopped. The reservists peered around from behind the airman. I crouched down behind the wall and looked through the gooseberry bush. Mother stood back from the mess and put her hands on her hips, her lower lip curled out and making her ugly.

The airman narrowed his eyes, looked down at the broken bowl and up at my mother again. Then he walked on through the spilled oats and the shards, the reservists following behind. He left a single line of bloody footprints down to the truck that was waiting at the bottom of the hill.

Next week Mother applied to be the town air-raid warden. They gave her a black greatcoat, a nickel-plated whistle, and a strange helmet with a long, flared front and back and two semi-circles cut out around the ears. It had a decal on it that said "AIR DEFENSE."

She made an oath to Adolf Hitler down at the post office and took a course in rifle shooting but gave up after the second day because she knocked out one of her front teeth. On the first day at the shooting range, she had only aimed through the front sight when she pulled the trigger, which made a ricochet off the back wall that sent the instructor running for cover. She gave up her pay to the Winter Relief Fund and borrowed a bicycle from Mrs. Müller down at the bakery.

Every night after sunset she cycled around town making sure all the blackout curtains were drawn so that none of the RAF bombers could use the town lights to guide themselves into Cologne. If someone's curtains weren't drawn, she wouldn't knock on the door and remind them. She'd stand in the street and blow a whistle until people started coming out of their houses to see what the matter was. Then when the offending family opened their door, usually having drawn their curtains and now faking innocence, Mother would say in a loud voice, "If Your Curtains Aren't Drawn The War Will Go On!" That was the slogan on the posters she was given to stick up, showing a giant black bomb heading toward a house with one window lit up.

She became the most unpopular woman in town after about a week of riding around town blowing her whistle. She came home at midnight, the greatcoat down to her ankles and torn from the times when she got the tail caught in the chain that locked the wheel and sent her off into a pasture or the ditch. And from wearing the helmet, her hair would be its normal curly self around the edges but molded like an egg on top where the helmet had been.

She started going out again after midnight and sometimes didn't come back until ten o'clock the next day. Then she'd sleep all afternoon and go out again after dark. She looked like a vampire, pale with purple blotches under her eyes.

I found out later that she used to catch a ride over to Remagen, flag down some car in her "AIR DEFENSE" helmet and say it was official business. She went to the antiaircraft battery, which had its guns set up on each of the black towers of the bridge over the Rhine. They let her sit in the control room and stare out the window at the tracers thrashing red lines across the sky. She liked the *pom-pom* sound of the guns when they fired for the half hour that the planes were overhead, fifteen minutes going one way and fifteen the other. Afterward she'd stand around with the gun crew, learning to smoke cigars, drinking apple schnapps, and eating cucumber sandwiches. They played Mozart on a Gramophone to the whole of Remagen through a bullhorn. They never shot down a plane. Mother said they just pointed the gun barrels up in the air and fired off all the shells they had because no one could see the aircraft.

Walther and I used to sit at the breakfast table before school, while she was still over in Remagen, eating uncooked porridge and firing spoonloads of flour mixed with water at each other across the room. I told him that if we ate lots of uncooked porridge and then drank hot water, we'd pop.

When we came home late in the afternoon, she'd have cleaned up the mess and Walther would bounce on her bed until she woke up. Then she'd tell us about the firing the night before, fists clenched over her head like she was shooting the gun, loading the shells, shouting orders for better trajectory into an invisible telephone held to her ear. Sometimes she took her helmet off the bedpost and put it on her head to liven up the story.

* * *

THE WAY it would go with the one Mrs. Hammacher called a milkmaid was that we would be introduced at a party. She wouldn't talk about true love, and I wouldn't mention guns or the coolness of the Messerschmitt. We would get along fine. She would be pretty. Round-faced and happy and shy. First she wouldn't say much, but after we had left the party or were back in her kitchen, she would talk all the time.

We'd meet after school, and I'd spend all my money in restaurants that looked nice but served bad food which she would be too polite to eat. She'd want to hold hands. She'd wear traces of makeup, but only traces, and no perfume. Sometimes we'd sit in a café, and she'd knit and I'd do my homework or read or get drunk with the waiters. She'd always be knitting me something, scarves mostly.

Soon she would start talking about true love. I would pretend to throw up, and she'd throw her knitting at me. Then when I wasn't concentrating and the names of a few gun calibers would fall out of my mouth, she would roll her eyes and go into a sulk.

She'd be afraid to kiss me because of the germs, so I'd pull all the money out of my wallet, wave it at the waiter, and tell him, please, please, to destroy me.

I would just stop being able to take it, and I'd find myself in the blackest part of the middle of the night standing in the field beside Lise Hammacher's house, staring at the windows for lights that were never on.

I HAD a lot of friends besides Benjamin, mostly from my Hitler Jugend Group. We heard a great deal about Brotherhood from the instructors. We heard as well the demand that we win. Every time we met up, there was always some kind of competition: obstacle courses, archery, shooting, singing. So someone was always the winner, and everyone else jealous of him, or the loser, who let the team down and was hated. If you stayed in the middle, no one noticed you, so it was always the way that we learned to win. It was winning by rules, with no lying or cheating, but winning by aggression against the enemy. So afterwards, going home through the streets, the instructors kept reminding us we were Brothers, but there were always hate and jealousy and pride and shame.

Benjamin used to listen to what I had to tell him about the Youth Group, and then he would get sad. He wheeled himself around in circles in his room, and after a while I would be quiet. Then he told me to keep talking.

Eventually he would start beating his legs with his fists and speaking in his own private language.

I T W A S a warm summer. At the end of August I packed two changes of clothing, some books, and a bottle of apple schnapps and took the train south with about half a dozen others from my school. The journey took three days. Most of the first day I was drunk from the schnapps, and after that my memory of the trip was mostly of standing with my hands in my pockets in a line waiting to get stew from a portable kitchen set up at stations along the way. It was always stew, out of tin pots with aluminum spoons. Sometimes the stations were jammed with people saying good-bye, people crying and getting trodden on. Often there was no one. We gorged on stew and fell asleep for a while in the sun on the concrete platforms.

We arrived at Bad Tölz in Bavaria at one in the morning in the rain, and the six of us were the only ones to get off the train. We walked around in the dark looking for someone to give us directions, and then a truck without its headlights on drove into the station yard. An SS sergeant wearing a helmet got out and asked us if we were looking for him. We guessed so. From the light of a match we could tell there was someone else in the truck. He told us to get in, which we did, and bounced around on the metal floor while he drove, because there were no seats. The SS men spent the whole time laughing at jokes they told each other.

I USED to think, when I was lying on my iron bed at the Camp after the lights had been turned out, that there would be no point explaining this place to Benjamin. What happened at the Camp would not make sense to anyone who had not been at the Camp. Anyone who came from the Camp carried the stench of it with them forever. You could tell from a hundred paces away that someone had been to the Camp. I looked for them when I was not at the place because I felt comfortable among them. All this could not be explained. I lay on my bed hearing the breathing of the other twenty people in the room and seeing the shadows of rain down the windows reflected on the ceiling, and there was the regular sound of the gates being opened, headlights of trucks shining through the room in a sweep, showing pale faces asleep, shadows stretched long and then suddenly gone. Brakes, boots striking the road as people got out of the truck, then the truck driving out again into the dark.

I knew then that when I got old and tried to look back on the time at Bad Tölz there would be only a scattering of pictures, and I would sit somewhere with my face gone saggy and remember only the fragments, perhaps the only real thing left: the blood group letter A tattooed on my armpit.

The first thing I remember anybody saying to me was that this time next year I would be lucky to be alive.

The next thing I remember was a gray-eyed man in a black uniform staring me in the face and telling me never to look him in the eye again. So of course I looked him in the eye. Couldn't help it. He took me out in front of the rank of boys in which I had been standing all morning in my new uniform, which was field-gray with no insignia, a plain black belt, and black ankle boots. We also wore helmets. He stood me in front of the line and struck me in the face with a riding whip. Then he yelled, "Strike me!"

"No, sir."

He struck me again in the face, and the lash of the whip spread across my head and down into my neck.

"Strike me!"

"No, sir."

Again. He struck me again and sweat was coming out from my clenched fists as if I had been holding wet sponges.

He yelled for me to strike him, I said, "No," and he hit me maybe five more times. Then he told me to get back in line and never to look him in the eye again. I stood in line, and my face puffed up while the man in black walked back and forth along the rank shouting at us.

He yelled at us that this was the end. We should welcome the end, he said.

All afternoon we stood in the line. The ragged hole of sun

faded away into the clouds and radiated pale light across the stone walls of the courtyard.

"You must be honest, decent, kind, and loyal to people of your own blood and to no one else." Sergeant Voss kept saying that. He was about twenty-five years old, a little shorter than most of us, but he seemed like a much taller man who had been compressed into a smaller space and was not happy about it.

He said he hated us because we were weak, and he said the only certainty was that the war would change us. Of everything we had learned in our schools, there was only one certainty: that it would wear us down on the outside, peel the flesh off us, and scatter the bones of our backs like dice.

It seemed Voss had been broken and torn up, stuck back together, his brain still raving mad, and he was only trying to figure it out for himself, walking up and down, spit flying from his mouth, and raging from his unseeable gray eyes.

IN THE barracks there was a boy called Handschumacher, and it was clear from the beginning that he thought he was going to run things. He walked around the dorm in his underpants telling us how to make our beds and fold our clothes. He was broad-shouldered and had red hair. Every place I'd ever been had some big guy in it who figured he could be boss just by being big. And I knew it was just a matter of time before someone else, some slope-shouldered bean pole would outthink him and ridicule him. There were recipes for this kind of thing. Every class, every school, every Youth Group had a Handschumacher. Every Group probably had a Westland, too, but I liked to think that wasn't so.

Von Schwerin made it clear that he should have been an officer candidate, that his brothers and father were officers, and that Handschumacher was a malcoordinate and an idiot. Then he sat on his bed like a Buddha and wouldn't speak to anyone. He had a small, sharp face. Talked as if his nose were permanently clogged. He was comfortable here. You could tell. As if he'd come a week before the rest of us and learned the feel of the place, so he could have the edge by the time the rest of us arrived.

Breder stood on the windowsill and announced we were all going to die. Just kidding. He punched me on the arm and called me buddy. He did the rounds, talking to everybody. Trying to get to know us. Shaking hands. How you doing, buddy? When he came to me, I answered only yes or no or mumbled, until he left, and I watched the chiseled angles of his head and shoulders until they went out of focus at the other end of the room.

There was no one from home. They had all been put in separate groups. Everyone stood around making things clear about themselves until they got bored and played cards. I lay on my bed and thought to myself that the only thing I had made clear was my name. I was going to assert myself. I had to find something to assert. Then I fell asleep.

I woke again just before they turned the lights out, when an old man everybody called Plem-Plem came in with a trolley on which there was a jug of ersatz coffee and aluminum mugs. We all got a mug of coffee, Plem-Plem turned the lights out, and we sat on our beds in the dark, sipping.

I MET Benno Posner in the eating hall called the Mensa. We sat opposite each other at one of the long wooden tables, and for a while we didn't say anything. The hall had a high ceiling with beams at the top. The walls were plastered stone and draped with banners and paintings of old generals. The windows were like those in a church except the glass wasn't stained. There were five tables down the length of the hall, and one table set apart from them where the officers sat. Most of the time it was empty. Steam from the kitchens was a fog near the counters where the cooks dished out food into aluminum bowls, which we ate from with aluminum spoons, and from aluminum mugs we drank the cold water they gave us out of pottery jugs. The food was all right. They cooked about as well as my mother.

Posner looked up from his soup, the blond blast of his hair sticking up from his head, and out of reflex I turned away from his eyes, in case from nowhere a horsewhip would come thrashing into my face.

"Westland."

"Posner. Haven't seen much of you."

"Come across anyone else from Bad Godesberg?"

"Not yet. They're around, though."

"I heard Dietrich broke his leg."

"How?" I tore a piece of bread from the lump I had been given.

"Obstacle course." Posner picked up his bowl and drank from it like from a cup. When that was done, he licked his spoon and stuffed it away inside his gray shirt. "I saw him being carried away on a stretcher."

"Too bad." My mouth was too full to say anything else.

"Are you having fun?" Posner wiped out his bowl with a piece of bread, and when he drank his water, I heard his teeth clinking against the metal mug. He stood up, put his cap on, the gray ski cap we all had, with a cloth skull sewn on the front. He stood there picking his teeth, which were small. The milk teeth of a child, wedged into the tough skull of a boy whose father was a circus strong man. He waited for me to look up, but I didn't, and he left. When he turned around, I raised my head and watched him walk to the counters, put his bowl down, and go out into the courtyard for a cigarette, red-eared with frustration that I hadn't talked to him. I watched the moving piece of my town leave the hall, then sat at the table until it was empty and the cook told me to get the hell out. I looked down the table at the spilled salt and the water patches, splashes of soup, and one bowl left out at the far end.

"Come on, boy. Get out." The cook put his hands on his head and sighed.

I pushed my bowl across the table to him and still stared into space. "You get out, instead."

"Anything you say, little hero." He waddled away into the fog, and I sat staring until they turned the lights off.

I had not thought about anyone from my hometown. I had barely even thought of my family, and then when Posner, whom I had known for more than ten years, sat down in front of me, I had nothing to say. I realized, as I climbed the stairs to the dormitories with the others, that the only picture of home that came back to me was of my empty room and the dust that would be settling, the clock that would have stopped, the cuckoo sticking out as it did when the spring wound down, like the tongue of a dead animal.

I WATCHED von Schwerin, on the bed opposite mine, take out a silver cigarette case, open it by pressing a button where the two sides came together, and take out a cigarette. Before he lit the thing, he tapped it on the flat of the case.

He saw me watching and held out the open case for me to take one.

"I have some of my own. I was just looking at the case."

He snapped it shut and threw it to me. It was warm from being in his pocket. On the front there was a running devil engraved in the silver. On the back was "Lafayette Escadrille 1917."

"My father got it off an American pilot in the last war. He crashed right outside where my grandfather was quartered in a farmhouse. He got out of his plane, walked over to the window, tapped on it with that case, and then put up his hands to show he surrendered. It was the first thing my father saw, so he took it. Do you have a cigarette case?"

"The pack they come in is usually good enough for me." I

threw back the case, took the crushed gray-and-white pack of ration cigarettes from my boot where I had thrown it.

"I like my cigarettes a little squashed," I told him. Then I had a smoke and didn't talk to anyone for the rest of the evening.

THE BLACK and white of Voss's uniform became the black and white of my thinking. I lived through daydreams that went on for days, while the rest of me marched and stood and ran when it was told to.

WE HAD to crawl along a course under barbed wire, through a stream, across a patch of grass, through a trench. They wanted us to go through a hedge of stinging nettles. Already that day we had been made to walk across a ploughed field in open file; ten paces, drop, pretend to fire our rifles, stand, walk, drop. So we were covered with mud, cakes of it on our elbows and knees. We had thought it was over with the field work for the day and were sitting in a huddle trying to boil water over a pocket stove von Schwerin had with him. It clouded over and started to rain in fat drops on our heads, so we spread our capes across the group of us, and, by the light of cigarettes, watched bubbles rising off the bottom of the water pot as it heated.

Voss tore off the capes and kicked over the stove, said it was illegal equipment, and confiscated it. Then he told us about this new course we had to do before going back to the showers. He said we were going to have to crawl because people would be firing bullets at us at waist level. We moaned. He asked us if we all understood about the bullets. Moan. We were all told to shut up and assemble at the starting point. We moaned over to the waist-high piece of string where it was all going to begin. On our faces, Voss told us.

"How the hell are they going to know what waist level is from over there? How the hell are they going to know that?" Breder was hissing into the grass at the starting point.

The course was marked out with white rope.

Voss shouted to us from somewhere over by the guns that when they started firing, we should begin, and the last one to cross the line would have to do the course again.

"It's not going to be me." Handschumacher nudged his way to the front.

He slept in the bed next to mine, and he talked in his sleep. When the headlights of the trucks that were always coming and going at night shone through the dormitory as they came up the hill to the gates, I used to watch the red of his hair suddenly appear in the glare, then disappear again. When he was not talking to himself in the night, he talked to me, hours of whispering.

It was only when I was talking to Handschumacher that I thought of home. He lived on the Austrian-Swiss border near a place called St. Gallenkirch.

In the beginning, he liked to round off the talks by telling me something he thought I didn't know: a new piece of farm machinery his father was thinking of buying, the way to set snares outside a rabbit warren so that the rabbit would kill itself quickly and not ruin the pelt in the snare wires. He'd tell me this, then roll over and pretend that he was trying to sleep, as if he didn't have any more time for me who wasn't in the know. He couldn't keep this up for very long because he didn't have enough things to nail me with that I didn't know about. I just let him talk, and he liked me better that way, and he wore himself out, and I liked him better that way, too.

"It isn't going to be me who has to run this again." Handschumacher shuffled forward of the starting line.

"It *is* going to be you." Von Schwerin tried to drag him back by the feet, and they were about to have a fight when the guns started up. It sounded like someone cracking a whip above our heads, and I heard the bullets strike the brick wall of the gym building. I pressed my face into the dirt and didn't move. Then Breder began scratching at my feet, and I crawled after von Schwerin's boots.

When we were going along the trench, von Schwerin's heels cracking against my helmet, and the side of the trench caving in, leaves from the trees above flipped down onto us as they were shot off branches. The whip cracking merged into a stutter, and after a while my ears hurt from the sound.

I kept spitting. I couldn't swallow. Oh, shit. Oh, shit. Oh, shit.

There were tin cans attached to the barbed wire, and when the bullets struck them, they spun around and hummed. The bullets whined off somewhere else. Von Schwerin and Handschumacher were punching each other, swatting awkwardly because they both reached the bottleneck of the wire at the same time. Then von Schwerin was through and moving like a cockroach across the patch of grass toward the stream. Handschumacher moved after him a little more slowly and babbled.

"You stop, Schwerin! Come back here!"

Von Schwerin slithered through the stream and crossed the finish line, but the guns kept firing until all of us were through. It was a shallow stream, barely ankle-deep, and full of rocks that met at a sort of dam where we had to cross. The water was warm, frothing with the rain. When the guns stopped, we looked around for a while before standing up, then with our knees aching we hobbled back to the showers; all except Breder, who was last and was supposed to do the course again. But it was raining so much by then, dripping from the visor of Voss's cap in a ring of bright water, that Voss said to hell with everything and let him go.

As we walked back to the showers, an old truck without a canvas roof passed us, and sitting in the back of the truck were two soldiers with the machine gun that had been firing at us. They looked very old, and their eyes were sunk into their heads.

They were old from being used up and scared, the way I re-membered Stein. One of them was draped with bullet chains, half-shining, heavy brass, around his neck like some African tribal decoration. The other used his belt to hold the gun steady on its tripod. He held it as if the gun were a dog which would run away if he let go. The bullet man looked up at us and stared, but the other kept his eyes fixed on the gun.

It was warm rain. We took our helmets off, let drops fall into our eyes and mouths as we walked without talking, dragging our feet, past the gym, to the showers. In the few minutes of the walk, with the very soft touches of raindrops on my face, I was at peace.

THE SAME time next day we were under our capes again, boiling water with the new stove von Schwerin had bought in town. It was still raining. The capes were triangular and printed with camouflage done in green, dark green, brown, and dark red spots. The SS camouflage was different from the Army stuff. The Army capes had blotches of green and brown, done over with little stripes of green, like rain. The blotches had hard edges, not rounded like the SS. The Army stuff made you think of a crop field in the winter on a rainy day. The SS was more like trying to make out the shadows in a jungle clearing but not being able to. Shapes that seemed to make sense and be things at first, but then when you stared at them they drifted and obscured themselves. I spent a lot of time staring at the camouflage pat-terns on the cape, staring at the stitching and the tightly woven fabric, the pale metal buttons, the shapes that came and went in the blur of the colors.

There was a hole in the middle of the cape to poke your head through and buttons along the outside to join up with other capes and make a tent. We always just threw the capes over us and huddled like cavemen.

We boiled the water and then didn't know what to do with it because none of us had any coffee powder. It was enough that we had boiled it without Voss kicking our little home apart and confiscating von Schwerin's new stove.

Another group was getting the treatment of the obstacle course with real bullets. Their NCO yelled at them to keep their heads down, then, like Voss, he ran down to the machine gun, and with the sound of the bullets coming in, we all crouched closer together.

There were two boys behaving just like von Schwerin and Handschumacher, punching each other to be first out of the wire, the others hanging back and whining as the walls of the trench caved in on top of them. We saw the pale flecks of branches as the bullets cut them apart. Red dust from the smashed brick of the gym wall, which the bullets hit, drifted about in a cloud.

I watched from the head hole of my cape, my focus changing from the muddy figures getting muddier out on the course to the clean tears of rain beading on the edge of my cape and falling when they became too heavy.

The gun stopped. Down at the end of the course you could see the man with the bullet chains around his neck playing with the bolt to get rid of the jam.

The boys under the wire and those still in the trench raised their dirty faces to see what was going on. The boy at the front of the group jumped up and ran for the stream, laughing. He hurdled the stream, and when he was in the air, the gun went off again. The boy in the air did a backwards somersault, his arms waving out to the side, and landed in the stream.

In our canvas house there was a sudden intake of breath. The others on the course didn't seem to notice and kept crawling. When the next one got to the stream, he started shouting, and by then the gun had stopped, the NCO and two gunners were sprinting forward.

We dropped our capes and ran, jumping the white rope markers of the course, over the trench to the water, where the boy was lying on his face.

The NCO took the boy by the arms and dragged him up onto the bank. There was a hole punched into the front of the boy's helmet. His face was red, in lines streaked bright crimson over the dirt on his pale cheeks. There was also a hole in his chest. The NCO held him up by the shoulders, and the boy's head fell back. The man put his finger against the artery in the boy's neck. We stood around and watched. Somewhere over by the gym a bell was ringing. The NCO made a noise in his throat and dropped the boy. The body fell over and slid a little way head-first down toward the stream. The boy's hands just touched the water, and red came from his sleeves, pooling in the palms of his hands and running away through his fingers, fast. The red washed down the stream and frothed pink where it went over the rocks, like the bubbles of a cartoon thought.

BAD TÖLZ was like a castle. It was a castle, really, turned into a Camp. The walls were thick stone and the roofs made of heavy clay tiles. The buildings like the dormitory were new brick, but the main halls and the courtyard were old. Dull gray. The courtyard and the alleyways were cobblestoned, and often for punishment we had to pick out the moss that grew between the stones. Another punishment was running the steps between the main castle and the dormitories. There were three hundred stone steps, actually three hundred and twelve, and we ran them in our hobnailed boots until it seemed our calves would pop out of our legs. The next morning the runners felt as if their feet were pigeon claws, and they could barely walk. There was a well in the middle of the courtyard that had a little slate roof and from which only the people who graduated from Bad Tölz could drink. Voss sometimes wound the bucket up from the bottom, stuck his head in the water, then dropped the bucket down again, the rope spinning on its wheel. Then he would shake his head like a dog, stuff his cap back on, and think of something new to yell at us about. There was a rumor that the graduates dropped their daggers down the well before they left the Camp. The daggers were chrome and black, about the length from the elbow to the tip of a person's fingers. The blade had a point but no sharp edges, and engraved on it with acid was "My Honor Is Loyalty." Every graduate got one, along with a piece of paper supposedly signed by Himmler saying we had to give it back when we left the SS, never to draw it without reason or sheath it without honor. Something pompous like that. I imagined a pile of hundreds of daggers going rusty and covered with slime in the dark at the bottom of the well. I had never seen one of the daggers.

VON SCHWERIN used to wait in the shower room until we were all finished before he washed himself. He sat on the bench with a towel wrapped around his waist and a look on his face as if he were waiting for a bus. Then he folded his towel over the tiled wall the showers sprayed against and stood by himself, scrubbing his armpits with soap which he kept in a wooden tub, rather than use the honey-colored stuff that dripped from dispensers on the wall.

It was the same with the latrines. Nobody ever saw von Schwerin taking a dump. And when someone was taking a dump, you usually saw them because there were no doors on the cubicles. When we asked him about it, he said he was saving it up for the Big One.

And the few times I made it to breakfast early, he was always first in line. We had half an hour in which to eat. Handschumacher and I usually arrived in the last ten minutes and gave ourselves indigestion. But von Schwerin was there before the doors even opened. He brought newspapers with him to read. They weren't always new ones because no newspapers were delivered to Tölz on a daily basis. Sometimes people's parents sent newspapers from home, for local news. Once a month Handschumacher got the *Niedersachsen Dairy Report* from his uncle.

The only thing that arrived regularly was *Signal*, which was a picture magazine put out by the Army. It got dumped in the smoking room every Friday evening. Von Schwerin made sure he got that first too. He sat on the couch with its horsehair stuffing coming out, or at the piano with the magazine propped up on the lectern as if it were music he was reading.

He also brushed his teeth after breakfast and not before like the rest of us. There wasn't really time between eating and parade for us to brush them. So we would see him running up the stairs while the rest of us were on the way down, doing up our buttons, pausing on the levels between the stairs to polish our boots by rubbing the toes against the calf of the other leg.

All this made Handschumacher angry. He coughed loudly whenever von Schwerin passed him on the stairs going up. In the showers he would keep turning around to see von Schwerin looking into space and waiting for people to leave. Handschumacher never said anything. Not to anybody. But it was clear he was annoyed, because he never looked von Schwerin in the face. He took pleasure in staring the rest of us down when he got the chance.

Then one day when I went to wake Handschumacher up, I pulled back his sheets and he wasn't there. It didn't occur to me until after I'd pulled the sheets back that he'd be anywhere but under them, since we were always the last two out of the dormitory, and I was his alarm clock.

I figured out on the way downstairs that he had to be sick and was wondering if I had time to slip some food to him before parade since the nurses at the Sanatorium didn't give you any food that you could eat. Nothing on the walls. Just gloss white paint. Smell like preserving fluid and bleach. The undersides of the wooden food trays scratched with dozens of names and rude things about the sisters.

When I got to the Mensa, I saw him sitting opposite von Schwerin, as if the hall were full and he had nowhere else to sit. Von Schwerin was ignoring him, reading a paper and sipping ersatz coffee out of a tin mug. Handschumacher rattled his knife and fork, blew his nose, and laughed at private jokes being told in his head, but von Schwerin still ignored him. This lasted until the first of two bugle calls, five minutes apart, for parade. Von Schwerin folded away the paper, took his tray back to the trolley, and went upstairs. Handschumacher turned to watch him go, then went out red-eyed and pissed off to our rank formation on the parade ground.

Handschumacher stayed in the shower long after the rest of us had gone. He turned himself into a prune and rubbed off half the skin on his face with the acidic soap in the dispensers. He looked around once or twice to see von Schwerin sitting on the bench cutting his nails with a little brass clipper. Handschumacher stayed in until the hot water ran out and then left. Von Schwerin showered cold, but made sure he looked as if he were enjoying it.

Handschumacher stood outside the smoking room until the *Signal* showed up, then read the magazine, clicking his tongue at the articles and making such a noise that people poked their heads into the room to see what was going on. Von Schwerin never showed up.

Breder went to the bathroom in the middle of the night and stood in one of the cubicles, pajamas in a pile around his feet, taking a piss. When he was finished, he heard a rustling sound, looked around the corner of the cubicle, and saw Handschumacher in the one at the far end, head peeking around to see if maybe he had finally caught von Schwerin doing the Big One.

The next morning Handschumacher slammed his tray down on the table in front of von Schwerin, then took his coffee and threw it at von Schwerin's newspaper. The paper fell apart in von Schwerin's hands.

"Is it just me?" Handschumacher poked himself in the chest. "Just me you're trying to tick off with all this first-out-of-the-shower, first-to-read-the-magazine, fucking never-do-a-shit-like-everybody-else? Or is it everyone? Are you the Better-Than-SS-SS man?" Handschumacher had stopped poking his chest now and by the look of it had forgotten what else he had rehearsed to say. I was almost sure he had rehearsed it. Otherwise he wouldn't have been able to talk so fast and make that much sense. "*Don't* be fucking with me like this!" He mashed his fist onto his food tray, the blood crushed out of his fingers, leaving a tangle of pale skin and bones. "I didn't come here to have people like you try to get one up on me."

It seemed he might explode, blow himself apart in a detonation of red hair and food tray and uniform.

I thought there might be trouble, and I pushed my tray slightly away from me, noticing as I did twenty other boys doing the same thing.

"Why didn't you come out and say it in the first place, Handschumacher?" Von Schwerin let the mess of his soaked paper fall on the floor.

"Some things shouldn't have to be said is all."

"And why do you have to spend the last week dicking around when I would have told you from day one that you couldn't win at this dumb little game you've started?"

"Why's that?"

"Because you're transparent like a piece of toilet paper. As soon as I saw what you were doing, I had you figured out."

"All right, so I'm transparent. So after this I go home and milk cows and you go sit in your castle on the Rhine and play chess with your Noble-Nose friends. But you're still making fun of all of us with your little shit-kicking games. You're equal with me here. You don't get above me by doing what you're doing."

"I'm not trying to be better than you. You just think I'm trying. And because of that I *am* better than you. You can't even take care of yourself, so don't try to take care of me. Now have we gone far enough or did you have a fight lined up for us? Is that what you were really looking forward to?"

Handschumacher was staring at his plate. Von Schwerin got up and went away.

ONE DAY in every ten we had leave to go into Eschenbach, which was the nearest town. We walked in or caught rides on trucks, dressed in our gray uniforms, which I decided must be universally ugly to all girls, especially the ones in the town, after generations of cadets from Bad Tölz.

They did it so that only one or two sections got leave each day, so the bars were never crowded with the universal ugliness of gray, but there was always a steady flow of it. The first day we had free, I walked to Eschenbach with Breder and von Schwerin. It took almost an hour, and when we got close enough to see the church spire sticking up out of the trees, a car pulled up, and an officer shouted at us to polish our boots, which had gotten dusty as we walked the road. Buzzards floated over the fields looking for food. We could smell the earth in the breeze.

We stopped at the first place we came to, which was a café and candy shop called the Ortsburg. We sat at one of the wooden tables outside and waited for someone to come out and serve us. There was an old couple at the other table, sipping their drinks and staring into space. I heard a click, and when I looked across, I saw Breder cleaning his nails with a switchblade knife.

An old woman with a body like a tree trunk, vaguely dented in the middle by her apron string, came out and told us to fuck off because she didn't like SS soldiers. Von Schwerin told her to shut up and bring us something cold to drink. She went away and came back with a big broom with which she began to beat Breder on the head, thinking it was he who had been rude. So we left. We found out later that the place was called "Chubby Trudi's," and soldiers weren't welcome there and never had been. Not in the First War. Not now. Chubby Trudi beat every person in uniform who sat at her tables, with a witch broom meant for sweeping the hearth. Didn't matter about being SS. It was the uniform. She was like an old bull who charged when she saw field-gray, except she was an old bull who wore an apron and lived in a house with bright blue painted shutters.

At the town square they were having a rummage sale for the War Relief Fund, tables brought out from the church into the square and piled with old clothes. There was a table for food made by the Women's Church League, and we bought rolls with jam in them, sat on the church steps stuffing our faces. It was all overpriced, and the clothes were ratty. Most of the women selling what was on the tables looked too bored ever to bother having drinks with us. There was one girl whose blond hair had streaks of brown in it and wound around her neck over her shoulder, and she was very beautiful. We couldn't help but stare. I hadn't seen a girl in about two weeks, except if you counted the huge Annette who worked in the Camp kitchens, and she was barely human, which was to be nice about her.

I bet Breder he couldn't get the girl to have a drink with him, bet all the money I had, against his switchblade. He walked over to where she was selling raffle tickets for a pram and a baby's crib, his hobnailed boots scraping on the stone. He said something to her, his back all stiff, and bowed slightly. She looked at him, a flash of eyes in her face, then looked at us. We shook our heads madly and pointed at Breder. She smiled and Breder turned around to give us the Death Stare. She said something to him, and even though we were far away and she was whispering, we stretched our necks out to listen. Breder pulled out his wallet and gave her some money. She smiled and put her hand on his shoulder.

"Shit, I've lost the bet. I lost all my god-damned money." I clicked my heels together and jammed another roll in my mouth.

"Ha, ha," von Schwerin said very slowly.

Breder turned around, sharply on his heel, and walked back to us. He stood in front of us, and I groaned, let my head fall forward until I was looking at his boots. Then I felt something hard slide down my back inside my shirt, and it was the knife. I looked up and asked what happened.

"She said she'd only go out with me for a drink if I bought some raffle tickets. So I did."

"So you won the bet."

"She's only going to go out with me if I win the raffle, and I never win raffles, and anyway I'd be so embarrassed to win a baby's pram that I'd only cut my wrists with the knife, so you have it, Westland. Hell."

We walked away from the square, and all Breder could say was "Hell."

Wirtshaus "Der Namenloser." The bar was low-roofed and warm, with a breeze coming through the open stained-glass windows. It was all dark wood and polish. We sat in a booth, and when the barman came over, wiping his hands on a cloth, von Schwerin slapped his money on the table and said we were all going to get drunk as dogs.

"An SS man behaving like a dog. Well, now, there's a change for you." The barman went off and tapped us some beer.

"We shouldn't let him get away with that." Breder was chewing his thumbnail.

"So go fix his wagon." I poked him in the chest. The barman was huge, and he could say whatever he wanted, as far as I was concerned.

"Maybe if we all jumped him at the same time."

"He probably says that to everyone."

The barman put the beers down in front of us, and as his hairy arm slid past I saw his veins like blue shoelaces under cheesecloth.

Then there was a long time of beers coming and going and us coming and going to the bathroom, von Schwerin singing, and suddenly the whole bar singing, the barman loudest of all, drying the glasses behind the counter and stacking them up behind him. More beers; full, half-full, empty, with the foam splashed on the sides; full, half-full, and so on. Breder was talking about the possibility of our being sent west instead of east. Von Schwerin and I said no chance. Then von Schwerin talked about his home near Hannover, and said if he didn't make officer his family would probably disinherit him.

His father was a colonel in the SS, quit his job as a bank manager and joined with the first handful back in 1923. He left after the Night of the Long Knives, because he didn't think the SA should have been treated as badly as they were. But he came back once the war started.

"My mother tried to stop him, of course, and he'd already lost half his friends by joining in the first place, because they hadn't figured the SS was the service for anyone named 'von' anything. But he was worried about the whole nobility thing from the start. He never did see himself as noble when he was working for the bank. He thought to be named von Schwerin ought to mean something, said every generation ought to earn that for themselves. The SS seemed the right choice for him. Always had. He was going to raise his family out of this Middle Ground he always talked about, make it noble again. When Hitler started talking about the Knights of the Empire that would last a thousand years, my father talked his way back in. I don't think he cares who wins the war. He's doing all he can in the place he put himself. He doesn't want any more than that. My papa's a very reasonable man about things that make sense to him. Quite a lot of things don't make sense to him, though."

Von Schwerin ordered a piece of apple pie, which was under a glass dish on the drinks counter behind the bar. He ate it in two mouthfuls, while Breder and I watched, our mouths chewing the air.

"Pie!" said Breder in a loud voice, the word popping out of his mouth like a burp, when the barman came with more beer. He gave us the whole pie, told us to choke on it.

Von Schwerin dabbed the crumbs off the table with a wet finger and ate them. "For me not to join the SS would be like changing my name. My papa never even offered me a choice. He held a surprise party for me after I left school. You know, all my friends, a couple of girls. Then about halfway through I figure out what the real surprise is when he pulls out enlistment papers for the SS, made out so all I have to do is sign. Everybody's clapping. Mother leaves the room. There wasn't a whole lot of choice involved.

"My brother joined in '40, won a Knight's Cross by '41. There was a bunch of partisans in some town in the Ukraine, and they were holding up the advance. The forward group he was in only had a tank and no shells to fire it. He ordered everyone out of the tank, then got in himself and drove it straight into the house. The house collapsed on top of the tank. House caught fire. End of brother. Still, end of partisans, too.

"My other brother died at Kursk. I heard he was captured and hung from a telegraph pole with barbed wire. Do you know what his regiment did in reprisal? Have you any idea? Twelve hundred prisoners and a town. That's what they did. There's a town out there on the Steppes that doesn't have any people in it now because of what happened to my brother.

"That's good enough for my father. Honor is very important in my family. If there's anybody left at the end, we will be very honorable."

"You'll make it." Breder nodded.

"You think so?" Von Schwerin looked hopeful.

"I'm not wrong about those things." Then Breder said it made him thirsty, predicting the future, and besides he was a good Catholic boy who deserved another beer.

Von Schwerin said he was a good Catholic boy too, so he had beers coming as well. They looked at me and I had to admit I was no good Catholic, no good church boy at all. They both looked offended, and I told them it was because my grandfather, my father's father, came back from the Great War after he had been shot, patched up, shot again, gassed and stabbed and he sat at the table with his family down the sides and his wife at the other end, said either God was there and He was a bastard, or He wasn't there at all. There would be no more praying in his house, and no more church. No more rosaries, crosses, or hymns. So there wasn't, and that was that, and I had another beer.

"But it doesn't work like that." Breder's mouth hung open, and from the expression on his face, it looked as if he were going back in evolution and becoming an ape.

"But it did." Across the room a group of people had broken out laughing at a joke the barman told. There was sweat on his balding head.

"What happened after that?" Von Schwerin snapped his fingers and we got more beer.

"He went mad." I got up, went to the bathroom, and peed for a very long time. When I came back they still wanted to know how my grandfather went mad, so I told them about the time he was up from Munich visiting us when we heard the war had started. I was in a sandpit that my father had made for me behind the compost heap in the garden. Bees hummed over my head and landed on the flowers that Mother planted by the woodshed. I was playing with some lead soldiers. Grandfather sat in a deck chair in the middle of the garden, wearing a Panama hat, undershirt, and his gray trousers with the suspenders hanging down over the sides of the chair. He was smoking a cigar and making a ship out of matchsticks according to some plans he sent off for from Berlin and got in the mail. All around the chair were broken match heads. He sang to himself all the songs about the sea that he could think of. The air was heavy with heat and quiet, the only sound besides the singing, my gun noises from behind the compost heap.

Then my father burst out the back door, walked straight over to my grandfather, took the ship off his lap and smashed it. When I saw that, I was frightened almost shitless. My bowels cramped and I hid.

My father screamed for a while at the top of his voice about what a fat lot of good Grandfather's war had been, his callings to God and God sent to hell in his failing hour, a fat lot of good his generation was, who lived in their mud holes on the Somme. Because now there was another war. It was going to start all over again, and a fat lot of good it did us not praying all these years.

He went away into the house and slammed the door. I poked my head up from behind the compost heap and Grandfather had the ship in his arms, rocking it back and forth. His Panama was on the ground, upturned like half an eggshell.

"But I was right. It only goes to show I was right. Oh, my God! Oh, Jesus Christ, what a waste!"

He had walked me through the woods that morning, moving on his careful feet with his voice sounding like a drowning man's because of what the gas had done to him. People would turn and stare at us, after we walked past, to get a look at the man with the water-logged voice. He tried to tell me about the Somme, then forgot what he was talking about, and when I reminded him, he exploded with more trench stories, his walking stick cutting the air over my head as he made the gestures.

"Whole woods turned to matchsticks, Sebastian. Can you see it? Can you even see one tree that way, and the ground nothing but mud and craters? You should have seen it. Matchsticks. What was I talking about?"

By 1940 he had gone out of his mind. My father stopped thinking it was the end of the world. The Wehrmacht had just pushed the British back into the sea. The Poles were charging Panzer tanks on horseback, waving their cavalry swords. Through all this my grandfather refused to leave his house on the outskirts of Munich. He walked around his garden in the middle of the night watering the grass, watering the rocks and the pathways, watering my grandmother when she came out to see what was going on. He set pieces of paper in front of him, talked to them, then sent them away as letters.

Then in '41, we went to visit them for Easter dinner, he at the head of the table, Grandmother at the other end, and the rest of us spread out between them.

Grandfather looked up, put his fork down, squinted across at Grandma, and said, "Who the hell are you?"

He had forgotten who she was, and he never remembered.

You could get away with talking like a drowned man from the phosgene stuck in your lungs, and you could mail off blank pieces of paper, even water the concrete pathway of your garden, but you could not look across at the woman you had been married to for thirty years and ask her who the hell she was. He was sent to an asylum, he died in the place, and there was no God in my house.

"Well, now—" Breder and von Schwerin sat back in the wooden booth. "Better hope it doesn't run in the family, Westland." Von Schwerin was trying to snap his fingers and get more beer, but he couldn't.

"No, _you_ better hope so, Schwerin." I went away again and peed for hours, and when I came back, everybody was pointing at Breder and laughing. The floor looked as if it were breathing. I found a cigarette and slumped against the wall while a stream of people went past me into the bathroom.

Breder had won the raffle; a pram and a crib. They had both been delivered to the bar. People were on the floor laughing. Someone poured a pitcher of beer on Breder's head, then dragged him outside and dumped him in the pram.

Von Schwerin and I paid for the beer, which took almost all

our money. We went out into the street, and Breder was in the pram with his arms and legs hanging out the sides.

"I won."

"Well done, Breder." Von Schwerin sat down on the sidewalk.

"What are we going to do with this stuff?" I was looking around at the dark houses and the crib standing in the middle of the road.

"Voss!" Von Schwerin jumped up as we saw Voss, and ran back into the bar. I ran after him, and Breder flapped his arms, trying to get out of the pram, but couldn't.

In the bar I looked around at the smoke and spilled beer, people passed out or half passed out at the tables. Von Schwerin wiped the condensation off the window to see outside, but it was old glass, and cloudy, and he wasn't able to make anything out.

"He'll kill us." I looked for a place to hide.

"He'll kill Breder. I can't see a damn thing."

"I feel sick already, Schwerin."

"Don't you let me down now, Westland. You stay on your feet."

We went outside, and Breder was still in the pram, smoking a cigarette.

"What happened?"

"Nothing."

"Why not?"

"He was more drunk than me. He walked by on the other side of the road, anyway, and didn't see a thing."

Von Schwerin turned the pram around and we wheeled Breder home, taking turns because he was heavy and some of it was uphill. A couple of trucks passed us, but no one stopped. We could tell they were SS trucks because they drove with their lights off. Army trucks kept their lights on. A lot of times we took breaks and sat down by the side of the road, von Schwerin and I sitting back to back sharing cigarettes from his silver case.

"Look at the stars." Breder was still in the pram. We lay on our backs, and there were thousands of stars in the sky.

It was almost dawn by the time we made it to the big hill that led up to the Camp. Von Schwerin was trundling Breder along the road, and a wheel fell off the pram. It tipped over, put Breder in the ditch and von Schwerin on his face. The pram lay on its side with the wheels spinning.

Breder came up out of the ditch, slapping the dirt off his knees and elbows. "Wasn't the girl going to have a drink with me if I won the raffle? She was, you know."

"Too late now." Von Schwerin carried the pram out into a field and set it down.

It seemed like they had both forgotten about the bet and the knife, and I didn't remind them, because it was a good knife, and I had always wanted one like it. So I kept it and shut up.

There was pink in the sky when we walked through the black gates of the Camp, and as we got into bed, the others long since back and gone to sleep, the colors of sunrise were spread across the walls.

TWENTY PAIRS of dull eyes stared at Voss when he came out of the guard's hut.

My brains were grinding at my skull, which in turn was grinding at the sides of the steel helmet on my head. Our faces all sagged down onto our chins, and it was too bright. Even out on the assault course in the morning fog it was too bright. The sound of the stream was like marbles bouncing off a corrugated iron roof.

The guard's hut was at the edge of the field by the gym. It was only a wooden shed where the NCOs could go to get away from us, suck at the hip flasks of alcohol they all carried, and smoke in peace. Voss had been in there by himself for about twenty minutes, while we stood in two lines of ten, swaying gently and all of us sick.

Voss walked out of the hut and slammed the door. With the noise of the slamming, he flinched, and from that, we all knew he was sick, too. He stood where he was, looking at the ground, rubbing his temples. Then he took a cigarette out of his pocket, lit it with a small brass lighter and took a puff. When he looked up, he saw us all smiling at his beaten-up-from-the-night-before face, and the cigarette drooped in his mouth. His eyes opened wide.

He started yelling. Anything he could think of, walking fast over to us, clenching and unclenching his fists.

"Are you all here playing Titty-Fuck or something? Grinning like apes, are you? I got a funny face?" He pushed his nose close to Breder's and asked him if he thought his NCO had a funny face.

"No, Voss."

"Get on the ground and do push-ups!"

We twisted our wounded eyes around to see Breder lying on his face.

"One!" Voss stood with his hands on his hips, looking down at Breder. Breder did one push-up.

"More!"

"Can't, Voss. Feel terrible." Breder was propped up on his extended arms, fingers dug into the muddy grass.

"Do more, Breder, or there'll be trouble." Voss stuck his cap on his head and sighed at the low-hanging clouds. Breder went down but he didn't come back up. He lay with his face in the grass and his elbows in the air.

"For God's sake, Breder. Is this the way it's going to be every time you get leave? Which one of you was it I heard was wheeled home in a pram last night? My God!"

"That was me," Breder mumbled into the grass.

Voss decided he didn't like Handschumacher smiling the way he was. Made him do push-ups, too.

Handschumacher did all the ones Voss asked him for, so Voss told him to do more.

"Think you can take it, do you?"

"I know I can." Handschumacher rose and fell at the earth.

"Are you strong? Do you have what it takes?"

Handschumacher shouted forty and jumped up to face Voss. "I wouldn't be here if I didn't have what it takes."

Voss was not bug-eyed with sarcasm as I thought he would be. Instead he looked a little sad. "Do you want more, then? Can you take more?"

"I can take what you give me."

"Then on your face." Voss didn't let him do push-ups for long. After a while he set his boot on Handschumacher's head and rammed the boy's face into the ground. "I feel sorry for you, Handschumacher, because I could make you do this until it killed you, and you would let me."

Then Voss raised his hands to the sky and said for God to give him strength, swore at Breder again and shoved Handschumacher back into rank.

He led us out across the field and through a gap in the tall hedges until we came to an embankment on top of which were railroad tracks. Beyond that, ravens and magpies clustered in a plowed field.

We sat on the tracks, which were rusted. No train had been on them for a while. The sun came up from the clouds, burned away the fog. We lay on the ties and smoked, ate what food we had in our pockets. Von Schwerin had a jam roll from the day before. It had a few bits of fluff on it, but we ate the thing anyway—Breder, von Schwerin, and I—while the others sat around in their groups playing cards and talking. Voss pulled von Schwerin's confiscated stove from his satchel and squatted over it like an Arab, trying to boil water for powdered coffee, which he drank from the aluminum cup attached to his water bottle. He licked the rim of it before he drank because the metal was hot.

He didn't say a word to us. We stopped talking, too, after a while. We realized it was a gift from him, this place to sit for a morning and be calm. I didn't try to make sense of his whipping me with his riding crop, and there was no sense to make of this either. He gave it to us so we took it, and did not thank him.

IDEOLOGY CLASS.

We sat at desks with our backs straight and hands folded on the desk because that is what we had to do, and listened to an ugly little man named Herr Fleps talking very fast without making much sense about the *Nibelungenlied, Götz von Ber-lichingen, Faust, Emilia Galotti*, Mozart, Beethoven, Wagner, *Egmont*, Maria Theresa, Schiller, and *Siegfried*. All these people were German and had become part of Germany, never to be forgotten by the German People. We sat glazed-over in our seats and heard him talk about the necessary expansion of the German People and the mopping up of the Slavic Empire to create the great Living Space. It was necessary to suppress Bolshevism in order to secure the survival of Greater Germany and the Germanic People. The Russians were corrupt and badly organized. The Americans were corrupt and evil. The British were corrupt, evil, and badly organized, and so on, with all the bad things he could think of eventually being loaded onto the French.

"So why did Stalingrad fall?" Breder asked the man.

Herr Fleps replied as if he had known before what the question would be and had not needed time to think about it, that it was because of cowardice, weakness, and Foreign Nationals.

He made us look at a glass case that had blobs of wax in it. The blobs were molds of different noses, eyes, and ears. German noses, Jewish noses, Anglo-Saxon noses. He tapped on the glass with the ring on his finger and said he hoped we were aware of the racial barriers that separated our different cultures.

That night Breder and von Schwerin snuck into Fleps's classroom and, on von Schwerin's stove, they melted the pink wax noses and ears one by one into separate piles of mush, then set them back in their labeled piles and left.

It was easy to do this because there were no locks on any of the doors. There weren't even locks on our lockers, because it was taken for granted that no one would ever steal. The locks would have meant that they didn't really believe in what they preached, and the whole Camp was geared on believing.

"Be true to the bread of the fatherland and our people will live forever," Herr Fleps always said.

MANEUVERS.

They put us in trucks, with all our gear on, and drove us into the hills. I slept lying on Breder's stomach, Breder on von Schwerin's, von Schwerin on someone else's. I pulled the collar of my greatcoat up around my ears and looked for a while at the gray insides of the truck, the shafts of white light coming in from outside. There were never any seats on these trucks. Voss sat up front with the driver, whose name was Kaslaka, and they were both looking at a map, trying to figure out where to go.

I woke up when everybody was leaving the truck. I jumped out, and my knees gave way when I hit the ground. I fell in a puddle.

We were in the middle of nowhere, a dirt road going from no place to no place, pine forests thick on either side of us. It was raining.

"I want you all to get on your knees and pray it stops raining." Voss stood in the road, carrying two ammunition cans.

"Where are the other trucks?" I was rubbing my eyes to try to get them in focus.

"They're off at other ends of the training ground. You'll bump into them later on." Voss and Kaslaka walked into the woods, and we followed, pine branches brushing over our shoulders and making them wet. Kaslaka carried a machine gun. He was much taller than Voss, fitted badly into his uniform, and he was bald, shaved his head every morning the way some of us shaved our faces.

It was dark in the woods, and we moved past rotting piles of logs, smelling the live pine in the trees and the dead pine on the ground. There was almost no sound, except the wind blowing through the tops of the trees. I lit a cigarette, and Voss walked back, slapped it out of my mouth, and told me I would smoke when he told me I could.

When the pine became birches and patches of soggy ground, we stopped. Voss sat on a tree stump and looked at his map. Kaslaka leaned on the machine gun as if it were a crutch, pulled a biscuit out of his pocket and ate it, the crumbs falling off his chin onto his jacket.

"This is the place." Voss stood and pulled his trousers up, which made the trouser legs come untucked from his ankle boots, and the trouser legs flopped down into the mud. "Shit. I always do that."

"Why don't we camp over here?" Handschumacher pointed to a thicket, a mess of brambles and holly bushes.

"Too obvious. That's where they'd expect us to be."

"Well, then, Voss. If they *expect* us not to be there because we think they'd expect us to be there, then we should go there and surprise them."

"You are tremendously fucked up, Handschumacher."

We made hovels for ourselves with capes and branches twined together. I already knew how to do them because I'd seen the blinds the hunters made in the Kottonforst near home. We put mud on the ends of the broken branches so no one would see the breaks.

Voss posted guards, and we sat around with nothing to do.

Handschumacher went into his thicket to take a dump, then ran out, trailing a long sheet of toilet paper, and said there was a body in there.

"N o w w h o do you suppose that is?" Kaslaka stood over the bones and rotten clothing, hands on hips, squinting at Voss for the answer.

It was a German uniform the body was wearing, what was left of it. We could still make out the SS belt buckle. The helmet, filled with water and leaves, the liner turned to slime and the paint almost rusted off, was right beside the head. The dead man lay on his back, flattened almost completely by decomposition. The head had nothing left of it but bone, gone moldy and breaking apart. There was fungus growing on the forehead.

We found a rifle a couple of paces away, the mechanism rusted shut.

Voss bent down and rummaged around the chest, put his hands through the material of the tunic, exposing the ribs, and found the oval dog tag. He rubbed it on his knee to get rid of the dirt.

"F.R.P. 12SS. O. 143778." Then he looked up at Kaslaka. "There's no other way he got here but on a training exercise. This is our training ground. This man is Hitler Jugend Division. Look, he's wearing jackboots. He's got the old-style helmet on, the kind without the flared rim. The helmet's got two decals on it. Nowadays there's only one. He's been here at least two years, I'd say." Voss rocked on his haunches, sighed, and stood up again.

"Do we bury him?" Von Schwerin leaned forward over the dead man to get a better look.

Voss didn't seem to hear. He put his boot on the corpse's chest and pressed down until something cracked.

Kaslaka went down on his knees, put his thumb between the corpse's teeth and pulled the lower jaw down until it almost came off. "Two gold teeth."

"You leave that." Voss kicked Kaslaka's hand away. "We don't have to bury him, but we don't have to rob him either."

Kaslaka went away and peed against a tree, shrugging and muttering to himself, imitating what Voss said in a squeaky voice.

We stood staring at the body. Voss got angry.

"What? You want him buried?" He picked up the helmet, poured out the water into the skull's eye sockets, then set the helmet on what used to be the face. "There. Buried. Now leave the bastard in peace. And forget about what you saw. There might be a good reason he ended up here, and it's none of our business trying to figure out why. None of you saw this. This man isn't here. Got it?"

VOSS TAUGHT us to start fires with the bark from a white beech. He also taught us not to eat the rations as if they were civilized food or anything. He told us just to mix it all together in a mess tin, heat it over the fire, using a stick to hold the pot, and keep the lid on so ashes didn't get in.

We sat over the fire holding out our sticks, like a pack of trolls going fishing.

"YOU'RE TAKING up all the room, Breder." Von Schwerin pushed him over toward the edge of the hovel we had made.

"Don't be doing that to me now, Schwerin. I was just getting comfortable. Besides, if we stick close, we'll stay warm."

"You're one of those homosexual-type people, aren't you?"

"All right. Enough. Go stay in your own damn hovel."

"I will." Von Schwerin stood up, ripped his cape off the top of the shelter and walked off. The shelter collapsed on top of Breder and me so we had to rebuild it. Then we warmed our hands over von Schwerin's stove, which he had forgotten to take with him. We ate a bowl of meat, rice pudding, mashed biscuits, a tube of cheese, margarine, bits of bread, and some lemon candy. It wasn't bad after the candy melted.

Yelling and screaming and guns going off. We crawled out of the hovel, and the place was full of people wrestling on the ground, more guns firing and their bright flashes putting suns in our eyes. Everyone wore the same uniform so you couldn't tell who was who. Three boys were trying to drag von Schwerin away so Breder and I chased them. They dropped von Schwerin, and when we got back to our hovel it was pulled apart, trampled on, and someone had bent our spoons into pretzel shapes. More people ran past us, shooting. I fired at them with the blanks I had been given. Rifle jammed. I picked up a rotten branch and broke it over the head of the next person who ran past. Wood chips flew everywhere, and he fell on his face.

"Sebastian!" I looked up, and someone was waving to me from the edge of the pines. It was Posner.

"Hello, Pos. That was a good job you did on us." Then I was kicked over and booted in the thigh.

"What the hell do you think you're doing chatting with the enemy, Westland?" It was Voss. "Get after them!" I got up and he kicked me in the leg so I fell over again.

They were gone. We stood in our hovel place, and it was a wreck. We poked around in the smashed branches and torn capes, then rebuilt everything, and von Schwerin came back because he said he was freezing and would sooner sit here with us peasants than get dragged away again.

"Sons of bitches. I don't ever want to see that again! You have to watch out because this is going to go on all day." Voss chased us out of our hovels and made us dig trenches in the woods with our shovels. The ground was soft, and it didn't take long. Wait. We waited.

After an hour we saw a line of men coming through the woods, slowly, tapping their way like blind men.

A branch cracked somewhere in the dark, then there was whispering.

"Fire!" yelled Voss.

"Eh?" Breder poked his head up.

"Fire! I said fire!"

So we all fired, deafening ourselves, and afterwards ran to where the whispering had been. I could hear only a far-off ringing because Breder shot his gun off almost in my ear.

I ran smack into a tree and fell over, lay still for a few seconds, my eyes filled with tears and my nose bleeding. I sat up and tasted the blood, touched my fingers gently to my nose to see if it was broken. I walked after the rest, seeing dark shapes moving, the flashes of guns making me blind.

I came to a hovel and belly-flopped onto it, figuring that would do for a start before I shredded the thing. The hovel was built around a tree stump, and it hit me so hard there was no air left in my lungs. I stood, trying to breathe, and Handschumacher tackled me, said this was for tearing his cape back at his hovel, and punched me in the ear.

"Handschumacher!"

"Knowing my name isn't going to help you now." He punched me in the other ear. "Damn Bolshevik. Damn Yankee."

"For God's sake, Handschumacher! I'm on your side!"

"*What* are you doing, Handschugoddamnmacher?" Voss pulled him up by the collar and threw him away. "That's Westland. Can't you maybe do that to the enemy? You mental fucking pygmy. Get out of here!" He kicked him away into the dark. "Westland, what are you doing, letting yourself get beaten up by a pygmy?"

"I—"

"Well, get up." Someone ran out of the dark at Voss. Voss

stepped out of the way, pushed whoever it was over me while I was on my hands and knees trying to get up. The boy landed on his head and moaned. Voss pulled me up by the arm and told me to get lost.

When we got back to our hovels, we found they had been flattened again. It went on all night—colliding with trees in the dark, wrecking hovels, punching strangers, and running away again.

When the sun came up, Breder and von Schwerin laughed at me because I had two black eyes and a swollen nose. Handschumacher said he was sorry about hitting me, kept bringing over cups of coffee and apologizing. He poked his red-freckled face into our hovel and asked how we were doing. Von Schwerin put his hand over Handschumacher's mouth and gave him a shove. Suddenly Handschumacher was back in the hovel again, freckles spread across his face so that it was all red now.

"Don't you fucking push me, Schwerin. Don't you give me the excuse of doing what I should have done a while ago."

Von Schwerin stared at him, a look on his face as if he were sorry for the boy.

Handschumacher beat the earth once with his fist, looked at me, then beat the earth again. "I said I was sorry." He didn't come back after that.

WE ROLLED up our capes and walked back to the truck, Kaslaka still carrying the machine gun, which never got used, and carrying the ammunition cans as well.

The truck wouldn't start, so we sat in the ditch eating crackers. It was a bright morning. It felt like a Sunday.

"Do you know"—Breder was running his tongue over his chipped front tooth—"I didn't have a clue what was going on the whole time."

"That's the way it is." I blinked out of my black eyes.

"And how would you know, Westland?"

"How would he know?" Von Schwerin sat down next to me and put his arm around my shoulder. "Westland was a member of a gun crew that shot down a bomber over his home. Westland knows what's going on."

"Really?" Breder opened his mouth wide and had his going-back-in-time-to-becoming-an-ape face on again.

"Sure." Von Schwerin lit himself a cigarette.

"Excuse me, then. I take it back." Breder stood up and walked across the road to talk to someone else.

"What did you tell him that pile of rubbish for?" I unhitched von Schwerin's arm from around my shoulder and rummaged in my bread bag for a can of food.

"Just to bother him."

"Just to keep him on his toes." I stretched and yawned.

"That's it."

"But he was right." I opened a can of meat by jamming my Youth knife twice into the top to form a cross, then prising back the sides. The Youth knife was what we were given in the Hitler Jugend: a blade about as long as my palm, with a hook at the knuckle guard. There was a Hitler Jugend black and red diamond stuck in the handle. I found out, after I had brought it from home, that it was a sissy thing to use your Youth knife after you'd left the Hitler Jugend, but I didn't want to use Breder's switchblade in front of him in case he asked for it back, and I didn't have another knife.

"What was Breder right about?"

"That none of us knew what was going on."

"Well, like you said, Westland—that's the way it is."

"Tell me the truth. Didn't you think even once about what this would have been like if it was real?"

"It is real, Westland." Von Schwerin took a spoonful of the foul-looking meat from the can I had opened. You got used to its taste after a while. It was blotchy red with white bits.

"Not real war, though."

"True."

"We would all be dead by now."

"Several times over. And you'd have been polished off by Handschumacher." Von Schwerin rolled around, laughing.

"It's not funny."

"No, it's not funny." Von Schwerin was sitting up and not laughing now. The stubble on his face was like pinpricks on his chin and upper lip. "But there's nothing we can do about it, Westland. Your father found that out. My brothers found it out. Most of the time there isn't a damn thing you can do. You want to be a hero, Westland? One of the Knights of the Empire who will last a thousand years? There are no Knights and there isn't much left of the Empire. There's only us. *We* are all that's left."

"So what the hell are you doing here, Schwerin? Tell me." Breder sat down opposite us. Beyond him, Voss and Kaslaka were still playing with the engine and trying to get it to work.

"I'm here because I want to be, and as long as I do my job I don't have to explain a damn thing to anybody. Isn't that right, Sebastian?"

"Don't bring *me* into it." I was angry at von Schwerin for calling me by my first name only when he needed me.

"It's rubbish. You're here only because your father wants you here." Breder nodded and pursed his lips to show he thought he was right.

"What about you, then? Tell us why the People's Friend Breder is hiding out in the Waffen."

And Breder couldn't answer. He said something about wanting to serve his country, a bit about not wanting to shirk responsibility. But he probably couldn't remember why he joined. It was pissing me off; people always wanting concrete reasons for this and that, when there weren't always concrete reasons to give. Breder probably took one look at the enlistment poster that said, "Your Comrades Are Waiting for You in the Waffen

SS," and joined because he figured he needed a few Comrades.

The truck started. We climbed in and slept again, twined like cats, the sound of the changing gears moving through our bodies.

I STOOD in the smoking room with my hands resting on
the windowsill, looking out through the small, diamond-shaped
panes at the courtyard and the fields beyond it. The windowsill
was cold, and rain leaked through the lead framing of the panes,
down the glass, and onto my fingers.

Handschumacher had pulled the couch up next to the radio
and was listening to Hitler making one of his broadcasts. He
sat on the end of the couch with his head in his hands, sniffing
now and then.

Between Hitler talking and the announcer making com-
ments, you could hear the crowd screaming, *"Sieg Heil!"* A sea
of them. Screaming.

When the broadcast was over, Handschumacher sat back on
the couch.

I was watching a woman in a blue dress walk through the gates, strutting in her stiletto-heeled shoes and not minding the puddles, the arc of an umbrella over her body. She crossed the courtyard and went into the officers' barracks.

"You know, I listen hard to those speeches. I listen, and I get all fired up, and then when it's finished, I can't remember what the hell he said." Handschumacher took out a cigarette case, removed a cigarette from it, tapped the white stick on the hardness of the case, and put it in his mouth. "Got a match for me?"

"Since when did you start using a cigarette case?"

Handschumacher whipped the cigarette out of his mouth, then paused, looking at the spit-shine on his boots, and put the cigarette back in his mouth. "I've had it a while. Actually, I bought it last week." He weighed the case in his hands, as if he wished he'd never shown me the thing. "It stops them from getting crushed in my pocket." He started looking for a loose match.

"And since when did you tap the cigarette on the lid?" I threw him a box of matches.

After he had lit the cigarette, he stood up, set the case on the floor and stamped on it one time, crushing it into something useless. "Better now? Schwerin the only one allowed to have a cigarette case? Schwerin the only one allowed to tap his cigarettes? Better now?"

I sighed and put my hands in my pockets, thinking I should have gone into town with the others, even if it was raining. I told him I didn't mean to hurt his feelings, knowing as I said it that it wasn't true.

"Don't you worry about me, Westland. I don't have any feelings to hurt. I'll keep my fucking cigarettes in the pack from now on."

After he had stamped out and slammed the door, I sat at the piano, smelling the sweetness of the old books falling apart on the shelves, the sweat smell of the horsehair stuffing in the couch. Then I played "Chopsticks" a few times and fell asleep at the keyboard.

Voss walked into the dormitory and stood there looking at us. "I'm going to be with you longer than I thought."

"How's that, Voss?" Handschumacher pulled his knee out of Breder's chest, as he was strangling him on the floor.

"I've just been told I'm being sent out with you. The Camp's closing down."

"What does that mean?"

"It means they can't raise enough people to take your place when you're gone. I guess that's what it means."

"How did you get to be here anyway, Voss?"

Breder took advantage of Handschumacher's being so interested in Voss and crawled away under his bed. Handschumacher often sparred with Breder, but not with the rest of us. He never touched von Schwerin, because if he did it would be the beginning of a fight.

"How did I get here?" Voss shrugged as if he hadn't thought about it before. "I just got the order. We pulled back from Normandy to be refitted, and I just got the order to come down here."

"What were you doing in Normandy?"

"I was a recruit. Just like you. We went off to Normandy from Bad Tölz, got smashed to bits, and then we pulled back. Before that we were stationed near Paris. I went there once." He put his hands in his pockets and glared at us. "So what?"

"Just wanted to know." Handschumacher sat back against the iron frame of Breder's bed.

"Now you know."

"How bad did the Division get hit in Normandy?"

"Doesn't Herr Fleps tell you those things?"

"Fleps doesn't tell us anything." There was a general sound of rude noises about Fleps.

"The Division was formed in 1943, made up of Hitler Jugend people, mostly, and was sent to Russia. It had ninety percent casualties in the first six months. After that it was reformed and sent to Normandy, and in the first month of that campaign it lost seventy-five percent and almost all its equipment."

Kaslaka walked in smiling and said nothing.

"Which means"—Breder stood up—"that if we joined in '43, we'd be dead by now."

"Chances are."

"And chances are we'd be dead if we joined up last year, too."

"Right."

"So is there any reason we should expect anything better this time around?" Breder stood on his bed accusing Voss with a pointed finger.

"Wouldn't count on it, my child. Of course, you could be like Kaslaka and survive it all right from the beginning."

"Eh?" Kaslaka looked up from where he had been staring at his boots, hands in pockets.

"Just saying you've been around since '43."

"Oh, yes. I have." He nodded and pursed his lips. I realized then that this was the man with the bullet links wrapped around him from the time when we did the assault course and they shot at us.

"Kaslaka got lucky."

"You got lucky, too." I walked past Voss, without looking at him, on my way to the bathroom.

"Not as lucky as Kaslaka."

"What now, Voss?" We stood in a circle around him.

"Get in the game, children."

When I was in the bathroom, I put my face in a sink full of water. Stared at the plug hole. Percentages mean nothing, I figured, and thought of Kaslaka, and told myself I was right.

"Now is the time for heroes!" Herr Fleps smashed down on his desk the pointer he used to indicate places on the wall maps. "You must be prepared to meet the sacrifice. Without it the sacrifices of those who have gone before you will be worthless. Understand that there is something more important than your own lives. Understand the sacrifice."

Bell. End of class. We tramped down the steps into the courtyard and stood by the well, smoking cigarettes before dinner. Saying nothing. Nothing to say.

"WHY DON'T you tell us what it was like in Normandy, Voss?"

"What's the point, Handschumacher?" Fat clouds were riding overhead in the duck-egg blue sky.

"Just to know."

"You wouldn't understand. I could tell you a lot of things, but they wouldn't mean to you what they mean to me. A lot of things only make sense when they are going on. It was very green in Normandy, and it was hot, and there were a lot of apples on the trees. Is that enough about Normandy for you?"

"So if that's all there was, how come the seventy-five percent casualties?"

"Because that's not all there was, Handschumacher."

VON SCHWERIN woke me in the middle of the night and pulled me over to the window. Down in the courtyard there was someone hanging from the end of a rope at the main entrance gate. A couple of people were trying to cut him down. The head of the body hung down onto its shoulders, and it swung as they cut at the rope. When the body fell, it landed in a heap on the cobblestones, and the ones who had cut it down dragged it away by the feet out of sight. We watched for something else to happen but nothing did.

The next day the rope was gone, and no one said anything about it. There were no announcements, only a rumor about a boy called Gunther Braun who was called away sick the night before.

I ALMOST never got mail. Mother sent me a pair of socks. I got one letter from Benjamin, who wrote about going back and forth on the ferry from Bad Godesberg to Königswinter by himself, getting drunk with Stock at the café. His family had to hire people to wheel him around town or through the woods so he wouldn't go mad. Mostly they were old ladies, and he annoyed them so much they quit after a few days. He told me to remember the great times I was living in, then signed his name with a small *b*. That was all. And of course there was never a breath from Lise Hammacher. Of course.

BEHIND THE gym were burlap bags, held above the ground on metal frames and filled with blocks of wood. One day a week we had to stand twenty paces from the bag, bayonets fixed on our rifles, and run at the bag, screaming as loud as we could. We had to stick the bayonets into the bags, still screaming, and, screaming, pull the bayonets out to let the next person in line do his bit. Sometimes a bayonet caught in one of the wooden blocks and you couldn't get the blade out, and Voss beat you with his horsewhip until you either fell over or freed the blade. We tore our throats with screaming, and almost every day we could hear the sound of howling, as if from wolves, coming from behind the gym.

We called it "Butcher's Hour."

"Something to write home about," said Breder.

"Nonstop Action Cabaret," said von Schwerin.

THERE WERE more maneuvers, nights of crawling around in the woods in the fog, beating each other up, and from these we learned that, for all the training, when things began happening the way they would happen, fast and loud and breathless, we wouldn't know what was going on. It became clear to us—the randomness of pain, the great fragility of flesh. For all the learning and talismans there was only one absolute: that either we would fall or we would not fall. There wasn't a goddamned thing we could do about it.

AND THERE were more nights of standing at the edge of town in the dark, trying to get a ride back to Bad Tölz after spending the day and the night and all the money at the Namenloser. It was always Breder and von Schwerin and me. Sometimes we asked Handschumacher along, but he stayed by himself, and he knew we didn't really care whether he came or not. Sometimes the three of us had to walk the distance back, and by the time we arrived, we were sober. Other times we got on a truck, bounced on the metal floor back to Camp, and carried our drunkenness to bed. Then the next day, if Voss felt as bad as we did, we went out to the tracks and spent the morning staring into space.

THE TRAINING ended after thirteen weeks. There didn't seem to be any reason for its ending except that the thirteen weeks were up. I was comfortable now in the rough wool clothes and in hobnailed boots, and comfortable eating from our aluminum bowls, being yelled at and obeying. I didn't cramp anymore in my bowels when they screamed at me. I just went blank. The tattoo had faded from black to blue under my arm. My hair had grown out a little, been cut, grown out a little again. I had permanent windburn from so much time outside. I knew the timing of the Camp and its stench and when not to try to make sense of what was going on.

We were issued insignia: a white eagle on black cloth, which we sewed on the left arm; two collar patches, one plain black, the other with two white lightning bolts. We also got black shoulder boards with white piping. Each of us received a belt buckle with an eagle on it and stamped around the eagle was "My Honor Is Loyalty." They dressed us up in that and sent us home for a week. No celebrations.

I caught a ride to the station at six in the morning. The sky was gray and hanging down over the trees. At the station I bought some soup from a caldron on the platform, good soup with carrots and bits of meat stirred up from the bottom, served by a woman I fell in love with while I sat on my pack drinking the soup from my mess tin, watching her not watching me. The scraping of spoons in mess tins was almost the only sound. When the train came I fell out of love with the woman, and found a seat by the window. We went north.

The sun came up red over the fields.

IV

I TOLD myself I would be busy. There were a lot of little things to do and no time to think. Maybe there were even enough things so that I wouldn't have time to explain over and over what it was like at the Camp. Perhaps they would just catch the stench of the place in my clothes and my hair and not have to ask.

Late in the morning an old woman woke me up by shaking my knee, then held out a basket of rolls with hard-boiled eggs in them. I took one, paid her for it, and ate the thing while she was selling more rolls to others in the compartment. It was good, the yolk still soft and warm, the bread steaming when I broke it open. I bought four more and ate them one after the other, drinking from the brown felt-covered water bottle I held between my knees. The water was still cold from when I'd filled the bottle at the bathroom taps. The old woman sold all her rolls and got out at the next station, pulling a shawl over her head to shield herself from the wind as she walked toward the station house.

I looked out of the window for hours: fields, woods, towns, cities. I walked up and down the corridor outside the compartment, stepping over soldiers sleeping like tramps, rolled in their greatcoats. The place was full of smoke, the smell of food from ration cans, the smell of sweat. The bathroom was filthy. You pressed a button on the floor and everything dropped away onto the tracks.

EVERY TIME I woke, there was a different person sitting in front of me. I wanted another old woman to come around selling egg rolls. At some station we came to in the afternoon, I got out of the train and bought the first thing I saw, which was a loaf of black bread and some cheese in the station café. I rushed in and people turned around to stare. I saw the bread and cheese under a glass dome on the counter. It was dark in the café and drafty from the door being opened and closed.

"How much for the bread and the cheese?" I asked the woman behind the counter, her face divided by two splats of red lipstick and her breasts like melons.

"Fifty pfennigs a slice, with cheese."

"How much for all of it?"

"I don't know, dear. I guess about three marks." She put down the mugs of beer she was carrying.

I grabbed the bread and cheese, paid, and ran so as not to miss the train, then sat eating the yellow cheese and the dark bread, trying not to catch anyone's eye in case they asked me for some. I stuffed it all in my mouth and swallowed.

*   *   *

AN OLD man was slapping me on the arm with his fat hand. He wore a brown overcoat and a brown hat. His trousers were tied with a piece of string, the kind farmers use to tie their bales of hay. "Hey, what's it like at the front?" He sat back in his seat, folded his arms, one chin smiling beneath the other.

The others in the compartment looked at me now; a man and a woman with a little girl sitting between them, the farmer's wife, if he was a farmer and not just a man who tied his trousers with string, a man with a thin face and Himmler glasses, who might have been a plainclothes policeman. They were all looking, waiting to hear about the front.

So I said, "It's rough," and pretended to go back to sleep.

THE TRAIN filled up so much that it was hard to breathe. No one wanted the windows open. A woman asked if I would give her my seat because her legs were tired from standing, so I did. I stood in the aisle with the other soldiers, mostly men from the "GrossDeutschland" Division. We huddled in our greatcoats. Mine was already coming apart. The buttons were dull gray with a pebbly surface, and two had already fallen off. I kept moving to let the train guards pass, my arm hooked around my pack so no one would steal it. After a while I stood up and strapped myself with my belt to a holding bar by the door and hung there like a scarecrow.

I made a sign out of a piece of paper and pinned it to my chest with two safety pins from my field bandage. It said, "Please wake me at Cologne." Then I let my head fall forward and stared at the floor, muttering at fragments of daydreams that dragged back and forth in my head.

A nun woke me at Cologne. I got out and walked around the platforms, trying to find the next train to Bad Godesberg. The train didn't leave for an hour, and it was already almost midnight. I walked up from the station to the cathedral square and saw the spires of the great church holding up the sky. Then I sat like a bum on a bench in the square, hoping there wouldn't be an air raid, smoking one cigarette after another and flicking the butts onto the empty concrete in front of me.

I WALKED home from the Bad Godesberg station at three in the morning. The stationmaster was in his office behind the wire grill, his head back and his mouth open, fast asleep. No one in the streets, and no cars on the road up to Pech. Only the sound of my boots on the road.

The front door was locked when I got to my house, so I went back to the garden and lay down in the woodshed, next to the lawn mower. The place smelled of oil and old grass. It was warm enough, and there was a bit of light through the spider-web-laced window at the back.

"BUT YOU shouldn't have slept in the woodshed, dear! Goodness me!"

"Didn't want to wake you up." My back was stiff from lying on the floor. I sat at the kitchen table, holding my head in one hand and a mug of milk sweetened with honey in the other.

"Well, you should have told us you were coming back. I'd have tidied the room. It's all dusty now. Goodness me!" Mother shuffled around in her nightdress. She was taking a week off from the Air Defense, since she'd sprained her ankle the last time she crashed into a ditch.

Walther emptied my pack on the floor, dressed himself in my spare clothes, then ran upstairs to look at himself in the mirror.

"How long are you here for?"

"A week."

"Is that all? I thought perhaps the war was over. Ha, ha."

"Yes, that would be funny, wouldn't it?"

"Are you going to tell me all about it?"

"That can wait." I stood, stretched, and went upstairs. The bed was bare except for the mattress. The cuckoo clock had stopped. Dust. I dressed in some old clothes and came back downstairs with a handful of ration coupons that I was given before I left the Camp. Mother put them in a jam jar above the sink. Then, because I was uncomfortable in my old clothes, I went upstairs again and put the uniform back on. I wasn't used to the feeling of not having a belt around my middle and the pinch of the buckle when I bent over.

"I'm going into town for a while."

"But I'm just heating up more milk. Sit down for a minute. I see you've put your suit back on."

"I'll be back in a couple of hours."

"It's so nice to have you home."

I turned as I walked past the house to the bus stop and saw her standing by the window, the mug of hot milk in her hands. Her face was impossibly pale.

I GOT out at Bad Godesberg and stood for a while in the street with my hands in my pockets, in front of the shop where they used to roast coffee when there was coffee to roast. The smell of it used to spread across the road and stop people in their tracks. Always around four in the afternoon.

Eva Weiden lived in a side street near the town square. I'd tried to convince myself on the bus ride down that I was looking forward to this, but that was a lie.

I couldn't try to get away from the Camp. The more I tried, the more my mind slammed me back into the place.

I walked past Eva Weiden's house and into a café.

I sat at a table by the window and drank a cognac. A man came up with a red can collecting for the War Relief Fund, and before he reached the table I stared him down. He stared back for a while, then nodded and didn't ask for money.

Out in the street again, I bumped into Mr. Weiden.

"Oh, *there* you are. Eva was convinced you weren't coming. So how's everything?"

"Good, Mr. Weiden."

We stood there grinning at each other.

"Well, you go ahead and get inside. I'm just off to get a newspaper."

"WHAT'S WRONG with you?" She leaned across in her pretty clothes with her pretty face, put her hand on my knee and smiled.

I had been sitting with my spine rigid for maybe an hour, holding a teacup in my hand and talking to her parents while they sat on their couch nodding and agreeing. I couldn't remember what I said. I only remembered the repetition of the image of the boy somersaulting back into the stream. And every time the picture surfaced, I batted it back down again. They listened, filling the teacup now and then, and setting little cookies on a dish, which I balanced on my knee. They listened and stuck in little questions to make it easier for me to talk. Then finally they must have caught a smell of barrack blocks and sweat, oozing from my forehead and my armpits. They caught the rotten odor of it and instinctively got up and left.

When her parents were gone, she centered herself on the couch, comfortable, and the curve of her hips clear under her dress.

"Are you sure there's nothing wrong?"

"Nothing at all nothing's wrong I'm right as rain all clear just fine."

"Good." She sat back and crossed her legs and smiled. "So you've been having fun?"

"Fuck, yes."

"What was that for?"

It felt good to swear, the word riding up on my tongue like a black ball of caviar which I pressed to the roof of my mouth and crushed.

"So there is something wrong. I knew it." She shifted, as if she had just off-centered herself on the couch and were correcting the error.

"You look very pretty today." The words fell out of my mouth, one by one, like stones.

"Thank you. You look well too."

WE SAT in the park near the opera house where I had gone and talked to the drunk after my father died. I was wondering how Breder and von Schwerin would rate her, how they would rate her hips and her chest and her mouth. We had a bench to ourselves. It was sunny and even a bit warm, people walking their dogs, boys flying balsa wood gliders, and pigeons hammering their beaks into the ground looking for food.

"You didn't write to me."

"I know, Sebastian. I did write, but I kept tearing the letters up. I thought about you all the time."

"Thank you." The pigeons waddled across the path toward us.

"Do you want to walk around some more? I have some money. We could go to Königswinter."

"Maybe so."

"It's so nice to see you. Will you be back again soon?"

"Of course." Then for no reason I could think of afterwards, I pulled Breder's switchblade out of my pocket, hit the button on the side and the blade flew out. I stretched my arm back and threw the knife at one of the pigeons. It hit the bird in the side and nailed it to the grass. I got up and walked over to the dead animal, its wings spread, pulled the knife out of its smoke-purple body, and walked back to the bench.

She got up and left. I sat by myself on the bench doing nothing for a while. Then I lit a cigarette and had a smoke.

She came back after a couple of minutes and held her hand out for me to take, at the same time looking away. She led me like an infant into town.

"WERE YOU treated badly at Bad Tölz?"

It was a small table at the restaurant, and the place was full. It was a room full of glass and really meant for summertime when the light makes bright dust trails in the air onto the tables and the faces of the people eating.

"I suppose."

"What do you mean?" I could tell she was fed up and just wanted to be gone. Perhaps she was embarrassed that I was SS. I wanted her to stay, thinking things would shape up in a minute or two.

"One day a man hit me with a horsewhip."

"My God!"

"Your God."

"I want to know all about it, Sebastian. Does that bother you?" She held the tips of my fingers in her cold hands. "Does it bother you, I said." She tugged at my fingers. "I want to know."

"You don't really. You think you do, or maybe you think it would be nice if you did, but you don't. So let's not start that."

"I understand."

We ate the food and went back to her house, and when I said I was leaving now she said she had tickets to a concert and more food for a meal she was going to cook herself tonight. She had even persuaded her parents to leave. It would be all very jolly.

"Don't you want to spend time with me? We haven't seen each other for months."

"I'll come back tomorrow."

"What about the concert?" She raised her arms and let them

fall again to her sides. Her dress was gray, and she was wearing a red patent-leather belt.

I walked to her front door and sat down on the mat.

"Is it other girls? Have you been out with other girls?" She came over and knelt down next to me.

"Oh, for God's sake. What girls? There aren't any girls down there."

"You've been off with other girls. I can tell."

"Stop with the fortune-teller acting. I haven't been off with other girls, all right?" I pressed my hands against the sides of her face and kissed her forehead.

I stood up to go.

"The trouble with you is that you don't care about my feelings." She slammed the door to her house.

I sat in the bus going home and saw everything and thought everything in the field-gray of my uniform and the black-and-white of the Camp.

I missed the sound of other people breathing in the room, of Handschumacher getting pissed off in his sleep. I waited for the sound of the trucks, the headlights on the walls, and the rattle of the gates opening and closing. When none of that came, and the ticking of the cuckoo clock became too loud, I went down to the kitchen and found a bottle of plums in syrup on the windowsill above the sink. The plums were very cold and sweet, and I spat the pits onto the wooden table.

When I woke up, I was still at the table, the grain of the wood printed on my face, and Mother was sitting in front of the fireplace stirring the ashes. Through the window I saw my brother in the garden. He was wearing my helmet, which came down over his nose, and he was running headfirst into one of the trees over by the compost heap. He hit the tree, bounced back, the helmet fell off, and he sat on the ground, shaking his head. Then he put the helmet back on and ran at the tree again.

*　*　*

A BOY named Müller came by late in the morning delivering milk. He used to be in my Youth Group, and when we graduated he didn't have to sign up because he was in charge of a local farm.

We stood leaning against his milk truck while women came from their homes to buy milk with their ration coupons.

He was tall, like a stork, and had no chin. He spoke very carefully and when he talked, his hands moved in front of him like birds chained to his wrists.

"It's like there wasn't a war at all up at the farm." He tore a bunch of coupons out of a woman's ration book, gave her a bottle of milk, nodded thank you, and turned back to me. "But things have changed for you, haven't they?"

"A lot of new people. Good ones, mostly. A lot of changes. Yes."

"It's just me and the cows at home. And the family, of course." He looked around to see if anyone was coming for more milk. The back of his truck was loaded with wooden crates filled with white bottles. "Does it look like it will end soon?" He raised his stork eyebrows and looked down at me.

"Couldn't tell you."

"Never mind." He gave me a bottle of milk without charge, then drove home, because Nachtigallenweg, our street, was the last on his run, the closest to the woods.

The houses in Pech were made of gray stone with slate roofs. In the winter there was only stone and mud and white sky, but in summer there were flowers in the window boxes, and the moss on the slate was bright green.

I walked through the woods to Benjamin's house, drinking the milk fast, spilling it on my coat and feeling it run down the sides of my mouth. When the bottle was empty I threw it away, hearing the glass bounce and not break on the pine-needle floor.

* * *

I WHEELED him up to the high ground above the town, not far from Müller's farm. It was raining a little, so he held an umbrella over us, switching from arm to arm as he got tired. It was a place called the Onion Field, because wild onions and horseradish grew there, and sometimes the poor people came up from Bad Godesberg to gather food.

We went to the field because Benjamin said a plane had crashed there last weekend, and in a couple of days it was going to be hauled away for scrap.

There was a long time when we said nothing, as I shoved the chair up the hill past the skeleton hedges that bordered the road.

"It's an English plane. Got shot down or something. I heard over at the café that it had engine trouble. There's a policeman up there guarding it, but at least we'll get a look." He held the umbrella forward and put his head back into my stomach and looked up.

"Sure."

"We can go home if you want."

"No."

"I said if you wanted we could go home."

"I heard you."

"Shall I ask you how it was at Bad Tölz or do we forget it?"

"Forget it for now. Later, maybe."

"Right."

"How are your parents?"

"They're at a wedding."

I saw he had put on some weight and had bought some new clothes, these clothes not green like everything else he wore. Little rubber tires of fat fell out over his new brown trousers. He still dressed in black cripple's shoes because he never wore them out.

The plane looked very small from where we stood at the edge of the Onion Field. You could see where it had come in with its landing gear down, hit the field and broken off its wheels. Then it had skidded across the old grass and mud, propeller bent into an *L* shape, and stopped in a hollow with its nose pointing vaguely at the sky. The cockpit was covered with mud and bits of grass sprayed up by the propeller. Someone had put a rope around it, the rope held up with iron spikes, but there was no policeman.

"It's called a Hurricane, that kind of plane. It was flying escort to some bombers." Benjamin wheeled himself up to the edge of the field, and I stood holding the collar of my coat close to my neck and feeling the rain on my head.

"What happened to the pilot?"

"He was taken away in an ambulance. He had a fur coat on and fur-lined boots as well. That's what I heard."

"I thought you said there was a policeman on duty."

"Probably went home because of the weather."

"So let's go." I reached down and picked him up out of his chair and even with his fat rubber tires, he still weighed almost nothing. He put his arms around my neck and I carried him across the field to the plane.

"We had to come to a place like this every day, Benjamin. We walk, drop, shoot the guns, and by the time we arrive at the other end we look like a bunch of Zulus. We get classes telling us about the Supreme Sacrifice, and people telling us how the Division has already been wiped out twice since 1943. I sleep in a dormitory with twenty others. Same age. They come from all over the place. We have one day free in every ten. Then we just go and get soused. This time when we go back they fit us up and we move out. That's it. That's all of it."

He didn't say anything while I carried him. His legs, through the cloth of his trousers, felt like sticks.

The plane was painted brown and green and had two circles on each wing, blue and red. There were letters and another circle on the side. We stepped over the rope, and I set Benjamin down on the wing, which was made of thin aluminum. The tail end of the body was made of canvas, and it gave when I pushed my hand against it. There was water at the bottom of the hollow, and I fell into it as I climbed into the cockpit.

"Someone's going to catch us." Benjamin looked around and drummed his fingers on the wing.

It was a leather seat with straps all over it to hold the pilot in. Half the Perspex of the canopy was gone. I got into the seat, which was wet and soaked my trousers. All I could see through the window was mud. There were pedals that moved the rudders on the wings, and a joystick in front of the seat, with a red button on the side. I closed my hand around it, and suddenly there was noise all around and the plane shaking, a little cry from Benjamin as he fell off the wing and out of the plane. Into the sky, bright arcing lights of tracer bullets going up and coming down. The smell of cordite reached me and filled my lungs. I let go of the button and it stopped. There was still smoke coming from the wing guns as I ran with Benjamin on my shoulders, him covered with slime from the bottom of the hollow he fell into, back to the wheelchair and down the hill laughing before the police came and found out we'd shot up Müller's cows a couple of fields away.

STOCK WAS a little drunk when we got to the café in Königswinter. He was very loud when he saw us, telling the rest of his customers that we were National Heroes.

He sat around drinking with Benjamin for the afternoon, and showed us the trick he had learned from Benjamin, which was to flip a full glass of beer upside down without spilling the beer. By the end of the afternoon we were the only ones sitting outside. Everyone else had gone into the main part of the café because it was cold and raining. We held our beers in one hand and umbrellas in the other.

Nothing new. It was the same beer: Steffi Pils; the same half-drunk Stock, same ferryboat taking me and Benjamin across

the Rhine, but the summer gone now, the water black, a perpetual ache in my stomach from something miserable that rose
up in me and fell away again before I could tell what it was.

MOTHER CROSSED her hands and straightened her back.
It was the end of the dinner, and the kitchen smelled of food.
"We were thinking of renting out your room while you were
away."

"Who's we?" I looked at her through a glass of water.

"Me and her," Walther said, with two bits of bread plugged
in his ears.

"Be quiet, Walther. Well, anyway, what do you think?"

"Sounds delicious." Walther pulled the bread out of his ears
and ate it.

"Shut up, Walther." She popped him on the head.

"Maybe I'll be back sooner than you think." I took out a pack
of cigarettes and set them on the table. On top of that I set a
box of matches.

"When's soon, dear?"

"I don't know."

"I suppose they'll take Walther next."

"Suppose so, darling." Walther ducked for cover.

"Where on earth did you learn to talk like that, you dirty little boy?"

"Darling delicious." He ran away upstairs in his pajamas.

"Go ahead and get a lodger. I don't care."

"Good. Then I will. It's so nice to have you home."

"I HAD all these things I was going to get done." I looked
up blurry-eyed from staring at the floor.

"Like what?"

"I can't remember anymore." We were in Benjamin's room,
looking out the big window in front of his desk at his mother

hanging up the laundry on a line. "I thought I had hundreds of little jobs to do, and now I can't think of one."

"Can't have been that important."

"They were at the time."

Benjamin wheeled himself over to the fireplace in the corner of his room and struck at the fire with an iron poker, as if beating back something that was rising from the flames.

SHE AND I came back from the concert holding hands. She had managed to change the tickets, and since I hadn't thought she'd be able to do it, I'd said over the phone that I'd love to go to the concert if she could switch them.

She was singing.

The flimsy chairs in the concert hall creaked every time I crossed and uncrossed my legs. It was a chamber group, two men and a woman, in a place lit by candles. In the pauses between the music, everyone coughed and sneezed as if they were in a gas attack.

"You see, I knew you'd like it."

"Yes, indeed."

"You did like it, didn't you?"

"But of course. I said I would and I did. Loved it."

We were standing in the little tunnel that went under the railroad tracks. There were old posters stuck on the walls, rotting, things left over from the summer, recruiting posters.

"Sometimes you are so cold. Not now, though." She was wearing her red patent-leather belt again, and I remembered I had given it to her as a present before I left.

It was she who was cold, her hands like little river stones, which I held and breathed on to make them warm.

THE FIRST thing a person saw when he walked into the Weidens' house was a suit of armor. It had been in their family for three hundred years. It was iron and ugly, the helmet looking like a pot with a slit for the eyes cut in it. There were scrapes and chips in the arm plates from where swords had hacked at the knight, and in the leg there was the flower-shaped puncture of a morning star: a ball with spikes on it attached to a chain. In the breastplate was a dent, like a fingerprint in butter.

This dent was from when the suit was new, and I had heard several times from Mr. Weiden how the blacksmith had taken the breastplate from the cooling water, still hot from the anvil and the hammer, and shown it to the knight.

The knight had asked if the plate would stop a musket ball. The blacksmith said of course it would. He carried the breastplate out into the snow and set it against a tree. Then he loaded a musket and gave it to the knight, told him to go ahead and shoot.

The knight told the blacksmith to put the breastplate on. There were things to consider, the blacksmith had said; the shock, the range. The knight told the man to put the plate on or he would shoot him without it.

From the shot, which blew the blacksmith over backwards but did not kill him, came the fingerprint-in-butter dent, and from the three centuries past, which turned Mr. Weiden's ancestor and the blacksmith to dust, came the armor, on which Eva hung her coat as she walked in the door.

Her parents had gone to bed, left us bread and margarine and two half-dried apples from their cellar at the foot of the stairs.

She went up to her room and ran a bath while I sat on the stairs and ate the food. She whispered to me from the top of the stairs to come up, so I went, swallowing the bread and killing the apples in a couple of bites.

She was still humming the music from the concert when she shut the door to her room, kicked her shoes under the bed, then turned to me and, with a movement so slight it was barely a movement, she shrugged her dress off into a pile of bright silk on the floor. Then she took off her underpants and her watch and there was nothing else to take off.

She told me to strip, walked into the bathroom, shut the faucets off, and lay down in the million soap bubbles frothed up in the bath.

It was very hot in the room, and I could feel my ears blushing as well as the rest of me, and I stripped without speaking, waiting for Mr. Weiden to kick open the door and find me wearing only my shorts and trousers and shirt, then only a shirt, and finally nothing at all to hide behind in front of Mr. Weiden.

She raised her red-painted nails from the bubbles and waved at me. "Are you coming or are you going to wait and stand there until my father comes in?"

I sank into the bubbles so that they flowed onto the floor. "Christ, do you think your father will come?"

"I don't know." She was giggling. "Maybe."

"Do you think they're asleep?"

"Ohhh." She grabbed a handful of bubbles and set them on my head. "I guess."

We stayed in the bath until the water was cold. The walls ran with condensation, and it was very late. Then she wrapped herself in a blue towel and put a white towel on her head, sat on her bed staring out the window into the dark.

I dried myself, then dressed, still feeling the imprints of the hot and cold taps on my back, and as I dressed, I felt the miserable thing rise up in me the way it had when I was crossing the Rhine with Benjamin. It rose up and I shoved it down again.

I saw her back as she dressed, the dimples of water soaking into her shirt. "So." She did not turn to me. "You're leaving now, are you?"

"Yes. I have to."

She handed me my coat, still wearing only her shirt. "And of course it's stupid to ask when I'll see you again."

"If I knew, I'd tell you." We were whispering more than talking. The last sounds of the bath water being sucked down the drain made us speak louder.

"And this number you've given me is all I have to use to get a letter to you?" She folded her arms and rocked slightly on her hips.

I wrote down the code again on the blotter on her desk.

"Brush my hair." She held out a brush.

I tried, but I didn't know how, and after a while she said very quietly, "Gently. Don't pull so hard."

"Trying."

"I'm just keeping you. You should go."

I stood at the door, and there was no more to say. When I hugged her good-bye, I breathed in the smell of her shirt and her hair and wondered if I could keep it for long.

Still numb from the quiet, I walked downstairs, trying not to make the wood creak. I heard her door shut.

I passed the living room, the fire fading in the fireplace. When I reached the front door I suddenly turned again and looked back into the living room. There was a hand, holding a wineglass, sticking out from behind the high-backed upholstered chair.

Mr. Weiden turned slowly, the wine stirring against the sides of the glass, and in the light it seemed his cheeks were hollowed out, his eyes only sockets.

"Be careful, wherever you go, Sebastian."

"I'M LEAVING tomorrow, Benjamin." I looked up from the table where we were playing Skat at the café in Königswinter. Stock was playing, too. Whenever anyone wanted more beer, they just threw something at him to get his attention. There was no other café I knew where people put up with so much from the waiter and stayed outside even in winter.

"They might call me up after all." Stock set his cards down and leaned back.

"Oh, yes? What for?" Benjamin paused for a long time as he drank his beer, then my beer, and finally reached over and tipped Stock's beer down his throat. "The Bird Watcher Corps?" Then he laughed very loud because he liked his joke.

"The Volksturm. The People's Army. They said they might take me."

"They're a bunch of idiots." I lit a cigarette.

"Who you calling a bunch of idiots?" A man walked up behind me and shouted in my ear. He was obviously a bit too old to sign up and must have been in the Volksturm, which were the Home Guard units made up of infants and old men equipped with First War guns or pitchforks or anything they could find. "Who you calling an idiot?"

"You, you fat side of beef. I was calling you an idiot. You personally." I had had a few beers. "Now go sit down and behave yourself."

The man put his hands on his hips, and I was thinking, oh, please go sit down. Please. Please. I didn't mean it. Then Benjamin wheeled back his chair and smiled.

"He's Gestapo, man. You're talking to the Gestapo." Benjamin kept smiling. The man walked back to his table, turned his chair away from us, and talked to his friends.

"Do you think that's the end of it?" I leaned across to Benjamin.

"Suppose so." He shrugged and laughed.

"I don't know how you think these things up."

"We should have a reunion." Stock took one of my cigarettes and lit it with a match which he struck on the buckle of his watchstrap.

So we made the time for one year from the day, toasted with our empty beer glasses, shook hands, and left. Stock waved goodbye to us from the ferry landing as we went across the river.

"You needn't worry about surviving, Sebastian. You have what it takes. Now is the time for heroes. We're all going to live forever."

We stood at the bow of the ferry, and the spray from the waves splashed against our faces.

"You'll come back with a trunkload of medals, and me—one of these days I'll just get up and walk."

"D o y o u have any use for this?" Benjamin's father came up from the basement holding a stick grenade. It was a hollow piece of wood about the length of a man's forearm. At the bottom was a screw cap and at the top a cylinder the size of a condensed milk can. This one was bigger than the ones we were given to practice with at Camp, standing behind a brick wall, and throwing them at specially dug foxholes. Unscrew the cap, unwind the waxed cord inside until you find the porcelain ball tied at the end, pull the ball and the string out, count two (one Amerika, two Amerika) and throw it so the thing cartwheels, then get down on your knees and hold your balls. Forget about your ears, because the explosion makes a vacuum and if the bomb goes off close by, you feel it in your balls more than in your ears.

"I've had it since the First War. Want it?"

"I'm sure they'll give me some of my own."

"I feel like throwing it at the neighbors sometimes." He stood in the doorway with goose bumps on his arms because he was wearing only his undershirt, trousers sagging at the waist, and suspenders hanging down the backs of his knees.

I gave Benjamin a hug, shook his father's sweaty hand, and the man was still shouting to me to take the stick because it was of no use to him as I walked off with my hands in my pockets.

I sat all night in a chair in front of my bedroom window, quietly singing marching songs, other songs, and nursery rhymes, and it seemed as if every color and taste and smell went through my head in a slow procession, never linking up to form something I could make sense of, never stopping, held back from driving me mad only by the songs I muttered to myself.

I s t o o d on the first metal step of the train, an Air Force boy jamming his pack in my face from the second step, and someone else leaning into me from behind. The smell of the train clogged up the air. Pretty soon the hobnails on my boots were going to slip and I'd fall back onto the platform.

I turned around, and Mother's face kept appearing and disappearing over the shoulders of the next boy in line. She waved and smiled, turned away, then turned back with her hands balled into fists and held to her cheeks. Rain fell from the roof of the train onto my neck, plipped on my helmet.

A train guard in a blue uniform shoved past me, and the Fly Boy used it as an excuse to hit me with his pack again, the greasy mess tin strapped on the side brushing against my cheek.

"Watch it with your pack, will you?"

The boy looked around, smiled, and turned away again.

All along the platform whistles were blowing. The train jolted, then stopped. People were crying behind me. Something tugged at my coat, and when I looked down, I saw it was Walther. He had squirmed through the line with a handful of money, which he put in my pocket.

"What's this for, Walther?"

He raised his face, and I shielded him from the jostle of people.

"Mother says it's for you on your trip." He hung onto my belt with his pink hands and blinked when the rain fell in his eyes.

"You tell Mother to keep it. I don't need it." I put the ball of notes into his shirt pocket.

"But you could buy me a present." In the little *O* of his open mouth, I could see his disappointment and the plan he had figured out: that I could spend the money on presents for him. So I took a bill, not looking to see what it was worth, and gave it to him.

"Tell her I took that much. All right?"

"Yes."

"When was the last time you combed your hair?"

"The last time Mother made me."

"It must have been a while ago."

"No, but me and some of the guys at school put paper glue in our hair so it would stick up straight and we'd be like Red Indians. Mother says you're going to get killed."

"Rubbish."

"She says she knows. She says she's seen it in a dream."

"Damn rubbish. Tell her Dad will take care of me. What are you going to tell her?"

"Dad will take care of you."

"Do you think he will?"

"Don't see how he can since he's dead."

The train jolted again. More whistles blew. The wailing on the platform rose, sobbing, and faded.

"You still going to buy me a present?"

The Air Force boy leaned back and rubbed his mess tin in my face, so I shoved him and he fell.

"I said one more fucking time, Air Boy, and there'd be trouble."

"I didn't hear you." He tried to stand up from the dirty floor, but people were treading on the tails of his greatcoat.

"Well, I said it, so you can stop leaning back on me."

"Fucking lousy-tempered SS idiot." He stood up, tore his coat, and shoved someone else.

"Passengers only now! Everyone else off!" the conductor in the blue uniform yelled in my ear. "You a passenger?" He looked at Walther.

"Nope."

"Well, off then. The train's going."

A woman half walked, half fell past us, makeup smeared down her face, crying. Everyone was crying or shouting.

"See you, Walther."

"See you."

"You're the chief now."

"See you, Sebastian." He unhooked himself from my belt and disappeared. I stepped into the train and heard Mother calling to me as the carriage jolted a third time and moved off.

"Sebastian! Sebastian! Bastiaaaan!" There were so many others shouting. The thunder of the engine cut them out. The door slammed, and there was only the noise of the train.

I saw the crowd on the platform go by, their arms outstretched toward the train, and as it speeded up, they became blurs. The platform vanished into brambles, the dirty sides of houses, and finally fields, plowed and rained on.

I took two paces down the aisle past the compartments, then someone grabbed me by the arm and pulled. It was dark inside. The door shut and it was darker. Lise Hammacher. She was wearing a raincoat and beneath that a dark red dress. Her hair was covered with a head scarf. Her hands pressed against the sides of my face. She took the helmet off my head and dropped it onto one of the empty seats. I moved my shoulders back, and the rucksack slid onto the floor. No words. Barely a sound except the hammer of the wheels on the tracks and passengers coming and going beyond the pulled-down blinds of the compartment. The motion of the train on my bare back coming up through the floor, her hair in my face and the strange shapes of the luggage racks, flecks of light coming in from outside but mostly the dark and quiet except for breathing, the distance from home measured on the muscles in my back, struck and shuddered by the motion of the train. The time of the train stopping and the platform turned into a place of wailing people, clunk-

ing in the halls, whistles and cold arms pressed against the door,
cold from air through the crack between the door and the floor,
cold air gone and the hammering back in my muscles and always her face very close, smell of perfume from her and canvas
and leather from my pack on the seat. Her mouth coming close
and light from her eyes when she raised her head, head going
back, stretching until the line of her throat barely stopped at
her chin, head twisting sideways, tendons in my neck racked
down across my back with the hammer of the distance moving
through the pebbles of my spine. Another station, slamming of
doors, and a woman carried past, screaming that her baby was
too young to go away; more doors slamming, the heat from her
arm hooked around my neck to raise it from the floor, the jolt
of the moving train, and it seemed to me then—love is still possible. The sounding of the engine's whistle and love is still
possible, faces moving in front of my closed eyes. I focused on
them, they disappeared, and her head went back again. She
breathed in all my air, breathed it back into me until I was dizzy
and my head twisted back, barely a sound, and love is still possible, and she knotted her fingers around my throat, bit at my
neck until blood came out. I couldn't feel anything, only taste
the metal tang of my own blood in her mouth. Another stop.
Raining outside. Why so many people crying? Why her crying,
eyelashes flipping angry tears at me, down here on the floor,
talking, her head going back again, the line of her throat a clear
plane up into the dark, and with all these people crying how is
it that love is still possible? Her eyes closed tight, squeezed out
the tears. Hands on my throat. Blood smudged on the side of
her mouth and bare shoulders, and she turned her head away
from me and cried. And love is not possible. Only the body
around me matters, and I will feed it and keep it and make it
work for me. It will always be this way. I will take the train and
leave and maybe someday I will see her waiting for another train,
but the good I thought was in me and in her is gone. Already

the memory of this is old. She smiled down at me, and her face was frozen blue in night.

"I HAVE to go."

"Go where? How long did I sleep?"

"You slept an hour or so. I slept, too."

"How did you manage to be on the train?"

"Your mother told me when you were leaving. I got this compartment for us. I had to bribe the conductor, and if there wasn't a war on, I could have arranged it for a damn sight less than it cost me now. He let me have this key for locking it from the inside." She held up a shiny *T*-shaped piece of metal with a square opening at the end. "I am leaving Bad Godesberg."

"Where? Tell me where so I can come and find you."

"I doubt you'll be able to do that." She stood up, put her dress on, and sat down to brush her hair.

"Don't say you doubt it." I buttoned my shirt.

"But I do. Do you want me to lie?"

"Where are you going?"

"Munich. I was up in Bad Godesberg selling the house."

"Why?"

"My husband and I are moving."

The train was slowing down. The conductor walked down the aisle tapping the glass and saying, "Munich."

"Will you at least write to me?" I put on my jacket and buttoned it up.

"If I can. I have to go now."

"You could stay."

"I have to meet my husband. Perhaps you could stay on the train and make things easy for me."

The train squealed and stopped. I could hear the station announcer's voice echoing in the glass and metal dome over the Munich station. The train doors opened, and I heard hundreds of voices. She took her suitcase off the rack, put on her gloves and her raincoat, and unlocked the compartment door.

"Be good, Sebastian."

"I'll be great. Please stay . . ."

"You know I can't." She kissed me on the forehead, then on the cheek. Then she left. I sat for a minute in the compartment staring straight ahead, then suddenly pulled on my coat, grabbed my pack, and ran outside.

It was bright from the station lights, and the place was crowded. There was no way to move. I saw dozens of splashes of khaki color that could have been her raincoat. I fell back against the filthy side of the train. An officer walked past and told me to button my coat. The faces in front of me were like pink cat licks. Hundreds of them, and the echo of their voices pounded my head. I got back on the train, and already the compartment was half full. It was eleven thirty at night.

I sat where my pack had been and watched the others unraveling bundles of bread and sausage to eat. I stared at the floor where I had been and where their feet were now. My eyes stung from the smoke. Some recruits came in who were going to Bad Tölz. We didn't speak, but it was good that they were there. We got out on the platform at Bad Tölz as the sun was rising.

CROSS-COUNTRY RUN. Every recruit in the Camp had to go. No excuses. Voss said we had become weak during our leave. He said we had gone back to our mothers' breasts. Now it was time to wipe the milk off our faces and get back to work.

"Very poetic," Breder said as we were leaving the dormitory, Voss checking our names off on a notepad at the door. For saying what he said, Voss kicked Breder down the stairs and made him run without boots. Twelve kilometers.

The rest of us wore undershirts, trousers, and boots. We stood at the main gate, slapping the goose bumps off our arms and huddling like cattle.

"Breder's all upset about something." Von Schwerin held on to the bars of the gate and rocked on his heels. "I rode back on

the train with him yesterday. Girl trouble." He rolled his eyes.
"I had enough trouble of my own."

"Like what?" I put my hands in my pockets and jumped up
and down on the spot to keep warm.

"I broke up with my girl friend just before I came to Bad Tölz.
We weren't getting along anyway. Her parents are Protestant
and mine are Catholic. Now I go back and she's gone and gotten married to a friend of mine. What do you think of that?"

"Don't know."

"Well, neither do I. Boom. Married. Won't even speak to me
anymore."

"Why not?"

"She wasn't speaking to me for a while before that. It was a
funny thing, Westland. I thought it was all over. Dead Beast,
and so on." Von Schwerin's face was pink from the cold, the
straightness of his thinking clear in the features of his face. He
took it very well and sportsmanlike that he would never be the
officer his parents demanded him to be. He never talked about
it except to joke, and only when he was drunk did it show that
he was angry. He controlled his manners and his anger with
the precision of his thinking. I looked at him, and all I could
think of was a clock that wouldn't run down. He had the Order
of the Camp already in him when he arrived.

"So I was at the club playing cards . . ."

"What club?"

"Oh, a club my father belongs to and where I go sometimes
to calm down. Anyway, playing cards and suddenly she walks
in through the revolving doors. Big thing at the club: revolving
doors. And no girls at the club. Goodness me, no. She walks
in past the old farts reading their newspapers and smoking.
You have to know this place. Ancient. All dark wood and felt-
covered tables, Oriental carpets and lamps with green shades.
I'm sitting at a table with three of my friends: Charlottenburg,
Zell, and Reichenhall. We all look up at the same time. Zell
drops his cards."

"Is she pretty?" I was leaning against the bars and staring up at the sky. So cold.

"Oh, she's beautiful, Westland. Anyway, she says she can't make dinner tonight. We were going to have dinner. I asked why and she said something had come up, so I sort of frowned and repeated what she said. As much as to say what the hell are you talking about? Then she just turned around and left."

There was the sound of an engine, and we saw it was Voss on a motorcycle, one of the huge Zundapps, painted gray. He was wearing a brown leather coat over his tunic, and he had on yellow-tinted goggles.

"If anybody falls behind I'm going to run them over," he yelled at us, and then his mouth twitched. That was one of his smiles. It was about all the jolliness you could get out of Voss. The gates opened, and we ran out, down the hill, trying not to trip each other up, Voss gunning his engine behind.

"So she left. Then what?" We were both in the middle of the pack.

"We started playing cards again, and five minutes later she came back in, past the doorman, past the old farts, and she wants to know how I could possibly dare cancel a dinner date with her. This time all three of us looked up and just gaped at her. It was she who canceled it, for God's sake. Not me. She sits down on a chair and stares at us."

"Strange."

"Serious."

"You're lying, Schwerin." We were at the bottom of the hill where it leveled out onto the plain. My throat was raw, and my lungs felt jammed with steel wool.

"I don't lie. I never lie. She just sat there, and when I asked her what she was doing, she said she could sit there if she wanted to. Actually, you can't, I told her. Would you mind leaving us alone and we'll have lunch or something? But no, she sits there and doesn't do anything. So we ignored her. Did a good job. Eventually she got up and started writing me a letter on a piece

of the club stationery. Scribble, scribble." Von Schwerin drew
scribbles in the air. "She stuffed it in front of me and stood with
her arms crossed waiting for me to read it. I didn't get a chance
to see what she'd written on it because she asked for it back
again. And I told her no. Told her . . . I believe I told her I'd see
her in hell. She picked up a chair and smashed it on the table,
and they dragged her out like a blithering idiot. Next thing I
know she's gone and gotten married to another one of my friends.
One of my not-honorable friends. He's on the Russian front.
German justice."

"Wonder what's wrong with Breder, then."

"Girl trouble. Has to be."

THERE WERE the stumps of wheat stalks in the field, and
Breder cut his feet up running on them barefoot. Voss rode behind and kicked him when he stumbled.

"Get up! I knew you were pathetic." He rode circles around
Breder, whose face was crushed from the hurt.

"I'm doing the best I can, Voss."

"Which isn't good enough." When Breder fell again, Voss
gunned exhaust in his face until he stood up. "I've treated you
well, Breder, and this is how you repay me?"

"You've treated me like shit." Breder's legs were splattered
with mud, and his hair was soggy with sweat. His head was the
wrong shape for the haircuts they gave us, shaved at the back
and sides with a little left to grow on top. He had a long face
and sad eyes, and in him there was no precision. His arms and
legs and his head all didn't fit together. By themselves they were
fine but not together. One piece didn't match the other. He was
no compact radical like Voss.

Voss rode circles around Breder and sprayed him with mud.
Some of us up ahead stopped and turned to watch, sweat dripping out of us like rain.

Eventually Breder just sat down and held onto his feet, rocked back and forth moaning. Von Schwerin and I walked over and picked him up. His feet were bloody, and his lips were bleeding from where he had bitten them.

"Leave him alone!" Voss sat on his machine with the engine idling as we held Breder up.

"We're just protecting you from him, Voss." Von Schwerin shifted Breder's weight.

"Me from him?" Voss lifted the goggles onto his forehead, which left pink welts from the pressure.

"We're just holding him back so you can get away before he loses his temper."

Then Voss laughed a little bit, the sound like a small animal choking, and drove off after the others. We took Breder back to the road, each gave him one of our shoes, then walked him up the hill to the Camp. Out in the field we saw the pram we had won, still upside down where Breder had thrown it. Breder didn't talk, and after telling him all the jokes we knew, most of which we had gotten from him, we stopped talking too. The guard let us in through the gate and we took Breder to Plem-Plem in his hole under the stairs, the place reeking of disinfectant and tobacco.

Plem-Plem sat him on a stool outside the hole, Breder with his head hanging down and hands gripping his knees. Plem-Plem fetched a bottle of some tar-colored liquid and said it would hurt, as he unscrewed the cap. He bent over Breder's feet. Plem-Plem's ears were like clam shells sticking out from his old man's hair. And it did hurt, because we heard Breder screaming as we walked across the parade ground to the showers.

It was good we were back first because there was hot water. Usually it ran out, suddenly from hot to cold so fast it felt like an electric shock. While von Schwerin and I were standing under the showers, Breder hobbled in, his feet stained the dark color of the disinfectant. Still he wasn't talking.

Von Schwerin got annoyed and left. I was enjoying the shower too much to leave, so Breder and I stood under the hot water saying nothing.

"I HEAR you got girl troubles." No point being quiet forever.

"Where'd you hear that, Westland?" He left the shower, wrapped a towel around his face and shook his head like a dog to dry his hair.

"Just heard."

"From who?" He leaned against the tile wall and slid down to the floor. I could see the cuts in his feet, the white slits in the flesh and trickles of blood still coming out.

"You got girl troubles or not? You've been acting rather dull lately."

"Well"—he pressed his palms together and looked up—"shame on me."

"Oh, all right. Hell." I got up off the bench where I'd been sitting, my knees pulled up to my chin and the heat from the shower steam stinging the sweat on my face.

"Have you thought, Sebastian"—he was on his knees with his hands on his hips—"about the chances of winning this war?"

"I thought you had girl troubles. Schwerin. . . ." I picked at my nails.

"You still listen to him?"

"So you don't have . . . ?"

"Not at all." He led me to his pile of clothes in the changing room and fished in his pocket until he found a map of Europe drawn on a piece of tracing paper. On the map he had drawn the Axis-Allied borders in '39, then '42, and then now. He shoved it in my face and asked me where I thought we stood. He got dressed while I looked at the map, and while he was pulling on his boots, I set the map on fire. I held it, burning, until the flame got to my fingers and then let it go. It was nothing when it hit the floor. Breder shrugged, put on his coat, and walked past me, slammed the changing room door so hard that paint chips flew off the wall. After a minute he opened the door again and hissed, "I made copies!"

I walked out into the courtyard after him. "So Schwerin and I stuck our necks out for that? No girl pregnant or run off with something else? We dragged you back here like a baby because of some fucking map you drew? It won't change anything, that piece of artwork."

He stopped and stood where he was, looking at the ground, a fine rain falling, freezing out the shower's heat.

"Last time I do a god-damned thing for you, Breder."

The rest of the runners were moving up the hill toward the Camp, like a flock of seagulls in their white vests.

Breder kept walking. I wished I had known when to leave off, as von Schwerin knew, and let Breder keep his maps and his ripped feet and his girl troubles if he had any.

A MAN arrived in a black car. He was a high officer with a black leather coat that had a red lining. There was a lot of saluting and heels smashed together and the man disappeared into the officers' barracks. Voss said it was Ramke, and Ramke was in charge of all of us. His showing up meant we would be leaving soon.

That evening Ramke was at the officers' table. The rest of the officers were there, too. Sometimes he raised his head and looked around, but it wasn't the kind of looking that saw anything. They made a lot of noise and drank beer from pottery mugs.

Ramke put me off my dinner, so I went out with Handschumacher to the courtyard. We sat by the well, smoking until it was time to go upstairs, briefly seeing Ramke and the others move across the yard to the barracks, leaving the smell of good tobacco and cognac in the air.

THE STORY OF RAMKE AS TOLD BY VOSS: There is no horror Ramke hasn't seen. There is no doubt in Ramke's mind about the Victory. Ramke is a professor of Sacrifice. He has sent more people up the line to die than he can remember. He is aware of Pain. There is nothing you can tell Ramke about Suffering that he does not know himself. War is only logic to Ramke. His blood cells are Swastikas and roll along his Autobahn veins to his great Teutonic heart. Ramke has been frozen and baked, beaten up, fucked up, trodden on, shot, stabbed, blown up, killed, and come back to life. He has sat in his bunker, knee deep in water in the Russian swamps near Lake Ladoga, polishing his boots while the bombs were falling outside. Ramke is acquainted with Grief.

All this Voss told us after he had drunk the beer left over at the officers' table, kicking open the door at three in the morning, the shadow of Kaslaka behind him, and telling us he had been at Thermopylae, Carthage, Troy, the sacking of Rome, the burning of the gates of Moscow by Napoleon, Waterloo, Verdun, Cambrai, and the Somme. He had been at Katyn Wood, Stalingrad, Tobruk, Normandy. Then he sat down in the corner under the coatrack and passed out. Kaslaka dragged him away by the feet.

WE WERE made to carry thousands of sheets of paper, in stacks tied with string, to a fire at the bottom of the steps and burn them. Then we walked back up, coughing from the smoke, as others came down carrying more papers. Black ash drifted up and scattered over everything.

We were told to pack our trunks, which would be sent home. There was a small list of things we were allowed to take with us. We had almost nothing anyway. Most of the trunks went home empty, except for Breder's, which he filled with rocks.

MAIL. Mother wrote to say she could see the bombers going overhead to hit Cologne by day and she could hear the ones that came over in the night. The Americans came in the day and the RAF at night. A couple of them had crashed into the hills by Königswinter. Stock joined the Volksgrenadiers. Was I getting enough to eat? And so on and so on.

Mail for almost everyone, as if it had been kept from us until the last minute. Von Schwerin's father wrote to him saying to make the best of it even if he wasn't an officer. Breder's cousin wrote from somewhere in Poland. The mess was indescribable, he said. There was no way to tell how it was. A couple of things had been cut out by the censor.

Plem-Plem wondered out loud what was going to happen to him when the Camp closed down. He tottered along the halls in the evening, wheeling the coffee trolley, talking to himself.

"WHEN ARE you going to figure out that we can't win?" Breder pulled out one of his copies of the map I had burned and showed it to von Schwerin. "These are the borders. This is where we really stand. Now tell me if you have any real hope. Westland here is just an arse-hole, but seems to me you've got some brains."

Von Schwerin stood up from my bed, where we had all been sitting, and walked to the other side of the room. It was a Friday night, and we had leave but didn't go into town because it was cold, we had no money, and it was raining. Everyone else went for a last binge at the Namenloser.

"You value yourself too much, Breder. I don't want to get killed any more than you do or Westland does, but there isn't a thing you can do about it unless you know some trick. You and I and poor old arse-hole Westland are in the middle of a country trying to build an Empire. If we keep fighting we'll win in the end."

"Enough talk." Breder raised his hands and showed us the pale white of his palms.

Von Schwerin had gone a little red, and he kept running his fingers through his hair to help himself think. "Why enough talk, Breder? Do you see I'm right?"

"You aren't right. You can't win simply by willing it to happen. I see now you're as ignorant as Westland. You think you need vengeance on anybody you can call an enemy to make up for your brothers' deaths. But what you really want is revenge on Germany, for sending them out to get killed in the first place. You want there to be nothing left. You're just waiting for the right time to die." Then there was no more talk because von Schwerin hit Breder on the side of the head and knocked him over the next bed onto the floor. He lay there for a while looking at the ceiling. Then some blood which was very dark came out from under the back of his head and ran across the floorboards until it reached a crack and dripped down into the dust between the boards. We picked him up and carried him to the sink, washed the cut, which he had gotten when he hit the corner of the bed rail. It wasn't a bad cut, but the blood soaked his back. Breder sat blinking for a few seconds, then got up and walked out of the dormitory, gently pushing von Schwerin away when he went to help.

Outside, rain was trampling on the cobblestones.

I sat on the windowsill with the lights out, alone in the room since von Schwerin had followed Breder to the Sanatorium or wherever he went. I smoked one cigarette after the other. From somewhere came the sound of a flute. I opened the window, and over the sound of the rain and through the veils of it I could see Kaslaka in the other dormitory block, playing the flute on a stone balcony that overlooked the courtyard. He was wearing a cape that shone like the skin of a snake, his bald head shone, and the flute was shining too.

In the light from the room beyond the balcony, his bald head was a skull. I could see nothing more than the dome of bone. The music of the flute was made more distant by the rain, slow music, and a strange quietness to come from him who had seen everything from the beginning, and stood blushing in front of us when Voss reminded him of it. But now with the man's head gone and the skull in its place, I saw he had always been that way, and Voss too, with his constant rage, the ugliness of his skull only vaguely hidden by a cap. The glimmer of the Death's-head, the way Stein's was and my father's must have been, and soon ours too, with no way to hide it, all of us merged into the one rank of the Sacrificed. It wouldn't matter if we were alive or not, because we would all be the same, the ugliness clear if you could see it and smell it.

"H E ' S G O T some stitches. I'm going to get punished." Von Schwerin sat up on the windowsill, and we both listened to Kaslaka until he got bored and went inside.

"Did they ask Breder who'd done it?"

"Yes."

"And what did he say?"

"Said he fell over."

"So what makes you think you'll get punished?"

"Because then they asked me and I told them the truth."

"You could have gotten away without saying it."

"No, I couldn't."

"Well, at least you've got brains. I'm just an arse-hole."

"So says Breder."

"We should have bonked Breder before all this started, or got him drunk or something. It only makes me nervous."

"And you know why it does that, Sebastian? Because he's right."

"Let's not start that." I went over and lay on my bed.

"Why not? Are you truly that much of an arse-hole that you think we can win the war not only by force of will but also by not talking about it?"

"What'd you hit him for, then?" I put my face in the pillow and breathed the smell of the linen.

"The bit about my brothers, I guess." The last thing I heard before I fell asleep was the sound of him cracking his knuckles.

THE LIGHTS were out. Everybody was back from town. The place smelled of cigarettes and beer. Von Schwerin was laughing, and Handschumacher was dancing with an imaginary person on his bed.

"She was quite pretty after about ten beers."

"How could you tell then if you were so drunk?" Von Schwerin was still on the windowsill.

Handschumacher kissed the air between his outstretched arms. "I could tell because she didn't say anything stupid. But her name was Hildebronn."

"No!"

"Yes, and already it's the beginning of the end. She's so pretty that if you only saw a little bit of her you'd still fall in love."

"What little piece? Ah, ha!" Von Schwerin had to stop himself from falling out the window.

"Like her upper lip, the way it curves up slightly, and her nose . . ."

"Only one piece!"

Handschumacher had crawled under his mattress. "The upper lip! I could marry it, fuck it, have kids with it and live with it forever!" He tipped himself and the mattress onto the floor.

"He's marrying a lip!" von Schwerin shouted down into the courtyard.

"I'm going to be so sick tomorrow. Possibly before tomorrow. Quite soon perhaps."

"Did you dance well?"

"We got thrown out of the Namenloser." He tried to put the mattress back on the bed but set it crossways, then fell on top of it and lay there because he didn't have the strength to do anything else.

The lights of a truck came and went in overlapping, oblong disks across the ceiling. Handschumacher's hair showed orange, then gold, then black as the lights caught it. The scraping of the gates as they closed. I thought for a second that I could have guessed the thoughts of each person in the room and been right.

"THERE'S GOING to be a ceremony tonight."

We were doing the obstacle course again, before breakfast, almost everyone ill from the night before. I was level with Handschumacher, him smoking a cigarette, as we crawled without enthusiasm under the barbed wire with the tin cans attached.

"What ceremony?"

"The one for us going away. This is when they give us the daggers and stuff. Ramke's going to be there. Good food. Bound to be."

"Food's not so bad usually."

"Well, maybe it's just that your mother can't cook."

We crawled across the open patch of grass toward the stream. Voss and Kaslaka were standing on the other side laughing about something. Kaslaka had rolled up the sleeves of his tunic, and I could see a line of purple scars across both his forearms.

We got to the stream and ran through it. Then Voss threw us back into it and told us to crawl. I landed spread eagle on my back in the stream and froze. After everybody had been thrown in, he made us stand in the foggy air in a line, water dripping off the ends of our fingers and our knuckles like marbles under the skin.

"It's all over, children." He walked away from us, then turned back, grinding his heels in the mud. "War's over. Ended this morning."

Kaslaka stood with his arms folded, looking the other way.

"You can all go home now." Voss spread his arms. "You can all piss off and go home and take a holiday."

"What are you talking about?" Breder's hair stuck out like the leaves of a clipped palm tree from the bandage the Sanatorium had put on him.

"It's over." Voss shrugged.

"Well, who surrendered?" Von Schwerin stepped forward.

"Back in line!"

"I want to know who surrendered." Von Schwerin stepped back.

"General Armistice. Now you can all go away. Home to your mothers." Then he went over to the NCOs' hut with its plank walls and tarpaper roof, and he and Kaslaka disappeared inside.

It was a strange feeling, this knowledge of the end of war, and Breder talked like a madman, showed everyone his map, flipping it in my face and calling me an arse-hole again. He danced in front of us as we walked back, frozen, to the showers, and he said he was buying everybody drinks. He told von Schwerin what an arse-hole he was to think it would go on like this. Senseless. Senseless.

And next to the gym where the dust from the bullet chips was still a pink paste on the ground, we put Breder against the wall, all of us. We kicked him and punched him and kneed him in the face when he went down on his knees, and we left him, because it had become suddenly clear to all of us except Breder that it was one of Voss's jokes. The strange feeling of the end had seeped out of all of us except Breder, where it had stayed, making him dance like an idiot. Heavy-bellied with the feeling that he knew he was right, he pushed it at us and we waited, all of us, for him to calm down and realize it wasn't over, and that Voss and Kaslaka were laughing at us like trolls from their hut. But our quiet made him louder, dance faster as the shadow of the gym wall came close. And then there had been enough waiting, we dragged him to the wall, beat him against it, and left. Because he had become the enemy. Because these things must be carried in silence.

After the showers we went to the Mensa for breakfast, took off our muddy boots, set them on a long radiator pipe that ran just above the floor. Voss took his boots off, walked past us, without smiling or speaking, to the caldron of porridge, and sat with Kaslaka at another table.

Handschumacher covered his face with his hands, as if he were trying to hide his freckles. "Did you hear what Breder said?" he mumbled out of his hands.

"He didn't say anything." Von Schwerin finished his porridge and went back for more.

But he had said something. He said: "Please, please, my friends," as if he couldn't believe it was we who were hurting him.

Von Schwerin and I left the Mensa, found Voss's boots on the radiator pipe, and pissed in them for a present. We didn't bother with Kaslaka's, and we didn't think he'd have noticed anyway.

ALL DAY from the kitchens there was the smell of food, the bitterness of wine being boiled down to make sauce, potatoes roasting. The cooks sold slabs of meat basted with horseradish on thick slices of bread. It was a bad deal because the meat cost two marks a piece, but there was nothing else to spend it on, and they weren't stingy, even took the meat back and cooked it some more if you asked them to. Then an officer named Heydt found out about it and stormed through the kitchens, threatening to punish everyone. We scattered back to the dormitories and the empty smoking room, heard him shouting, far down in the courtyard, that heads would roll.

HEYDT RAN about with a checkboard marking things off. Now and then he stopped, took off his cap, pressed his forearm to his face to wipe off the sweat, then stuck his cap on again. It was made of gray material with a black brim, white piping on the crown, aluminum skull on the band, and a small eagle above it. The cap spring, used to keep the shape of the hat's crown, had been taken out and the sides flopped down around his ears.

WE WERE put to work carrying a piano from the smoking room on the second floor down to the courtyard where it was going to be loaded into a truck. We got it out onto the landing and stood around trying to figure out the best way to move it downstairs. While we were doing that, Handschumacher leaned on the keyboard and the whole piano slid across the first step down the stairs and out through the bay window at the next level. Strange and airborne, it glided somersaulting onto the parade ground, where it smashed to pieces in a spasm of snapping wires and struck notes.

When we got to the window, Heydt was staring up at us, his head tipped to one side, the fingers of one hand pressed against his lips.

Breder came back in the afternoon from the Sanatorium and said the doctors couldn't figure out why he kept falling downstairs. He had a new bandage on his head, a black eye, chipped tooth, and bruised ribs. He sat with us in the smoking room on packing crates filled with books, and made jokes as if he really had fallen down the stairs, believing maybe somewhere inside him that it wasn't I who picked him up by the collar, and von Schwerin who punched his face, or Handschumacher back-handing him so that spit flew out of his mouth and his head smacked against the wall. After a while we were all making jokes about it.

Other sections were being made to carry more boxes down to the fire. They were the records of everyone who had ever been at the Camp, all the money spent and everyone involved with the Camp. Each boy who carried a box down managed to read some of the stuff on the way, and from that we put it together what the papers were. The smoke was the size of a rain cloud above our heads. Voss wasn't around. We had no work to do. Probably no one trusted us with anything except paper carrying after we sent the piano out the window.

We went up on the roof through the attic and stood with our feet braced on the gutter, leaning back on the red tiles and looking out across the countryside. There was a cold breeze that smelled of pine and wet earth. The church bell clanged in the town. Even with the breeze, the tiles were warm from the sun. Von Schwerin pulled out a piece of meat that he had stuffed in his pocket when he heard Heydt on the warpath. He threw it down and bounced it off someone's head.

"GENTLEMEN. GENTLEMEN." Ramke stood up, wavered, then banged his beer mug on the table to get our attention.

This business of getting drunk. I was silly in the face from the beer, wine, and breaths of cigarettes that got sent down the line and threatened, while the smoke stayed in my lungs, to pass me out through a black wall and leave me unconscious the way Posner was at the opposite table, his legs on the bench and his head on the floor.

I wiped my plate with brown bread still hot from the ovens, through the red wine and mushroom gravy that was poured over the broiled chicken and roast potatoes, served to us in small portions and eaten too fast, beer blowing bubbles in my stomach, coming back up my throat, followed by the stagger to the bathroom, the piss that lasted for years, focusing and unfocusing on the tile wall, staring for a few seconds at the dead-looking face in the mirror, the good feeling and more beer possible to drink now, who ate my roast potato Handschumacher you mental pygmy more beer the bubbles brothers of other bubbles finding the road to my stomach and my head turned to gibberish by Pilsner and Beaujolais what did Ramke say is it him moving or the whole of Bad Tölz spinning like a top?

The windows dribbled with condensation from the heat inside and the cold outside. The paintings of generals on the walls had moved to the edges of their frames in their bright uniforms to peek down on the tangle of uniforms and cooks trundling between the tables. The roof beams crossed and uncrossed themselves in the dust of cigarette smoke rising from the floor. Every time I looked up, my brain almost sliding out of my head like sand off a plate, the beams seemed to be in different places.

Couldn't remember the beginning of the meal. Couldn't remember a damned thing except I kept having to get up and pee and sometimes we were all singing, sometimes talking to ourselves like senile men. It wasn't a big meal but a special one, the wine going away fast, the bottle seeming to drink it up by itself. This business of being drunk.

"GENTLEMEN!" RAMKE banged the mug on the table, and it broke at the handle. "Gentlemen, quiet!"

There was no more noise from anywhere. I could see him vaguely at the head of the room, surrounded by men dressed in black with silver buttons on their chests like armor. He was wearing his cap, which he took off, wiped sweat from his forehead with a napkin, and set the cap down on the table.

"I owe it to you tonight to say that I do not know how things will turn out, and if I can't, no one can. In a day or two we leave in convoys for the Belgian border in the Ardennes, from where we will move against the Americans, through them, and on to the Meuse River. We have almost no fuel, not enough equipment, and you haven't had the training time you deserve. I trust you understand that none of this comes easily."

Then he sighed, and we raised our heads to see him looking down at the table, the hall lights shining on his slicked-back hair. Then he said the German people were too obedient for their own good, and the eyes of the officers popped a little. They started to sweat. He said the Germans had always answered their leaders' bad rulings with satire, in music, literature, in the humor of the back streets. Why had there never been a German revolution? What was it, he asked out loud, that made us so incapable of change? What was it that put us constantly back onto the same path? It happened because we had faith. Faith like no one else's on earth, and since we were the children of the Later War, which he didn't say but tried to, we knew that it took more than faith. One day we would fight no more forever. Quoting from an American Indian. We will fight no more forever.

Then he sat down, and we clapped, pounded on the tables, broke our mugs on the tables and waved the handles in the air, yelling. Ramke. Ramke. Ramke. We chanted until we went deaf. A fog-eyed Voss told us to line up beside the table.

Then out of new wood crates stacked in the corners of the room, they brought packets wrapped in brown wax paper, tied with wire and tagged. Ramke took each one of us by the hand, staring straight through us, smiling white teeth and moving on. Voss handed us each a packet, which we unwrapped. Inside we found the daggers.

They were black and silver, the length of a forearm, black scabbard with chrome fittings at each end in half-moon curves, an eagle and two lightning bolts engraved in the wood. The blade had engraved on it: "My Honor Is Loyalty." New steel. We carried them out of the hall and threw them down the well, a few at first, then a clattering multitude of bright flickers down into the water. It seemed a terrible waste, as we crowded around the well, throwing away what we had just been given.

A while after, Ramke came outside, surrounded by the officers, muttering and laughing. I went up to bed and felt the wine rolling like a ball bearing in the white dish of my skull.

WE WERE issued rifles from the armory, and long trench knives with clip scabbards for attaching to the inside of boots. Anything we had that was ruined they replaced.

The armory was a small, one-room building with steel doors, poorly lit and smelling of gun oil. Racks and racks of Mauser rifles, held in their stands by iron rods that ran through the trigger guards and were padlocked at the ends. Mortars and the fat propellered bombs they fired were lined up in green wooden boxes with yellow writing on them. Stick grenades. Bayonets. Brown rectangular boxes of bullets in chain links. Waxed-paper bundles of bullets not in chains. Helmets, messtins, water bottles, capes, stacks of field-gray tunics wrapped with hemp rope and tagged "clean," sniper uniforms dappled pink, brown, two shades of green, no insignia, leather tank jackets which they used to issue to U-boat crews when there still were any, now handed out to the SS.

Steiner, the armorer, was a man getting old, with black lines under his fingernails. And he wore brown, always brown and nothing but. He was a civilian, so he didn't have to wear gray. His desk in the corner of the shiny-green-painted room was covered with acquisition slips, with nuts and bolts and cleaning rags.

We took our rifles, bayonets, and mess tins and a bundle of bullets each. Handschumacher got lumped with the Spandau, which Steiner took from a trunk and gave to him because he was the tallest. He walked out to the Orderly room, swearing and staggering under the weight.

Steiner pushed acquisition slips stained with the grease of his fingerprints across his desk to each of us. We wrote down the serial numbers of the rifles and checked off on a printed list what we had taken.

Steiner was wearing a brown shirt, open at the neck, with a pointed collar. His eyes were watery, always flooded as if he were crying. I saw him only in the armory, when we went there to collect rifles for the range, or in the Orderly room drinking ersatz coffee. His wife was rumored to be a Hippo of Immense Proportions, his children like oxen. All of them probably the shade of a sepia print.

K98-7811R. K98-7811R. I repeated the serial number of my rifle to myself as I left the armory, thinking that someday we'd all be lined up outside again giving the rifles back and swearing to Voss as we came out: "I have no live rounds in my possession, sir." K98-7811R. Then we'd go home.

We stood in the courtyard, loading the bullets into the black leather ammunition cases we carried strapped to our belts. They gave us gas-mask canisters, gray fluted cylinders, but with no gas masks, so we put our rations in them instead. The cook gave us loaves of bread, and sausage, and each of us a bottle of dark beer from the cellars. We sat around our rifles, which were set in pyramid stacks, and we stuffed our faces. The high walls of Bad Tölz were bright in the winter sun.

Voss sat down next to us.

"Nice joke about the war being over." Breder was trying to open a can of stewed pears with his bandaged hands and a can opener.

"Thought you'd like that. And funny how you keep falling downstairs and hurting your stupid self." But he knew what had happened. It was ugly to keep so much hidden when we all knew what was going on.

"Funny thing. Yes." Breder stabbed a hole in the tin with his bootknife and sucked the juice out.

"And funny thing me jumping into two bootfuls of piss when I come out of breakfast."

There were hawks in the sky and clouds like giant teapots. Already Plem-Plem was pulling down the blinds in the dormitory windows. The building looked as if it were blinking.

"Hello, Plem-Plem!" Voss yelled up. Then everybody started yelling, "Hello Plem-Plem!" We took out our handkerchiefs and swung them back and forth above our heads. Plem-Plem looked out and down at us, at all the white flecks of the handkerchiefs, everyone calling his name. He stood on the windowsill and bowed. We cheered the old man for a long time until he began wondering what all the cheering was for and pulled the blind shut.

THE TRUCKS came in a long convoy from the depot, backed up one by one to the gate. There were benches fitted in them now, so we could at least sit, back to back.

Most sections had to share a truck. They filled ours with ammunition so there was room only for us. The tailgates were shut and the canvas blinds pulled down, and the benches were freezing.

Through a gap I could see Plem-Plem again, in the front doorway with his hands in his pockets and the cooks standing outside the kitchen.

We had to brace our legs to keep from sliding around at first. It warmed up and we took turns peeking out the crack in the canvas. Gears changing. Diesel. I pulled up the collar on my greatcoat.

"I was at Cambrai! I was at Troy, Carthage, and Waterloo!"

Handschumacher started shouting. Then he banged on the rear of the truck's cab, and after a minute a little door slid back and we saw Voss, a cigarette in his mouth, peering in at us. In his hands was a map, transparent in the light.

"What?"

"I was just telling them you were at Cambrai, Troy, and Waterloo."

"I certainly was." We got another one of his half smiles, then rammed back in the dark when he slid the door shut.

VI

I WOKE up in the tent wedged between two people, with a
third sleeping on top of me. The air was bad, and I sniffed at
the cold blowing in through the open tent flap. I lit a match and
groped for an arm, found out the time from the watch on somebody's wrist, then snuffed out the match. Von Schwerin said we
had driven maybe two hundred kilometers. We were someplace between Nördlingen and Schwäbisch-Hall.

There was thick mist outside left over from the rain. I trod
on our mess tins getting out of the tent. They were still half full
of the soup they'd given us the night before and told us was our
breakfast as well. All around the meadow stood the clumps of
other tents, made up of our capes buttoned together and held
up with rifles. The trouble was that to make a tent you needed

four capes and there wasn't enough room for that many people inside.

I pissed into a bush, at the same time trying to light a match so I could have a smoke. Then I squatted next to a tree, my nose itching from the first puff on the cigarette, and watched the night and the mist coming and going in front of me like the static on a movie screen. Fat drops of water shone on the ends of the branches.

L AUGHTER F R O M somewhere. I followed the sound, stopping to listen, then moving on.

I watched from the fog in the meadow two men silhouetted on a rise. They were both trying to do handstands, both failing and dropping out of sight. Then one of them stood up, drank from a bottle, and passed it to the other.

"Do another handstand."

"Can't. Oh, no."

"Go on."

"No. All finished." One of them sat down with his arms crossed. The other rolled him over and down the hill toward me. More laughter. The sky was vaguely rose from the dawn.

The man rolled to within a couple of paces of me, then stopped. He stood up, smiling, saw me, stopped smiling, saluted and stayed with his right arm jutting out in the air. It was Voss.

I inhaled deeply on the cigarette, knowing he would see my face in the glow.

"You little fart. I thought you were an officer." He sat down on the grass.

"I am. I've been promoted."

"Go back to bed, little boy."

"You go back to bed. You look more tired than me."

He stood up and leaned on my shoulder. From up on the hill there was a pop.

"He's opened another bottle." Voss ran up and became a silhouette again.

It was Kaslaka with him, and they let me drink some of the good champagne they had. It was sweet with no bitterness, and I drank until they took the bottle away from me.

"Did we wake you up?" Kaslaka lit a match in my face to see who I was. "Westland?"

When Kaslaka spoke, his voice came from far away inside him. It was not an unkind voice. It was a bit like my father's, if I could truly remember that. Probably not. If I thought about it, only fragments came back. The words "Hello, lads" as he walked into the house when he came home from work, or "Jesus God," sounding like "Yaysus gott" when he dropped his coffee mug, bounced it off his knee, then his elbow, and finally let it fall to chips on the floor. I remembered almost nothing of his voice, and his face left only strange echoes in my head, somehow woken up by the voice of the bald Kaslaka.

Kaslaka and Voss sat back to back and drank the rest of the champagne. Both of them would ask me questions and then not wait for the answer. They talked to me and didn't care what I said. They both lived in their own private world from which they had nothing more to learn and no one else to care about. They were old men really.

"Where'd this come from?" I picked up one of the empty bottles and saw on its orange label that it was "Veuve Cliquot."

"Some woman had it in her house when we were sent there to billet the officers. So we took it."

The officers got to sleep in houses, and we stayed in the field.

"Yeah, so we took it."

"She watched us walk right out the door with it."

"Probably burst into tears after we'd gone."

They laughed their troll laugh, staring off to opposite ends of the sky.

Then Voss sighed and looked up at my sad face, which had

become sad as I thought of the woman in tears in the doorway of her house, and he told me he knew what I was thinking— that they had no right to do that. He told me I should get in the habit of taking what I wanted from now on, because the Great Mother of the Camp was no longer there to wipe my face, and out here no one liked what we stood for. No one wanted their neighbors saying after it was all over that they had helped the SS. If a finger was going to be pointed, no one wanted it pointed at them. So I would take what I wanted. Understood?

He thinks the same way as Breder, I was thinking as I went back down into the fog of the meadow, and if Voss who has been where we are going has no faith left, then what faith is there for us? I tripped over a rabbit hole and lay on my face, breathing hard and thinking about it.

I took what was left of the soup in the mess tins which I hadn't tipped over and divided it among the empty ones, so I wouldn't get blamed. Then I crawled back into the tent and fell asleep among the sighing bodies, hearing the tick of a watch close to my ear, someone whispering in his sleep, my eyes open and dried out, champagne and smoke in the spit at the back of my mouth.

THERE WAS a girl leaning out of a window with her arms folded across her chest, no shirt on, her breasts barely hidden, and she was staring right at us with empty eyes. She had hair still messy from being asleep, or from being boffed severely by whoever else was in the room. I saw a girl like that at a bus stop once, bought her flowers and ran away before she could say anything.

Handschumacher tore her out of the magazine and set her on fire. He had bought the magazine and then was ashamed for having done it.

"It's the humane thing to do, really. Really it is, really." The paper burned on the floor, and her face and her arms folded away into fire and ashes. "We'll all go mad if we stare at that much longer." He was acting as if it was our magazine and not just his.

We nodded like idiots and searched the rest of the magazine for more girls to set on fire.

I THOUGHT maybe being in the truck would give me time to think, but it became instead a review of nightmares and stupid things I'd done, so stupid they made me cringe. None of the long talks and singing I'd thought there'd be. We sat on the benches or tied ourselves to them and stared into space with cigarettes hanging out of our mouths. I spent two hours watching Breder drool in his sleep. The engines of the truck were too loud for talk, and even though we barely moved all day it tired us out.

I never knew where we were. There was no real day or night, only the darkness of the truck that spat us out in the red sunsets and sucked us back in at dawn. We lived like vampires in the night. We looked for smiles from the village people and saw nothing, for the slightest sign of anything, and there was nothing. We were also getting sick of each other. We stank. The food was bad. I lost my comb and my hair was dirty. I was sick and tired of lugging around the Mauser and the twenty bullets. From staying out too long my hands began to cramp in the mornings. My inner thigh was chafed raw from the wool of the uniform trousers. Pissed off all the time.

We lined up half asleep on the side of the roads in the cold, other trucks going past and splashing us with mud. Standing for ages at attention while Voss went away to "see what was going on." I saw cities in the distance, and mountains, but always in the distance, and the places where we stopped belonged to some middle ground, where people hid in their houses and never came out.

Once, as we stood waiting across the road from a cluster of houses, a blue ball bounced into the street and a baby ran after it on rubbery legs. A woman ran after the baby, grabbed it, and darted back into one of the houses. The baby's arms stuck straight out forward, still set to pick up the ball. The woman turned to us before she disappeared, wide-eyed, and bared her teeth.

"What was that all about?" Handschumacher took off his helmet and ruffled his ginger hair, scratched at his face as if he were trying to rake off the freckles. "I live in a place like this, and I have a ball like that, and nobody runs away from me when I stand in the street at home. I'm not that fucking ugly." He went across the road and started yelling at the blank windows.

The wind was moaning around the curves of my helmet, and I couldn't hear what he was saying. He picked up the ball and punted it off down the road, then stalked back to the truck.

"Well, *I'm* not going to stand for it."

"You sound like a fishwife." Von Schwerin was talking through clenched teeth, and quietly. Since we'd left Bad Tölz, he had pulled into himself and become obedient almost to the point of stupidity. The pupils of his eyes had shrunk permanently to the size of black pinpricks.

"I'm not going to take this from these peasants. That's the way they want to play, fine. That's the way it will be played."

"Poor old Handschumacher." Von Schwerin again.

"Why, because I come from a farm?"

"Because you should never have left it. That's why."

DAYDREAMS OF Lise Hammacher. All day. The whole impossibility of it.

BREDER TOOK the boredom of the truck better than the rest of us. He slept all the time, dribbling great streams over his chest and the person next to him. I could see him as a small boy falling asleep in a room full of stuffed animals. No more talk about the maps. Voss left him alone, said he was a bad asset.

He looked surprised whenever he woke up, peering around the dimness of the truck. It must have seemed that he was still asleep and all of us would disappear the next time he opened his eyes.

The nightmares came crashing down on me. I dreamed of moving across a frozen landscape, snow up to my thighs, frozen rivers, dead trees, and across all this someone was chasing me, a man in rotten clothes I could see only from the corner of my eye. Sometimes he would catch me and we would fight on the ground, the snow turning red under us. Then suddenly he would be chasing me again. Nightmares like a freak show filed in front of me as I stood in soup lines or sat on mossy walls watching the tents being set up or taken down. At last one time the dream overtook me and I shouted out as the man-shadow lunged from the red gloom of my closed eyes. It was a soldier from the Great War, moldy Pickelhaube on his head, the spike broken off. No face. No eyes.

Von Schwerin leaned across Breder's body and gently slapped me in the face.

"I dreamed. . . ." I looked around and tried to figure out where I was.

"I know what you dreamed." He handed me a cigarette from the silver case he kept in his breast pocket.

Handschumacher despised the people in these villages. He barged an old woman off the sidewalk when she passed him going the other way. Her clothes and hands were filthy from being out in the fields where she'd been digging up potatoes, which she carried in the lap of her skirt, held up so we could see the ruins of her legs. Her face hung creased like a piece of crepe paper.

We had been looking for some fresh milk, completely sick of

the powdered stuff that clotted in our coffee and stuck to the roofs of our mouths.

When the woman hit the road, potatoes bouncing around her, a boy maybe fifteen years old came out from a house and shouted at Handschumacher in the strangest German accent I had ever heard.

"My God, these are real peasants," whispered von Schwerin.

The boy wanted to know what the hell Handschumacher thought he was doing shoving decent people around.

"I didn't hurt her," Handschumacher mumbled, and turned around to see if she was still there.

"You don't go shoving ladies around is all, Red Top." Then the boy gave Handschumacher the slightest push.

Handschumacher threw his hobnailed boot into the boy's shin, and to save the boy from dying, we dragged Handschumacher down an alley. We held him like a madman, which he had become, babbling and swinging his arms. We stuck his head in a cattle trough and held him under until he blew bubbles. He was calm after that, after he'd gagged a few times.

"Well, you shouldn't go shoving women around." Breder said this as if the argument had been revolving inside his head since the moment she fell.

"I hate these people. These people are filth. Have you ever seen it like this? Is it like this where you live?" Handschumacher raised his hands. "Is it?"

The water in the cattle trough rocked heavily, reflecting the dirty sky.

A WOMAN wearing a flower-patterned apron handed me a pitcher of cold milk from her front door. I saw a fire burning inside and a chair draped with a blanket pulled up close to the hearth. The place smelled of soap and old fires. I had been sent to tell her we would be camping at the bottom of her field. She had watched me from behind a lace curtain as I came close.

She handed me the pitcher before I could say anything. I was too busy thinking how, if I could sit by that fire for ten minutes, my hands wouldn't ache and my feet would be dry.

I sat on the doorstep while she walked down her garden path to see the trucks unloading at the bottom of the hill. I drank the milk as fast as I could, feeling it splash in my stomach and spill down my chin.

"Is that where you're spending the night?" She pointed one of her long fingers at the trucks.

"I'm afraid so. I was sent to tell you."

"I see." She wiped her hands on the apron, crumpling the linen flowers. "Am I going to have people staying in my house?"

"I don't think so." I looked up and saw she had very pale eyes. The milk was a balloon inside me.

"I see you've drunk all the milk." Then she stared long enough for me to get embarrassed and look at my feet.

"Haven't had milk for a long time. . . ." A quiet, guilty voice.

"Are you hungry?" She kept her eyes on me as she bowed her head forward and untied the knot her hair was in, so it fell down over her shoulders. I realized she was younger than I'd thought. She took off her apron as she walked back to the doorstep where I was sitting. "I asked if you were hungry."

"I suppose. Usually, I mean."

"Would you like a piece of cake?"

"Cake?"

"Yes. You know what a piece of cake is?" She threw the apron over the railing and disappeared into the house.

I breathed the smell of the milk from the empty jug, stood up, my bottom wet from the damp stone, put the jug just inside the door, and when I turned around, she was standing in front of me holding out a piece of sponge cake filled with jam.

"Thank you."

"You looked hungry." She was wearing one earring, only one, silver with a blue stone in it.

"Usually."

"If you come back tonight, I'll cook you a meal." Then she shut the door in my face.

Von Schwerin's birthday. He announced it as we buttoned our capes together to make a tent at the bottom of the hill. It took a while to figure out what to do for him. It looked as if we were going to ignore it, and von Schwerin began to sulk, but then we shoved him in the tent and told him not to come out, took one of the ever-present cattle troughs and lit a fire under it with old wood gathered from the hedges. Boys from other trucks came to see what we were doing. It took half an hour to get the fire started, von Schwerin mumbling could he come out now, and eventually we used gunpowder from bullet cases with the bullets tugged out. There was barely enough wood to keep the fire going, and we stirred the water like soup, steam pouring into the cold air.

When the water was hot, we called von Schwerin from the tent, and he emerged with his cheeks stuffed like a hamster's with candy from his ration pack. He said later he was timing how long it took a whole packet to dissolve in his mouth. He saw the trough and the fire and the steam, and without any word from us he stripped, throwing his clothes in all directions until he was wearing nothing but his oval zinc dog tag, but still held his hands in front of his privates.

The people who had come to watch applauded. Voss and Kaslaka sat on the hood of the truck and stared. The kitchen vans came sliding down the muddy slope, and no one paid any attention to them.

By the time he reached the bath, his skin was covered in goose bumps and his ears had turned red.

"You didn't have to do all this."

"And would you have let us forget it if we hadn't?"

We put out the fire when it seemed we might be boiling him

to death. He lay in the bath, in the veils of steam, sometimes letting his head sink beneath the surface so that when he came up his head became a plume of smoke.

We brought him his dinner. Voss brought him a cigar. The sky went black and stars came out. The wind picked up and blew the teapot clouds away. Soon there were nothing but stars and the hard cold and von Schwerin not wanting to get out of the water and make the run back to the tent.

From somewhere among the huddles of tents came laughter, and sometimes in the dark I made out the odd suns of cigarettes.

I DIDN'T know what I could tell Breder and Handschumacher not to make them suspicious, so I didn't tell them anything and walked up the hill to the woman's house, pausing for a second in front of the door, wondering how bad I smelled.

I SAT on a frail chair in the kitchen and squinted at her now and then as she stood with her arms folded, leaning against the sideboard. My chest was thundering.

"I like the name Sebastian." She had changed into a dark green skirt and a white collarless shirt that was too big for her. Probably belonged to her husband. Probably coming home soon from the late shift. *Wunderbar.*

"Did you like the dinner?"

"Yes, very much." I had almost forgotten that anything except stew existed. My stomach was still holding on to it and not digesting, trying to figure out what it was. But the rest of me knew. Duck. Duck with plum sauce. Okay to digest now. Please digest NOW. Duck, plum sauce, carrots, and Brussels sprouts.

She said she had killed the duck herself that morning, got it with a sling shot in the field at a range of ten meters. I said, "Really?" and she laughed. Seemed plausible to me.

We ate it at the kitchen table, the room full of the smells of cooking, Mozart on the Gramophone in the other room. *Nachtmusik*. And the sound of the tap dripping. And her talking sometimes fast and sometimes not at all, Berlin accent, apologizing for the lack of wine, discussing the merits of flambé, getting up suddenly and setting her meal, carrots and everything, on fire with a match and a dousing of plum brandy, waiting until the flames went down, close inspection of the remains, then loud laughter and her throwing the whole mess out the window. She wanted to flambé mine too, but I wouldn't let her.

"You can't *still* be hungry?"

"No. Not now."

"And it was good?"

"No question."

"How old are you?" She turned away to the sink, poured herself a glass of water, drank it, and I watched the curve of her neck and the pulse of the water going down her throat, the earring swinging half alive from her earlobe.

She reminded me of the women I used to see walking their infant children in the park. That age. That out-of-reachness. What the hell am I doing eating roast duck with plum sauce in a strange woman's house in the middle of the night? This has all happened ages in the past. That's right. This is a mirage from the memories of my ancestors. This woman with her red-blond hair has long since grown old and died, and she has not pressed her hands to my face and breathed into me; there is no pale light close and out of focus from her eyes, no pressure from the back of the chair on my spine. Already I know the smell of her sweat.

"Don't be scared. There's no one around, Sebastian. Sebastian."

* * *

SHE SAT cross-legged in front of the fire, the cuffs of her too-big shirt draped over her forearms. She braided her hair and talked. She wiggled her toes.

I sat against the stone of the fireplace in my gray shirt, my baggy trousers tucked into my socks. The boots stood saluting almost in the flames. My coat was still in the kitchen, helmet outside the front door.

"There." She had finished braiding her hair, and she took from my hands the bottle of plum brandy, knocked back a mouthful. "I'm so bored."

"Now?"

"Not now. Every other day of the year."

"What about your husband?"

"Oh, so you assume I'm married, do you, Sebastianovich?"

"Yes."

"Well, I am. My husband is a prisoner of war in England. Have you been to England? It's very pretty in June."

The hall clock struck eleven.

"You think you'll be a prisoner of war?"

"No. I don't think anybody takes the SS as prisoners." The right side of my body was warm from the fire.

"Do I seem to be boring you?"

"No, ma'am."

"How old do you think I am?"

I shrugged and drank more plum brandy. She looked to me like she used to be a debutante, and she was shipwrecked here. I began to have a fear of the forests and the hills as places where Handschumachers and pretty women went mad in the quiet, the kind of quiet that city people sought out for their holidays but returned home from before the mutterings of their city lives had ever finished ringing in their heads. So they never heard the quiet. Never froze so still they could hear the hissing of the mist. These were the people who went window-shopping in the middle of air raids.

"No idea how old you are." I stood up and went to the window that looked out over the field.

"I'm sure I'm younger than you think. Does this mean you have to go?"

"Sometime soon." I turned around. "You understand."

"Of course. I don't know you at all. I don't even know if your name's really Sebastian. Last name. I don't know that either. Don't know where you're from." She took a slug at the brandy, spat it at the fire and it burst into flames.

"Bad Godesberg. Last name is Westland." I walked up behind her, put my hands on her shoulders and rested my chin on her head.

"Don't tell your friends where you've been. Please. I don't know why I asked you in. Just lonely. Please say you understand."

I said anything she wanted to hear. Then I went away.

VII

THE WIND blowing around the corners of my helmet made me deaf to almost everything else. I walked down the middle of the road beyond her house, past a closed bakery, butcher shop, and post office.

Should have asked her the name of this place. This Place.

I sat at an empty fountain, which was a memorial to the Great War dead, perhaps a dozen names and a statue of a man in one of the coal-scuttle helmets of the later war, not the Pickel-haubes they had at the beginning. It was cold and bright, and the stone was blue in the light of the moon.

A Kubelwagen drove out of the dark, SS plates, four people inside, back into the dark, the smell of Ramke's cigars and diesel left behind.

Numb in the face and hands in pockets, I went back to the

field and stood with Posner, who was on guard duty. We were there most of the night. He said there were rumors the offensive was off, which made me ill because it had to be a joke.

"Where do these rumors come from?" I said it imitating Fleps's voice; he had told us always to ask where rumors came from. We were to disbelieve all rumors of war. But we never did.

"Our NCO says we're going for the weakest link in the American lines. He said the weakest link wasn't very weak, however."

"Someday someone will tell me something hopeful."

"How about this? They say it's going to snow soon." Posner hated wearing his helmet. Every chance he got he took it off. Now he had it stuck on a fence post.

"Big snow?"

"Rumors." He nodded and coughed, trying to smile.

"It's so cold."

"Which reminds me." He brought out a pair of fingerless gloves, hand-knitted of thick wool. He wiggled his fingers in my face. "Sent from home."

"What news do you have from Godesberg?"

"Apart from these nothing. It's like the lights went off when we left and they haven't come back on yet."

"It's nice to think so."

"You know, I don't think your NCO ever sleeps. He always seems to be creeping about in the middle of the night." He pointed to a shape coming down the hill, squelching the mud and singing to itself. "I heard he won a Knight's Cross in Normandy."

"Seems that way."

"You should ask him about it sometime. That was a hell of a place to be. Nothing like the east, of course, but you know, after a week or two in Normandy, the Division had about one tank left. This was defending an aerodrome at a place called

Carpiquet. Didn't have enough trucks to pull their field guns away so they had to blow them up and leave them behind."

"So how do you know all this? Not Fleps . . ."

"No. My brother was there."

"Didn't know you had a brother."

"Sure. He works at the ticket office at the Bad Godesberg station."

"What? Not the one . . ."

"The one with no legs. He was lucky they didn't shoot him there in Normandy after he was wounded. It's a bad habit the German Army has gotten into. The almighty Waffen SS. Brother said they shot anyone with a head or stomach wound. Amis used to find them lined up on the side of the road."

Voss walked past us, swinging his arms and not looking at us.

"Who goes there?" Posner mumbled.

"Voss."

"The Carpiquet Aerodrome."

"What?" Voss stopped walking.

"I said the Carpiquet Aerodrome."

"What about it?" He came close. "Westland? You again. You never sleep? I'm beginning to associate you with the night. What about the Carpiquet Aerogoddamndrome?"

"I just heard you were there is all." Posner offered cigarettes again.

"So?"

"My brother too."

"What's his name?" Hands on hips. Voss was showing his teeth like a dog.

"Posner, Helmut. Scharführer. 25 Panzer-Grenadiers."

"I know him. I thought he was dead. Posner. Well, well." He gaped in Posner's face.

"He's fine."

"Wasn't when I was with him. Him and Kaslaka and me all came out of Normandy together, just the three of us."

"How's that?" Posner sounded surprised that Voss didn't seem to care whether his older brother was dead or not. Oh, but you have to know Voss, I felt like telling him.

"We put on English uniforms and walked out, dressed Pos up as an officer even, put him on a stretcher and walked out." He smiled. I figured he had to be drunk.

"Where'd you get the uniforms, then?"

"Took them from the dead." Voss coughed and spat into his hands, then held them up to his face. "I keep spitting blood. I don't know what's wrong." He stretched out his hand, and I could see the darkness of the blood mixed with spit in his palm.

"How so the English uniforms?" Posner switched his rifle to the other shoulder and turned his collar up against the wind.

"I just remember"—Voss made the motion of picking something from his teeth—"I took a half-hour nap. I was so tired I had to sleep a little. We dug holes under the hedges, like a bunch of rabbits. Then at night we used to come out and get as many of them as we could. No more organization. Radio contact gone. Maybe three tanks left for the whole Division, and you know, all I'd had to eat for three fucking days was crab apples. It looked like the Canadians were going to break through, and this was after days of trying to hold and them always telling us reinforcements were coming. And there's dead people all over the place, and dead people in the ditches, cows dead in the fields puffed up like balloons. We'd take the aerodrome. They'd take it back. We'd shoot their prisoners and they'd shoot ours. Never saw so many dead. Seemed like every time I shut my eyes someone wakes me up and says they're coming again. There was a stream over at the edge of one of the fields where we got our water. We figured either they didn't know about it or they were letting it alone out of some sense of decency 'cause we had to drink something. So Knöchlein—he was in charge, even though he's addicted to morphine and wounded in the head—tells us to go get water; me, Kaslaka, and Pos. So we set out at one in the morning to be back before sunrise, crawling across the far end of the airstrip, enough bodies there that you can play dead if the flares go up. They're camped over by the aero-drome building, big corrugated iron thing. We were there be-fore and we thought it was safe, but they cut the throats of our guards and got us by surprise, shot us out of the rafters like pigeons. No one in there after that. We got to the stream with-out them seeing us, dragging the water bottles, and lay there for a while to see if anything's up. Nothing. No one around. So we got down to fill the bottles. It was a hard place to catch any-body. I filled some bottles and stuck my face in the water to cool off, and suddenly there's this almighty bang and I've swallowed half the stream. Couldn't see what was up. My lungs were full of water. Kaslaka drags me out of the stream and into the hedges, and I'm still gagging with water. There's flares going up from the Canadian side, but they can't see you if you lie still. You only see what's moving. Kaslaka jams a handkerchief in my mouth and tells me if I don't shut up coughing he'll kill me himself. Seems Pos either trod on something or someone threw a bomb at us. Can't tell which. So we wait there all night to see if someone's going to throw something else. Sure enough, about dawn a couple of bushes start crawling back to the Canadian lines. Couldn't tell they were people even when they were mov-ing. Must have been fucking Red Indians or something. And Pos waits all night in the mud by the side of the stream, half in, half out of the water, put a bandage on himself where he got hurt. Didn't say a word for a while when we dragged him out. Then he said someone else put the bandage on him. Said the Canadians did it. We say damn rubbish, Pos, they just fin-ished trying to kill you, what they want to put you back together for? After a while he starts saying an angel did it. Vision in white. Kaslaka says for an angel he did a pretty bad job, then he asks me if I think we should shoot him, right in front of Pos, and Pos says, 'Fuck you, Kaslaka, I wouldn't shoot you.' Kaslaka tells him he's just joking, but Kaslaka doesn't know what a joke is. We just had orders to shoot all nonwalking wounded. Just wanted to know if we were still following orders. Posner says if we're going to be Bolsheviks about this he'll walk home on however much of a foot he's got left. Not much. Not much of either. And it's too light to make it back. Canadians got sniper rifles so good sometimes a man standing next to you just falls over dead and you don't hear the gun go off. We'd never have made it across the field. Pos decided he was going to go delirious, so we dragged him to a hole, an old hole from the week before when the lines were different, a good hole, a safe hole. There were a couple of blankets inside, a crate of apples, and we stayed there all day hearing all sorts of shooting. This hole was a good two meters underground. Kaslaka went up to the mouth, and when he came back he said the lines had changed again, Canadians broke through. Maybe we retreated. Don't know. We were in the hole two days with Posner singing to himself. Nothing but apples to eat. On the third night we crawled out and found some dead men on the bank downstream. Everybody's gone. It's all quiet. Starry night. We stripped the bodies and dressed ourselves and Pos up like Canadians, same as the English in their god-damned scratchy wool suits. Made a stretcher and just started walking. Figured fuck it. No other way to do this. Got to live to be older than twenty. In the evening of the next day we got to the Canadian lines, no one bothering us, and we just went around the side of them and swam across a river they had stopped at. We had our German tunics underneath the other ones. It took us another day to find anybody friendly. We passed by a village with no one in it except bodies hanging from the gutters on lengths of rope. Seems Knöchlein got it in his head they were collaborators, lined up everyone he could find and made them count off: one, two, three, and so on, up to ten and every third person he hangs. Rest of the village heads for the hills. We found five boys from the Division in a barn. They were only sixteen years old, most of them, the ones Knöchlein saved for kitchen duty so they wouldn't get in the way. Seems Knöchlein found out there were no reinforcements coming so he ordered everyone split into small groups and told them all to do as much damage as they could on the way out. He wished them all good luck and blew his brains out. You know, a couple of weeks earlier we were walking the streets of Paris. I rented a little wooden toy boat at a pond in the Tuileries Gardens and spent all day pushing it around in circles with a stick. I swear it broke my heart to be in Paris. I don't know what it was. Carried my heart around like marbles in a bag. Then a couple of weeks later I'm more filthy than I've ever been before, I've killed half a dozen people, one of them with a shovel, and I'm dragging Pos around in the dark wearing a Canadian uniform. We got him to a field hospital. Then Kaslaka and I began the Great Retreat, got back to Germany any way we could, avoiding the military police. We called them 'chained dogs.' And when I'm home, for some reason, they give me a Knight's Cross. Not quite sure for what. Man just said Knöchlein recommended me. So Pos is alive. I knew his legs were gone, though. He's alive. Say hello to him for me."

He walked away looking old and drunk. I sat with Posner on the fence, smelling the smell of the woman in my clothes, watching the house on the hill for signs of her life.

I WAS leaning against the wall in the weak sun, breathing the damp air blowing down the street. I watched Handschumacher explain to whoever was listening, which was everybody in the truck, how to clean and cook the fish he had caught. He was pleased to be teaching us something.

We had found a fishpond at the back of a broken water mill, bordered off by wire with a sign saying: "No Fishing by Order of the Mayor." Handschumacher crawled under the wire and squatted on the bank for a while, staring at the black pond. Then he took a half loaf of bread from his satchel, broke crumbs off, and threw them out into the center.

After a while we could see the ripples where the fish rose to take the bread. Sometimes we saw the oily skin of their backs. Handschumacher threw the crumbs closer to shore, and closer, and we watched from behind the wire like a herd of cows. He took off his jacket and rolled up his sleeves, pulled a long knife, which none of us knew he had, from a sheath sewn into his tunic, and set it in the ground beside him.

The fish were slicing the pond, looking for more bread, gulping air and water when they surfaced. Handschumacher let a few crumbs fall through his fingers and when the fish rose he took the knife very quickly from the ground and flipped it into the mass of fish bodies. The water frothed, and in the dark we could see a silver side rolling downward. Handschumacher grabbed and pulled it from the water, a fish as long as his forearm, streaming blood from the spike through its belly and the knife breaking the sheet of its scales.

He did not take any others, although it seemed he could have cleared the pond that way because the fish had come back for more bread even as Handschumacher held the bleeding silver thing up to us and smiled.

We were almost back at the truck before we saw Handschumacher winding a handkerchief around his hand, having sliced his palm on the fin.

Now he had scaled the fish, and the sides of its belly were clean and open and gutless. He pried the hubcap off the truck with a crowbar from the toolbox, washed it in a puddle, and set up three cooking stoves in a triangle. He rested the hubcap on the stoves, lit them, and dropped a piece of butter from one of the ration tubes into the bowl of the hubcap. He waited until the butter turned brown and sizzled, then sliced apart one of the onions he and Breder had dug up a few days before, set the white rings in the butter, and the rest of us slobbered without shame at the smell.

"Don't use up all my fuel." Von Schwerin pursed his lips and frowned at the stove he had lent Handschumacher.

"Use all you want," Voss said from somewhere in the darkness of the truck, only visible from the light of a cigarette.

Handschumacher filleted the fish very carefully, cutting it almost in half, then peeling back the skin and setting loose new drops of blood from the trail of its spine. Then with the two slices of meat, off-white, half pink like an opal, he set them in the butter and they hissed. The rest of the fish, watching everything with its marble eyes, lay on the road with only its skin attached as if it had suddenly exhaled all its flesh.

It didn't take long to cook. The sun came and went and came back, and you could tell from the dampness of the air that it was winter coming. Handschumacher turned the fish slowly with his knife, and the butter bubbled around the shriveled onions.

I could feel the saliva welling up from under my tongue. Without thinking, I had dug my hands into the half loaf of bread in my satchel and crushed it. I put a piece of lemon candy in my mouth, spat it out again, and it stuck on the brick wall.

"Who wants a piece?" Handschumacher looked up and ran his eyes over us, twisting the knife in his hand. If he had given us each a bit, it would have been divided into segments the size of half a thumb, but he had to offer it.

No. You eat it. Go ahead. Eat the damn thing. We waved away the idea with flips of our wrists, and afterward sat by the empty hubcap smelling the butter go cold, while Handschumacher stood in the road, smoking a cigarette, his back turned to us out of some sense of decency.

"Your name Westland?" I turned around and saw the face of someone I vaguely knew from another company, and, in trying to place him, I didn't answer. "Well, is it or isn't it?"

"Yes. Westland. Me."

"There's a woman over there says she wants to talk to you." He jerked his thumb over his shoulder.

"What woman? Where?" I stood up and felt pain in my knees.

"She's over there somewhere. By the square. Might be your mother for all I know." Then he breathed out in some sort of laugh and walked away.

"Oh, Westland, your mother." Von Schwerin shook his head. "She's been tucking you in every night, hasn't she?" Breder hugged himself.

"Not funny. Do I have time to go see about this, Voss?"

"Take the rest of your life. I don't care," said the voice in the truck.

WHAT ARE you doing here, I was going to say when I saw her. How did you find this place? What is it? Is everything all right? Where's Walther? You're going to get in trouble if you hang around here.

I got to the place the boy had pointed to, a crossroads cornered by four small shops, all closed.

NO ONE.

Fuck. I fell for it. Didn't they do this to someone just the other day? Fuck. My mother, indeed. Idiot.

Then I turned back, spinning the steel plate of my boot heel on the sidewalk and began walking back to the truck. I saw a woman walking toward the crossroads on the other side of the street. I stopped and looked, and she stopped and looked, and I turned to carry on because it was not my mother. My mother didn't wear men's raincoats with the collar turned up like a gangster. Whoever it was, it wasn't my mother. Then the woman crossed the road, looking down at the ground. She got to the sidewalk, and I caught a breath of her perfume. I saw who she was, and a drop of sweat pooled on my upper lip.

She pushed the drop over my lips with her finger, looked very serious, which I knew meant she was about to laugh. And she did, so loud that I put my hand to her mouth. I walked her very quickly up the street to a bar, she trying to stick her tongue through my fingers and giggling, putting her arm around my waist and pulling me to her.

The lights were off in the bar, and all the chairs were on the tables except the one in which the barman sat, drinking coffee from a demitasse and smoking.

"Closed." He rolled forward on the meat of his belly.

"No, you're not." I put two chairs upright, sat her down and sat down myself. "Two cognacs." I looked at him. "Please."

I took out a pack of cigarettes and slid them across the table to her. "Smoke."

"Light," she said and slid the pack back to me, so I lit two and gave her one.

"I thought I'd never catch up with you, Sebastian. But I did. I couldn't pretend anymore."

"Pretend what, Mrs. Hammacher?"

"Call me Lise like you used to." She breathed the smoke out of her mouth and back in through her nose.

"What then, Lise? What? Pretend what?" I was standing outside the train again in Munich, looking for her in the crowd and sick for her, the officer telling me to do up the buttons on my coat, and she gone back to her husband.

The barman set the cognacs down in huge bowl glasses, a good amount of the honey-colored alcohol. He stood at the door with his hands in his pockets, sighing at the empty street and fogging up the window.

"I love you." She picked up the glass with both hands and smelled the cognac.

Then I laughed and she hissed, told me she didn't come all this way and leave her husband and friends to have me laugh at her.

"I left everything for you. You owe me more than your laughing. You knew I love you. You knew I couldn't leave you. But you knew I had to try, didn't you?" She stubbed out the cigarette, jamming it hard into the pale blue ashtray as if she were breaking the neck of a small animal.

I was going to tell her then that I used to stand in the field outside her house in the middle of the night watching for her, but it never got out of my throat.

"I've decided to wait for you, Sebastian. We can make a start again when it's over. Right here if you want."

"Not here. Oh, Christ, no."

"I don't care. You don't seem to understand. Anywhere. Africa. I'll wait in the jungle in South America for you if I have to. I have nowhere else to go except with you." She stood up, looked down on me. "I—love—you."

I blew smoke in her face. "You'll love me forever for a week."

"Not like that. No." She lowered her voice. "I'll rent a house. I have money of my own to make a start. It's gold, too. I have a plan. I want to spend the rest of my life with you."

"How did you find me in this place? I should have asked that first. No one's supposed to know where we are."

"My husband asked a friend, who asked some friends. He was right on target."

"How did you explain to your husband that you were looking for me?"

"Well"—she drank and the ball of violent honey went down her throat—"I told him I was leaving him and that I wanted to be with you. Then I asked him if he could find out where you'd be."

"And he did?" I did not look at her. I watched the barman standing by the door, quietly singing a song about sunshine in Mexico, rhythmically picking his nose.

"Yes. He said he was glad to see me go. He wished us all the best. He even let me keep the car."

"So my mother knows." She would track me down like a rabid wolf and club me to death with a rolling pin.

"Well, she will eventually, love. Eventually everyone will know."

Hate bubbled up in my face from the dark wood of the table, then faded away again. Every time you think it will be different this time, until what you are left with is so patched and ugly that you don't want to see it anymore.

I kept reappearing in the Munich station, shoving through the crowd to find her, turning people around like shop mannequins, sick from the foul breath of the night-train people who hung from the carriage windows.

This sickness.

"How long do you think you're going to have to wait?"

"As long as it takes. I don't care. As long as you come back to me."

Another cognac and another, and eventually the man just crashed the whole dusty bottle on the table and left it there.

Voss would have left in the truck by now to find a good field to sleep in.

Damn this dream of the crowded place returning and returning, and I can't see her goddamned face even when she's there in front of me. Has she been talking? Is she just staring at me?

We had stood up, but I didn't remember doing so. I blinked at the barman as we left, and it was she who led me now, down the road to a side street where her car was parked. It smelled the same. I opened the glove compartment and remembered the little light and the hard candies she put there in a can. It was the same struggling out of clothes and windows steaming up. Heat, hair in my face, hands clawed into my shoulders. While she told me that she loved me, I looked out the window through a space on the glass I had wiped clean of the fog, looked at the empty street. And then she was crying, saying she'd even knitted me a sweater. She climbed, half-dressed, over me into the back seat, the skin of the back of her thigh smooth down to the wrinkle of her knee, her foot pressed against the rearview mirror, drawing accidental lines on the misted glass with her toes.

It was a brown sweater with a blue line along the V neck and my initials stitched on a label at the back, and it fit me in a baggy sort of way. She wasn't crying now. She was telling me how she'd knitted it, and I nodded, watched her underpants hanging from the steering wheel.

She was behind me in the back seat with her arm around my throat, talking about how our new house would be decorated. She had books with designs in them on how to do it.

I drank some crème de menthe from a flask she handed me, and when she saw I didn't like it, she took it back in her own mouth and swallowed.

She told me about her trip, about asking at farmhouses if we had come through in our trucks. She hadn't stopped thinking of me. She didn't know what she would have done if she hadn't found me.

She asked if I remembered all the times when she drove me home from school. I said, of course I did, and arched my head back to look up in her face as she leaned over the seat, the smooth space between her breasts still touched with sweat.

There was thunder far away over the hills, and a while later rain on the roof of the car.

She fell asleep on my lap, and I stared out the windshield as the fog disappeared, the rain beaded on the hood and rolled off. I watched a light go on in a house across the street, then an old man carrying a candle in a dish made his way downstairs like a fat firefly until the front door opened, and he set a milk bottle on the step. The candle went out. He lit it again, shut the door, the door knocker rattling twice. The glow climbed back up the stairs and vanished.

I woke her up and told her I had to go. She asked me when we'd meet again and I said tomorrow. Said we were staying another day. Told her noon at the bar.

I love you. I'll be with you forever. I can't live without you. I'll see you tomorrow. She said all that, and I left her in her steamed-up little car trying to find her shoes under the seat. And I ran through the rain out into the fields, looking for Voss and Breder and von Schwerin, this ache in me as if my eyes had rolled around to white.

I FOUND the camp about two o'clock, nearly three kilometers down the road, and I fell asleep next to Kaslaka in the truck. And at six in the morning, as I had known we would, we packed up and left, driving northwest toward the Ardennes. At the time she would have arrived at the bar, I was asleep on Breder's shoulder in the truck, him dribbling on my head in his dreams, the shudder of the always-changing gears running up from the floor through our bones.

PICTURE: The angled, metal mass of a half-track moves quickly over the cobblestones, cracking them with its treads. The machine is green-gray, with pine branches twined around the fender and the tow ropes lashed onto the sides. I can see the heads of boys my age looking out over the top of the steel canopy, and one boy I watch as he watches me: his high cheekbones red from the wind and his eyes almost closed. I am standing beside a cow in a paddock which Handschumacher is trying unsuccessfully to milk. As the half-track passes, I see a shield surrounding a lightning bolt and a key done in white paint on the side. It is the insignia of the Hitler Youth Division. The only face I see is the boy's and that for only a few seconds. The cow moves and steps on my foot, then steps off mumbling. Von Schwerin gives it another face full of the long grass we pulled up. When the half-track is gone, only the diesel fumes, the smell of chipped stone, and the marks of the tracks are left.

"That's the rest of them. The rest of the Division. They've been trained in the north, and now we're meeting up." Von Schwerin slaps the cow gently on the side of the head.

Handschumacher shoves aside the ballooning udder of the cow and looks up from under the black-and-white Friesian belly. He wants to know what's going on.

"The Division's been split up and trained in fragments. That's because this Division isn't supposed to exist anymore. The fact that those lot just came through means we must be close to the Ardennes." Von Schwerin is still the quiet-talking mechanism he became a few days after the trip began. All speech leaks from him as involuntary whispers.

A column of trucks follows the half-track, canvas roofs pulled shut, no license plates. The column goes on forever.

End of picture. Darkness follows.

"Do you mean to tell me you've been rolling around with a woman twice your age?" I was riding up front in the truck with Voss. That morning Kaslaka had refused to get up from his spread-eagle position on the grid floor, and Voss liked company while he was driving.

I shrugged.

He shook his head and snorted. I noticed a piece of his right ear was missing.

"And you left her back in . . . whatever? That right?"

"Mm."

"She wanted to marry you or something?"

"Shouldn't have told you." I scrunched into the corner against the door and folded my arms.

"It's all right." He looked across. "I won't *tell*. Maybe she'll come after you some more. She hasn't got much to lose."

"Maybe she'll kill me in my sleep."

"Most dangerous thing in the world is a pissed-off woman."

"So says Voss."

"So I says. So says Kaslaka, too. Reason he's in the SS is because of a woman."

"Kaslaka doesn't know the difference between a woman and a lamppost."

"Nor do I when I'm drunk."

I raised my hands, palms up, and blew a raspberry.

"It's true about Kaslaka. Who else that you can think of shave their heads?"

I blew another raspberry.

"Think, Westland."

"I don't know."

"Communist Party members. That's what Kaslaka used to be."

I didn't argue much because I was thinking about food, a craving, like a pregnant woman's hunger, for onion soup with French bread and cheese on top. Maybe I hadn't heard him right, anyway.

"Kaslaka is from one of those Germanic colonies in Rumania—Bessarabia. He used to be in a little group of Communists in a town called Svetslana. You know, one of those half-arse operations where they held their meetings in the basement of the local milkman. This was back in the thirties, and the town Fascists and the town Commies used to beat each other up in the bar and break shit until everyone got fed up with both sides.

"He said there were only twelve members: farmhands, the milkman, postman, a couple of radical schoolgirls, and Kaslaka's the baker. They had a budget that wouldn't have kept a horse in hay. The only thing they had worth looking at was a red flag, and the milkman's mother turned it into a pair of pajamas for the man's birthday as a surprise. Kaslaka said that all they used to do was get drunk and go home after they had their meetings, and all the time the Fascists were recruiting in the mines and the farmers' unions. Kaslaka started banging one of the female Party members, and pretty soon he didn't give much for the Party himself.

"So one day the milkman, named Borodok, came back from a holiday in Austria and said he'd hooked up with the Central Communist Party in Vienna and he needed someone to go in and pick up money. He started talking about a new meeting place, maybe some uniforms, a flag. Pretty soon everyone is all gung ho and pointing the finger at Kaslaka because he's the only one besides Borodok who's ever been to Vienna and Borodok has some excuse about being recognized by the Gestapo. But Kaslaka doesn't want to go—said the day they broke the news to him he'd been up all night boffing Comrade Big Breasts in every room in the house, including the bakery downstairs. All Kaslaka wanted from this world was to make loaves of bread and make little comrades. . . ." Voss pinched the bridge of his nose. "Can't remember what he said her name was.

"They tell him he's got to do it for the Party, for his country, really"—Voss's clenched fist waved at the steering wheel—"nailing him with the Great Patriotic Spiel. They want him to sign over the bakery to this man he really hates called Soleki, but he won't do it. Goes home and hides in his bakery.

"But the woman started working on him, telling him it would be like a holiday. What's he got to lose from a few days away? She probably told him that while they were lying on the bakery floor all covered in flour dust and he with his head on backwards from boffing all day. So Kaslaka gives in and says he'll go, signs a paper saying the bakery is in Soleki's hands until he gets back, packs his things, and meets Borodok and the girl at the station.

"Borodok gives him a blurred photograph with a ring penciled around the head of a person in the picture, tells him that's the Supreme Comrade or whatever, gives him the name of a hotel and a room number in it. Time, date, all there, and they just sit drinking soup until . . ."

"Soup?" I opened my eyes as if I were coming out of hibernation.

"What? What do you mean? Soup. Yes, I guess. I'm only telling it like he told me."

"Suppose it was onion soup?"

"Westland, you are retarded."

"I've been dreaming about onion soup for days, Voss."

"You spastic."

Quiet.

Nothing.

Silence.

"So did he go to Vienna?"

"Yes."

"And what happened?"

"He got there, got to the hotel, and meanwhile there's lots of German soldiers in the streets since it's '38 and after the Anschluss, so he gets nervous. Decides to go up the back way to the room, climbs the fire escape, and peeks into the room. But there's no Comrade there. There's two SS men in black uniforms sitting on chairs in the middle of the room. He said that's all the furniture there was. Two chairs. They had their backs turned to him. You see, Borodok had set him up so that when he didn't come home, got all his ribs broken, and then drowned in a toilet bowl, they were going to keep his bakery. That's the way they were going to get their money for their People's Party of Svetslana."

"So what's he doing in the SS after that?"

"Because they turned him inside out. I mean, before all he wanted to do was be the village baker. And he'd probably still *be* the village baker if he hadn't gotten messed up in all that political crap. But they turned over something in him, flipped on the red lights, so all he can do is pile up the hate. Man, I never seen someone so full of hate as Kaslaka. This way, in the SS, he thinks he's getting back at them every day of his life. I never seen so much hate in a man."

Quiet.

"Fucking Communists." I stretched like a cat.

"They're all the same, Westland. Fucking Fascists, fucking Commies. Maybe they want something different in the end, but the way they want to get there is all the same. I swear to Christ, people hurt people like you wouldn't believe. I know it's the fifth oldest story in the universe or whatever—that it's all the politicians' fault—but they don't think of the ugliness. What they need is to know the details, these high and mighties. They lie and cheat and steal. You take one, say one of the blithering idiots who thinks he's running the Russian front. They're so concerned with the neatness of their maps that every time a salient appears, they throw away ten thousand people trying to close it again, when the truth is, they should leave it where it is. That way the poor Reds get shot at from both sides until there's none of them left. Something simple like that. Take one of those men and make him sit in a bunker through a two-hour barrage, then make him fight his way out with a bayonet or a shovel, and you won't have the waste. It's just the waste I can't stand."

Quiet.

Nothing.

One minute. Two minutes.

"He went home to Svetslana, took Soleki and threw him in the bread oven, and he took the girl and crucified her. Hammers and nails. Like god-damned Jesus Christ. Stuck her out in the fields like a scarecrow, which is what everyone thought she was until it came to harvesttime. By then he was in an SS training camp in Austria. They didn't have his name. They didn't know he used to be a Commie. You'd never think it. He's such a simple man. He's got the face of a village baker."

Rain.

Winter fog.

Lightning across the smokestacks of a factory.

"But he kept his head shaved."

Voss stuck out his lower lip and shrugged, and we both flinched at the thunder howling down from the clouds.

VIII

FOUR COLUMNS, five deep, six rows across. I was second
column, second from the left at the front. Breder was next to
me, and Handschumacher was on the other side. We were slow-
marching through a town. Making a show of it this time for
some reason. All part of the grand strategy. I never figured these
things out. Six days on the road. I think.

And for once I knew where we were.

I had come here with my parents about ten years before and
listened to an oompah band a friend of my father's was in. The
band was all dressed up in green suits with shorts, high socks,
and feathers in their hats. My father laughed all the way through
it and kept sighing loudly, sliding back in the pew of the church
where the concert was held. I remembered fragments of streets,
the ceiling of the restaurant where we had dinner, and dapples

of color from the windows of the church. The rest of the place was blanked out, but I remembered the name Bad Münster-eifel when we drove past the black-and-white sign on the way into town.

We lined up by the train station, high hills on both sides covered with evergreens, and the houses vaguely Alpine with their painted window boxes. We were in the trough of a valley, and the town had old fortifications around it, which the town had spilled out of, so the walls were surrounded on both sides by houses.

We filed down the main road running through the center, fat chipped cobblestones, and the main guard tower with its rotten wooden doors, looking as if it had been hacked from pieces of moldy bread. We passed by a small stream, above which the street was raised. It was knee-deep and had weeds in it.

Above us on the left was some sort of ruined castle, which I couldn't see because I had to be staring straight ahead. There were bridges crossing the stream and benches on the bridges. It was early afternoon, and all I wanted to do was lie down on one of the benches and sleep. If I had run for it then, broken rank and fled, I could have been home in three days on foot. They would never have caught me, not after all the things I had been taught. I knew we were only a day's ride from Belgium, maybe two, and that the Eifel Mountains we were in stretched out and up, giving the farmers fields and orchards, keeping some of the land to itself in thick forests. The Eifel gave way to the Hohe Venn, more mountains claiming more of the land with its woods, hiding villages and deep lakes, a place where people tucked themselves away when they went to be alone. After that were the Ardennes, and the rumors of Belgian towns appearing out of tiny, rained-on valleys, wild boar and deer running their black wood trails, smoked meat and cheese in all the shop windows, the draperies checked white and red, the houses made of gray stone. All I knew of the Ardennes was rumors, like I knew Paris had a Tower and Rome a Colosseum; I knew the Ardennes hung red-and-white checked cloth everywhere, that the people were foresters and ate smoked meat.

We went through the town in a few minutes, out of another gate, and halted between a gas station and a convent, which looked more like a barracks than the Camp.

I was thinking they must sell a lot of ice cream here in the summer. Why hadn't we come here more often?

Some men walked out in front of us down the road, carrying satchels, looking like auto mechanics in their blue overalls. They stopped halfway across the road and pointed at us.

Voss was talking to Ramke, leaning on the door of the Kubelwagen, nodding at whatever Ramke was saying.

"So where's the bar?" Handschumacher whispered to me.

"I don't know. Did you see one?"

"You said you'd been here before."

"Yes, but about ten years ago. I didn't go around looking for a place to get soused at that age."

Handschumacher squinted at me out of the corner of his eye, then stuck his tongue out. "Schwerin!"

"What?" All whispers.

"I'll give you five marks if you can give yourself an erection in thirty seconds." Handschumacher rocked on the balls of his feet.

"Wouldn't want to take your money."

"Why not?"

"I've got the fastest Willy in the West."

"I'll bet you anyway. Breder, you be the judge."

"Can't see from here."

"I couldn't take your money."

"Why not, Schwerin?"

"I already have an erection."

* * *

"WHAT ARE those two doing?" Breder stood up on his toes and stared at the men in overalls who had stopped to look at us.

"Trying to get a better view of the Great Thirty Second Erection." Von Schwerin.

Then I watched as one of the men took something from his satchel and threw it at us. I saw the thing arc up in the air and then come down on someone's helmet. A shout. I was buying summer ice cream far away inside my head. Something else fell down on us, more shouting, and I turned as another boy turned, holding his face and falling.

Acid like a phosphorus explosion, throwing its white burning branches, spread inside me as I saw a gash in the boy's cheek, first only a deep tear, then suddenly bleeding, blood everywhere, and things coming down on us from the garden of the convent.

I saw more men, others in overalls, throwing bricks and stones and bottles. They were behind us by the gas station and up on the town walls. Glass breaking. A brick smashed on von Schwerin's helmet, and the red stone powder puffed into my eyes.

People were running for the convent garden. NCOs screamed in the effeminate shriek that comes from yelling louder than it is really possible to yell.

Von Schwerin went down on his face, and I heard Voss, then saw Voss as he appeared in front of us like a goblin, waving his arms, commands pouring from his mouth. He pot-shot at the men with the Luger he carried, without appearing to hit anybody. The phosphorus dissolved in my bones and sent me running for cover, but I tripped over Breder and fell. A bottle turned to tiny fragments on the pavement. Breder said, "Shit," and covered his eyes. I looked at a sliver of green glass stuck in my knuckle, then slowly picked it out.

"Doctor! Get a doctor!" someone was shouting.

"Get . . . up . . . you . . . fuckers!" Voss was dead pale with anger, kicking us off the ground.

Slowly we were getting up and running. The Kubel had a broken windshield. I saw Ramke walking toward the convent in his long black leather greatcoat. A couple of boys were smashing in the door with rifle butts. White faces appeared in the windows. Nuns.

"Find . . . them. Bring . . . them . . . to me!" Voss kicked me behind the knee, and I fell, hitting the ground with my face. I felt blood run over my lips as I stood up again and ran after Breder, turning to see Kaslaka dragging von Schwerin over to the shelter of the Kubel.

Breder dove over a low wall into the garden of a house made of stone painted dull yellow. So I dove after him, and we lay in a dead rose garden, hearing footsteps everywhere and shouting. Rifle fire echoed around the valley, making it sound as if someone in the hills were shooting back.

I pushed away Breder's hand and the handkerchief he offered me, and poked my head up over the wall, tasting blood like steel wool in my mouth. I picked three bullets out of the ammunition pouch on my belt and stuffed them into the Mauser. I felt completely weak. Breder pointed, and I saw a man in overalls running from behind the house down a side street. The gun went off in my hands and shot a hole through the front window of the yellow house.

We chased him, me with my rubber legs, hurdled the walk, and stopped at the side street, which was the back lane to a row of houses and a place where people parked their cars. It looked like the room of a fairground haunted house, with dozens of doors and nothing else. They all led to people's gardens, and we couldn't see into them because the walls were too high.

The man was running down the middle of the alley, panting, his head back. I raised the gun, slipped the *V* of the foresight in front of his head, and pulled the trigger with a rubber finger, but nothing happened because I had forgotten to chamber another bullet.

"Wait a minute." Breder was just standing there.

I slammed the bolt back and forward again, aimed at the man. Breder pushed me against the wall, shouting something, and I shot a line along the bricks a few meters down the alley.

The man skidded to a stop, turned, raised his hands, and when he saw me look away from him and kick Breder in the balls, he climbed the wall and disappeared into a garden.

I left Breder on his knees holding his balls, and ran, not rubber-boned anymore. Pissed off now. Wondering what I did to deserve having stones and bottles thrown at me.

It was a greasy green-painted door he had jumped over, and I smashed it twice with my boot, leaving imprints of the hobnails like a waffle-iron in the wood. Then I opened the door like a human being, with the latch, and ran in as fast as I could.

The back door of the house was open, and when I ran inside, my hobnails skidded on the stone floor of the kitchen. I slid past the stove, the sink, and crashed into an ironing board. When I looked up from where I had fallen on the floor, there was another man in the doorway to the next room. He had brown trousers on and suspenders over an undershirt, bare feet, bald head. I pointed the gun at him. He yelled, "Oh, my God!" and ran away.

When I got to the door, I saw the man sitting at a table with his wife and two small children. The wife yelled, "Oh, my God!" and covered her face with her hands. One of the children threw a boiled potato at me. They were having dinner, pot pie by the look of it, with canned peaches for dessert.

"What for the love of God is going on?" The man bug-eyed me with his hands flat, raised slightly off the table. "What do you want? Has my house become a fucking Autobahn?"

"Shut up! Shut up! Shut up!" the wife yelled from behind the mask of her hands. Another boiled potato hit me in the chest, then bounced onto my boots.

"Hey, knock it off," I said to the little girl, who had a shower cap on and was wearing her nightdress.

"What . . . what is . . . ?" The man looked as if he were trying to swallow his lips.

"A man in a blue suit."

The father jerked his thumb down their hallway and out the front door.

"Oh, my God! Jesus fucking Christ!" The woman was pulling at her hair. The father snapped his head around and stared at her.

"Jesus what?"

The front door was open, and I went out in the street, which was empty. I looked at all the black windows and got spooked and hid behind a wall again. Nobody. No one at all. I walked down the sidewalk, trying to look dangerous and wondering what had happened to Breder and von Schwerin. Then in the middle of that I laughed, because all of us had been hurt and only one by someone other than ourselves: von Schwerin, who looked as if he only had a hangover, anyway, when they dragged him off.

I jumped the wall at the yellow house, suddenly very tired, and saw Breder crouched in the garden of the house next door. As I came up to him, he waved me down to cover, and we both saw, at the end of the alley between two rows of houses across the road, Voss and the man in overalls, the one I had been chasing.

The man was on his hands and knees from where Voss had knocked him with a rifle butt. Voss put down the rifle and kicked the man in the stomach. The man rolled over and tried to stand up but only got to his knees. He put his hands in the air.

"How are your balls?" I whispered, getting ready to stand up.

"Quiet." Breder put his hand on my shoulder and pushed me back down.

The man in overalls stood up slowly, still with his hands in the air. I couldn't see his face, only the brown curly hair at the back of his head. Voss stood with his hands on his hips, spat against the wall of the alley, and jerked his head at the man, who backed up two paces. Voss waved him away, like a schoolmaster shooing his pupils out of class. The man backed up two more paces and said something. Voss shouted at him to go.

I watched the man turn and run, then suddenly trip and throw his hands in the air, stagger on a couple of paces and fall, the crack of Voss's Luger sounding around the houses, boxing our ears and fading into barely audible clicks. Voss held the gun out for a couple of seconds after the man fell, as if he couldn't move his arm. Then he walked very quickly over to the blue overalls and shot the man in the face. The man's head bounced up from the pavement and down again. Voss put the gun back in the holster and jogged toward where the Kubelwagen was, past where we crouched behind the wall, holding our breath.

"He'll tell them the man was trying to escape." Breder stared straight in front of him.

I breathed in very deeply and then out again.

"I should have let you shoot him. At least that way he'd have had a chance. Voss executed him. Remember Fleps told us only the Russians did that? No." He shook his head. "I wasn't going to let you shoot him just for throwing stones. I don't care who he hit. And my balls feel like hell, thank you very much. So." He stood up, using his rifle as a crutch. "What the fuck." Then he left, and before I followed him, I looked for a while at the lump in the road. It seemed as if it had half sunk into the cobblestones, the boots sticking up like the stumps of small trees and the open hands waiting for raindrops.

VON SCHWERIN was sitting against the back tire of our truck which had driven up in the meantime. He was smoking a cigarette, his helmet on the ground beside him. There were people standing in small groups. Smashed brick and glass on the ground. Someone was brewing coffee on a portable stove. I trod in a small puddle of blood as I walked over to von Schwerin.

"You okay?"

He nodded, closing his eyes and breathing out. "Just shook me. How about you?"

I touched at the dried nosebleed, the hard clogs in my nostrils. "Voss did this, believe it or not."

"Voss just shot a man trying to get away." Von Schwerin peered over at the Kubel, and I followed his gaze to where Voss stood at attention in front of Ramke, who was looking away and scowling.

"I'll tell you about that later."

"What do you mean?"

"I mean I'll tell you later. Who are these people?" I pointed to half a dozen men lined up facing a wall, some of them in overalls, others in different work clothes.

"French workers apparently." Von Schwerin held his cigarette up to me. I took a puff, then flipped the stub over my shoulder. "You know, ones they deported to work in German factories. Apparently some of them just decided to start throwing rocks at us."

"Maybe they have a grudge." I sat down next to him by the tire.

"Well, they're fucked now, I can tell you. Ramke's pissed off about his windshield."

"Where's Breder?"

"He walked past a minute ago. Boy called Braun got his face cut up pretty badly, broken nose, jaw too, I heard."

"My little gossip merchant." I patted him on the head. "Where do these rumors come from?"

"Heard it in the breeze. Can you imagine the grief we're going to get? We just lay there. If they'd had guns, we'd all be dead."

"We're only human."

"Takes more than that. We're supposed to be beyond that point."

A man in a sloppy suit with the gold chain and medallion of a mayor around his neck drove up in a sky-blue Volkswagen and jumped out. Then he started yelling at Ramke, who looked at him for a little while as if he couldn't figure out where the noise was coming from.

"You take your trench manners and your bunch of savages and get out of here. I just drove past a man who'd been shot in the head. He was shot from this close." The man touched a finger to his head. "THIS CLOSE!"

"Stop shouting." Ramke. Quietly.

"I could see the blast marks. He was executed. I don't care what happened. This isn't the Russian front. Now get out. You aren't welcome. God, and these are boys! How old are they? What are you? Barbarians? Have you crawled up out of the Dark Ages?" The man was red in the face, his moustache twitching.

Ramke said something to his Kubel driver, a short man with a neck like a pink log. The driver picked up the mayor and shoved him back into the Volkswagen. Then he bent down and said something through the open window, drumming his fingers briefly on the hood. The car drove away.

"Is that what happened, then? Is that what Voss did?" Von Schwerin sat up and hooked his arms around his knees.

"Just that."

"Did he see you?"

"No."

"I'm afraid we will become that way."

"It's my ongoing nightmare." I sat up and copied von Schwerin, hooking my arms around my knees.

"Do you know, I can still smell the fish Handschumacher cooked in that hubcap."

"Where is he?"

"He chased down one of the Frenchmen and beat the crap

out of him. But then, get this, he let him go again. Ramke himself comes storming up and asks him what the hell he thinks
he's doing, letting one of the Frenchies go."

"What did Handschumacher say?"

"He said he thought he'd taught him his lesson."

"And Ramke's going to kill him now, right?"

"No. Ramke laughed. Handschumacher honestly thought
he was doing the right thing. You could see it on his face. Not
even Ramke could hold it against him. Now he's guarding the
rest of the Frenchmen who got rounded up. He's trying to show
Ramke he's not a complete moron."

Handschumacher stood in front of the men in overalls,
pointing his rifle at any one of them who moved. Now and then
he looked over to where Ramke was, leaning against the front
of the Kubel talking to his driver, to make sure Ramke could
see he was doing a good job. In a loud voice he told them all to
get back in line. They shuffled obediently, but they already were
in a line and had no place to go.

Breder walked past on the other side of the road, dragging
his rifle like a toy.

I WENT into the woods to take a dump, an old newspaper
rolled under my arm. From the hollow calm of the countryside
I would have said it was a Sunday. We were not far from the
town of Gemund.

Breder walked with me out of the camp, moping, shuffling
with his hands in his pockets, and his moping made my skin
crawl.

"Something on your mind, Breder?" I stopped dead in the
dirt path leading down to the woods, rutted by the trampling
of cows. I didn't turn around.

"No. Just walking. All right?"

"I'm going to take a dump."

"Good for you."

I turned around, and he was staring off back up the hill as if to see no one else was coming.

"I'm going to take a dump and you want to come watch me? Is that it?" I snapped the newspaper open, the way my father did at the table after dinner, which was the signal for everyone to leave him alone and let him read and smoke in peace.

"I want to talk to you."

"Can't it wait?"

"Don't want anyone else to hear." He tapped his boot on the ground, then raised his head slowly back, closing his eyes, suddenly whipped a handkerchief out of his pocket and sneezed into it.

I had been looking forward to my dump. It was about the only chance I had to be alone. Sometimes I sat for more than an hour, back against a tree, my forearms resting on my knees, and there was only the sound of the wind in the tops of the trees. Sometimes I could see other boys the same as me, staring off into space in their own corner of the forest.

Only Breder would have followed me off on my dump run. I thought everybody knew dumps were sacred. No one but Breder bothered anybody with private talks.

"So what is it?" I sat down against a tree and dug my fingers into the pine needles.

"I don't want any part in this, I've decided."

I made a movement as if playing the violin.

"Think I'm fucking joking, don't you?" He stood up, and I found myself looking at his boots, turned up slightly at the toes, the steel toe plate scratched shiny on the road, the leather chafed white. "I know you all think I'm a bad asset. Bad fucking asset. I know you're all fed up with me. Maybe you think I've forgotten all the stuff I said about the war being lost. Think maybe you beat it out of me against the gym."

I looked up and sighed.

"It hasn't been easy or anything, trying to pretend the whole lot of you didn't beat the shit out of me." He screwed his fist into his eye. Then he sat down. "Been a lot less easy trying to get someone to *like* me around here. You get this"—he slapped his hand on his thigh—"brand, and then you can't shake it. That's why I hate these little groups. Stand back and look at it and it's like looking at a pile of insects crawling all over each other, chewing each other up. It's fucking ugly, like a fucking scab you pick off every day and it gets full of pus. And I don't want to play anymore. What the hell right you think you have shooting a man like you tried to do yesterday? What right anybody got to take him away from his home? That's the way I been thinking. Sure, it's easy to ignore that. *You* didn't take him away. Isn't *your* fault. And after what we saw Voss do yesterday. Count me out."

"So you're fed up. I'm fed up too. Think I like dumping in the woods like a bear?"

"The amount of time it takes you, I'd say yes."

"So are you finished now with your lament, and can I take my dump, which I enjoy so very much?"

"I want to know if I can trust you."

"Yes." Sigh. "Why?"

"It's your turn on guard tonight. I'm taking off. I need you to give me a couple of hours."

"Then what you going to do?" I could feel a headache coming.

He shrugged. "Live off the land. Don't worry about that."

"No. You worry about it. It's winter coming up, and if you desert—that is the word, Breder, *desertion*—no one is going to take you in. The Field Police will track you down in a couple of days and pop your skull like a balloon, probably in public. Then they'll leave you to rot, hanging from a tree like in the Middle Ages. You're not going anywhere. You goddamn take your chances with the rest of us. You coward."

"No, I'm not. I didn't run away when you beat me up. If I'd thought that Frenchman deserved to die, I'd have spread his brains on the pavement myself. But he didn't. And I just don't feel like killing anyone." He was on his knees with his face close to mine. The careful rise and fall of his Adam's apple.

"Oh, why didn't you take this to Schwerin or someone apart from me? Why didn't you just fucking go?"

"Need a headstart. I've thought this out."

"You always do." Wind in the pines.

"So what are you going to do? I tell you I'm going and that's that. Are you going to give me a chance? I'm only asking for a chance." He was crying down his cheeks to his lips.

I leaned over and pushed his tears away with my thumb. Then he grabbed my wrists, smiled, and threw them away again.

"I don't feel like I'm deserting. Don't feel like I'm doing anything bad. Just fed up is all. Not desertion. Just changed my mind." Then he stood up and held out his hand for me to shake. "Good-bye, then, Sebastian."

"I didn't say I'd help you."

"But you will. I trust you." He took my hand from where it rested on my knee and shook it.

I sat for a while after he'd gone, drawing patterns in the pine-needle dirt with a twig, making faces and crossing them out. A few raindrops made their way through the branches. Outside, it was falling hard. I had meant to ask him why he'd ever signed up for this. Could have gone for something else. There are ways out if you're smart. Probably joined in the same fanaticism he's leaving with.

I was going to have my dump, no matter what. I sat in the woods like a bear and tried not to think. Raindrops. Lightning through the trees.

STANDING IN the food line, I smelled the stew and the stale aluminum smell of my mess tin and scraped some goo off the rim with my fingernail since sometimes the cooks wouldn't give you food if your mess tin was dirty.

I had lost all my eating utensils except the spoon. It was all anybody used anyway, since there was never meat in the stew that you couldn't eat without cutting.

The stew was so boring and so bad that it did not make me want something different to eat; it made me not want food at all.

Handschumacher boiled up some pine cones as a soup.

Von Schwerin said worms were good nutrition.

Handschumacher said the woods were crawling with deer and set up a snare, but only caught Breder, who trod in it while he was walking around in the dark looking for a place to pee.

Von Schwerin said we should consider this carefully and figure out what was actually in the stew: water, beets, potatoes, sometimes a carrot, bones, some meat, gristle, fat, grease, pine needles, sometimes blobs of lard. We figured it out and looked to von Schwerin, whom we expected to make some grand statement, but he had gone to sleep, so there was no statement.

A Kubel pulled up and two men in raincoats got out, slammed the doors so everyone turned to look. They wore chains around their necks with the half-moon metal shield of the Military Police. On the shield was an eagle and a swastika covered with green-yellow paint that glowed in the dark. The coats were gray rubber with green collars.

"We're looking for Sebastian Westland."

"Oh, fucking hell." I couldn't help it.

"Must be you, then." One of them smiled at me.

They drove me away in the Kubel, me in the back seat holding my mess tin like a begging bowl and almost in tears because I didn't know what I'd done wrong. They kept their helmets on, and, when the Kubel went over a bump, their heads smashed against the roof.

We stopped at a crossroads at the outskirts of a village. The two men got out, one tossed a pack of cigarettes to the other, then they stared at me in the back seat with my eyes wide like a rabbit's and asked me if I was going to sit there all day.

"This is just for our personal information." One of the MPs leaned against the Kubel and folded his arms over the half-moon shield.

"Whose?" It took all my energy to say the one word.

"Mine and Klaus's." Klaus was out in the middle of the road holding a stick with a flat circle on the end like a lollipop, which had green on one side and red on the other, and "Stop" and "Go," and he was out there looking for traffic. "Last night we stopped a woman called Hammacher and she said she was looking for you. You know her, yes?"

"Yes." Sickness like a black ball was rising from nowhere into my guts.

"She said you were engaged to her."

"No, sir."

"Did you know she killed her husband?" He was older than I, with blue shadows on his chin, cleft down the middle like clay run through with a knife. Eyes the color of walnuts.

I could feel my bladder aching when he said her husband was dead, as if some troll were standing inside me with a crowbar ready to open the floodgate and make me wet my pants. Trolls ran up and down my rib cage in their hobnailed boots. "No, sir. I didn't know that. I swear."

"She poisoned him with rat poison. We took her to the local police and they checked up on her. She's been driving around after you for a while now. You know anything about it?"

"Am I in trouble now?" I meant to think it and not say it.

"No. No trouble. Me and Klaus just wanted to know. I mean"—walnut eyes close by—"it's pretty strange."

"What happened to her? Where is she now?"

"Still in the station, I suppose." Friend of Klaus shrugged and shook a cigarette out of a packet, handed it to me. Klaus ushered past an old VW, twirling the lollipop like a pro. "Don't go down there, though. I mean, you're all right now. Not in trouble. But if you go make a fuss, you're liable to end up in a murder trial."

Klaus threw the lollipop up from one hand and caught it with the other. Then he threw it over his head and caught it behind his back.

"Me and Klaus just can't figure out why she's following you. I mean, she's a bit older. Sounds a bit"—he jiggled his outstretched hand—"strange."

"I—" It was all I could think of and all I said.

"I don't know what she thought she was going to do when she found you. Maybe she was going to marry you, whether you liked it or not. Taking them young. Klaus says he's all for that. None of our business, of course, but, you see, just interested."

"What's going to happen to her?"

"What happens to people who kill other people?"

"They get medals."

"Not this time, Bright Boy."

I should not have tried to be funny. I should not have tried to make friends.

"She was pretty hysterical when we turned her in, saying we had to let her go and all. Saying we'd all die horrible deaths if we didn't."

"What if I went to see her?"

"You'd get brought into it is all. She's in civilian hands now. They won't bother the military, which means they won't bother you, before a big offensive. Worst they could do is accuse you of having something to do with his death, and you were probably in your camp when that happened. You've got an alibi. You'd only have to deny it. But don't go in there and mess it up. Not if I were you." Friend of Klaus patted me on the arm.

Klaus fought a duel against ghosts with the lollipop.

"Is it all right if I go back to my group then?"

"Sure. Need a ride?"

"No, thank you."

"Westland, she gave us this to give to you." He reached into the glove compartment and pulled out the sweater she had knitted for me, which I had left in the car. "We were just interested is all, Westland."

I stood in the road with no one around, put the sweater to my face. Teeth clenched tight enough to crack. She left me to rot, and I was rotten now. She taught me herself what I did to her.

This black and white I had made for myself was worth nothing. It was only the most fragile frame of mind.

I looked at the town, like a clump of rocks in the middle distance, with the blade of the church spire in the center, and I went there. It seemed like whatever had been the best thing to do, we had never done it. No chance. Never was.

She knew I was out here. She probably didn't want me to find her. She threw herself headlong away from everywhere she was supposed to go. She had gone on a quest to find a place where she had no one and nothing, some empty plain with nowhere to hide.

And this was it. This had to be the place; the clarity of nothing towns and cafés, the clarity of fog and rain. I was only a part of what she looked for—a private, smoking fragment of the whole.

I left the sweater hanging on some barbed wire at the edge of the road.

"LET ME SEE." The policeman stood up from his desk and searched along a row of nails, on each of which there was a key. He talked like a homosexual. At first he wouldn't let me into the jailhouse, babbled and peered at me through an iron sliding piece built into the door, wanting to know what business I had coming to the jail, then telling me he had orders that no one was to see the Hammacher woman. So I gave him all the money in my wallet. He made me give the bills to him before he would open the door. I held out as many Reichsmarks as there were, and a wooden hand with brass joints at the fingers clunked through the opening.

No one else in the jail. Only four cells, and two of them with no bars on them, the space filled with crates labeled AM, which I knew was canned meat. Every can of meat in the German Army had AM stamped on the bottom.

"She had to be sedated." He turned, blinked, then turned back to the keys, tapping the wooden hand on the plastered brick wall. "She's got a mouth like a garbage heap, that woman. God, I daresay even *I* learned a few new words today."

The whole place was painted light blue, the same color as at a hairdresser's my mother used to go to.

She was lying on a small metal-frame bed and had a gray blanket pulled up to her throat. There was a suitcase of hers at the foot of the bed, and her shoes were set together beside a chair at the other end of the room. A small hole in the wall at the top let in air from outside.

"I don't know if you'll be able to wake her. Doctor came and shot her full of something, and it shut her right up, I can tell you." He was wearing one of those early-war police tunics that was too big for him, and red slippers instead of boots. "Want some coffee? Ersatz, of course. I just boiled the water. I suppose you've paid for it." He giggled and slapped the knuckle side of his wooden hand into the palm of the other.

"Fine."

"Are you the one she came up here to see?"

I shrugged and watched the shape under the blanket to see if it was moving.

"She killed her husband, you know. Did it the old-fashioned way and poisoned him, I hear. No one's allowed to see her officially until she's questioned. God knows how anybody even knew enough about it to stop her. We've had to send away for someone to do the questioning. We're strictly amateur around here. Never anybody in this prison."

"Coffee? Yes?"

"Yes." He flipflopped down the hall to his desk in the other room.

I hissed, "Lise," through the bars, and for a while nothing moved under the blanket. Then a hand with a wedding ring on it slipped from under the gray blanket and grasped the bed rail. She stretched and her feet in their stockings stuck out at the end.

She sat up and rubbed at her face, yawned and put both her hands over her mouth.

"Lise."

Her eyes, drugged, flicked up at me behind the bars. Then she laughed, a snort of air through her nose, and lay back on the bed. "Oh, Sebastian. I'm in so much trouble. These last couple of weeks have been like a dream. They still feel like a dream. I've been in prison before, you know. Drunk and disorderly. That was before I got married." She had crooked her right arm over her eyes. "Our plans to meet again went a bit wrong, didn't they? I stayed waiting for ages and only found out later you had left. I suppose they didn't give you time to tell me. Was it because of an emergency that you had to leave?" Now she was looking at me, a little glassy-eyed.

There was a clang down the hall, and I saw the policeman standing over a puddle of coffee with an enamel mug in the middle of the mess. His wooden hand was held out, grasping nothing.

"This blasted thing doesn't work!" He bent down and picked up the mug with his good hand. When he saw I was watching him, he stood up and laughed. "I'm trying to get used to it. It's supposed to work like a normal hand if you bend it in the right position."

"Why do you have it?" I took out a cigarette and tapped it on my thumb before putting it in my mouth.

"Africa," he said, as if it were the last excuse for everything. "I think it must still be out there someplace. One minute I had it and one minute I didn't is all I can tell you. Got me home, though." He swung the mug on his finger and told me he'd go fetch more coffee.

She was dabbing at her face with a makeup brush and looking at herself in the mirror of her compact.

"I think he's queer," she whispered, without taking her eyes from the mirror.

"I had to bribe him to get in here."

"Did you? That's sweet of you." She stood on the bed, the springs creaking, and raised her face to the tiny open window, breathed in a few times, then sat down again. "Have they told you what I did?"

"You mean, your husband?" She looked very small and frail in the cell, and I realized I had been afraid of her almost all the time except now. I was wrong to have come. I was only opening old wounds. She wasn't going anywhere now. Nothing more to say.

"Yes. I didn't quite divorce him. It wasn't quite as amicable as that. I don't think he was in any pain." She raised her head. "I can't stand these bars. It's the worst part of this damn dream. I keep thinking I'll wake up, put on my coat—his coat, actually—and drive into town to pick you up from school."

"Not in school anymore."

"Yes, but you see, that's not how it seems right now."

"I can't stay very long."

"You never could, could you?"

There was another clank in the hall. "Shit! Fucking tree branch! God-damned bundle of twigs. One more time and you're going out the window, into the garbage. *Fini!*" This time he hadn't even made it past his desk.

"He's talking to his hand, it sounds like." She was smiling. When she smiled, I forgot how much older than I she was.

"Sounds like. Yes."

"So tell me, was it an emergency that day you didn't come to me?" She sat on her hands and bounced a little on the bed.

"You seem very calm for someone who's just killed someone else."

"I didn't 'just' kill him. If you want to be dramatic, you can say I killed him a very long time ago. But it was a couple of weeks actually. And I'm not calm, Sebastian, I'm drugged. I'm sitting on my hands because the fucking things are shaking." Her eyes weren't foggy now. They were back to boring their trails through my head. "Why don't you pass me a cigarette?"

I was afraid of her again, somewhere beneath the surface. I fished the ration-pack cigarettes from my pocket, gray pack with two white lines running across it. She caught them in one hand and had the lighter ready in the other. Then she put two cigarettes in her mouth and lit them.

"I already have one." I raised the smoking stick to show her.

"Oh, I know. These are both for me. Can I keep the pack?"

"Sure."

She was still on the bed. Wouldn't come close to me.

The policeman came back, holding the mug with his wooden hand, leaving footprints from the puddle of cold coffee. "Take it. Quick, before I drop the bastard." He laughed.

"Do I get some, too?" She talked from a white cloud.

"Um . . . think you're not supposed to have anything after . . . um . . . whatever they gave you. Make you sick, I believe."

"I don't care."

"Well, all the hot water's gone." He stuck out his lower lip.

"So boil some."

"Why don't you do it yourself?" He smiled at her, then at me, then went back to his desk.

She breathed out the smoke from her nose and her mouth, then said, "Arse-hole," very quietly, to the floor.

"What's going to happen to me?" She flicked the butts one after the other at a bucket in the corner of the cell.

"I don't know." I put the mug down on the floor between the

bars so she could get at it, but she didn't move from the bed.

"It's funny you are going away to kill people quite legally, and here I am behind bars for killing someone probably far worse than anyone you'll run into." Then she laughed and said, "Jesus Christ! Why don't you talk to me?"

"I don't know exactly what's going on. I don't know what to say to you."

"Before you used to say you loved me."

"Yes. I think I said that just before you left me on the train in Munich. I tried to find you in the crowd."

"So you don't love me anymore?"

"Didn't say that. I wouldn't have come here if I knew I didn't."

"Oh, and spend all that money getting in here, you mean."

"No."

"You left that day on purpose without telling me, didn't you?" She had lit another cigarette and spat out the smoke like she was spitting out blood.

I looked at the floor.

"Didn't you?" The hard voice of Lise Hammacher the murderer.

Then suddenly, "DIDN'T YOU?" screamed loud and close, and her body smashed against the bars, her hand clawing out, and I backed against the wall, wide-eyed, the coffee kicked across the cell. She held onto the bars crying fat tears, her lips pressed tight together. Quiet for a while.

"Didn't you, Sebastian? How could you leave me? I've ruined my life to be with you. Look what I've done. Look at where I am now because of you."

"Not because of me."

"It is!" Another scream, and I knew the policeman would come to see what was happening.

I shook my head. "I have to go now."

"No, you don't. You're just leaving me because you don't love me anymore. I'm too old. Too much trouble."

"Not that."

"What then?" She wiped her eyes on her fists curled around the bars.

"You used to leave me every day of the week. You left me in Munich. You told me I was too young. Then you take it all back and later tell me all the same shit again. I love you and I have to go now."

"No." Tears and blue eyes melting.

"Is there anything I can get you?"

"What?"

"Nothing. I'm going now."

"You can't. You can go away from me, but you can't leave me. Not the way you think you can. No."

I leaned forward to kiss her, and, faster than I would have thought possible, she had her hand behind my head and rammed it at the bars. Now with her face close she snarled at me, voice coming from somewhere down in her throat.

"You're not *leaving*, Sebastian. No more than I'm *leaving* this place. Because you can't forget. You didn't forget this." With one hand she undid two of the buttons on her shirt. When the third got stuck she ripped it off, the button rattling on the floor. The smell of her nakedness touching my face. "This much I know you didn't forget. You try sleeping with your milkmaids and you'll see my face. You go as far away as you want, but you try to leave and I'll rip your heart clean out of your body, Sebastian," she spat at me. Her fingers dug into the back of my head. "Now, you go to hell, before I fuck you and kill you at the same time." She let go, then pushed me away. "Now go. Get lost. Get him out of here!" she screamed when the policeman came back, and I left, with her still screaming, down the blue halls, the policeman staring. He watched her with his head tipped to one side, a blank expression on his face.

IX

FIVE A.M. Guard duty.

A column of tanks went past in the dark. Mark IV Tigers like houses with tracks on them. Out of the turret of each tank I could see the commanders standing, vaguely illuminated from an orange light inside. They wore leather jackets and side caps, and wires from their headphones snaked around them like vines. The howling of the engines rose and fell as each machine went past. The famous Maybach engine. The Giant Mouse squeaking of the tracks.

I counted twenty-four tanks and twelve trucks, then a few armored cars and two Kubels. I sat on a tree stump drinking coffee from a tin cup as they went by. They must have been the same ones we saw a couple of days before, who made up the rest of the Division.

Then I remembered Breder. I hoped he would have the sense to run for it where I wouldn't be able to see him. A wave of arguments began in the back of my head, and I began whispering, "Fuck you," to little people running around behind my eyes telling me I should turn him in. Loyalty to the cause. Loyalty to Friends. Be honest, decent, kind, and loyal to people of your own blood. If I turned him in before he left, he'd say I was making the whole thing up.

I sat on a tree stump rattling the trolls around in my skull, trying to make them leave.

Someone walked through the woods at my left and out onto the road where the tanks had gone past. The person looked up and down, talking to himself. He was too short for Breder.

I stood up and walked into the road.

"Who's there?" The person took a couple of paces toward me. "You're on the perimeter. You can't go past this point."

"It's me, Schwerin. Is that you, Sebastian?"

"Yes. What's up? It's not your turn to take my place yet, is it?" I was thinking maybe I fell asleep before.

"I can't find Breder." He started walking toward me. I walked back to my tree stump, and von Schwerin followed. "You haven't seen him, have you?"

"There's no one here but me." I sat down on the stump.

"He's been gone a whole hour. Said he was going to talk to Voss, but Voss hasn't seen him. He took his cape and his gun, his whole pack. I was half asleep, not paying attention. You don't think he's gone and run away?"

"Don't suppose." I shrugged and felt sick.

"I bet he has. Silly fuck."

"No one's been past here that I saw."

"Well, he could have gotten past you easily enough. Could have gone out on the other perimeter."

"What are you going to do?" I looked up at the shadow of his head in the dark.

"Don't know. Voss says he'll send out squads to find him if he's not back by sunrise. I hope he didn't do something stupid, Sebastian."

"Don't worry about it."

A LITTLE while before dawn I saw the first groups moving past the perimeter, capes draped over their shoulders, the bumps of rifles underneath making them look like squadrons of hunchbacks. A few trucks pulled out along the road. I knew they wouldn't catch him. It would have been like trying to find a deer, one particular deer. I was only hoping he would last the winter. I imagined him living in a log house in the middle of nowhere, clothes rotting off his body and a beard sprouting up off his face, creeping into towns in the dark and listening at people's doors for any sound that the war might be over.

I was glad to have been gone when Voss raged in his own form of epilepsy, ordering out the squads. For Voss never to have seen a man as angry as Kaslaka meant he had never seen himself. And Ramke would have quietly ordered the camp to stay put while the search went on, orders whispered to his driver Bauer as if to an interpreter.

EVERYONE BUT Voss and Kaslaka had gone when I got to our truck. They had made a sort of table for themselves by tying the corners of a cape to three different tree trunks with rope. They were playing cards on it. The cape was tight enough so that Kaslaka could rest a small mug of brandy on it. The bottle was on the ground between the arches of his feet.

They looked up and raised their eyebrows when they heard me, hopeful that maybe I was Breder.

"Do you know anything about this?" Voss screwed up his eyes.

"What? About Breder taking off?"

"Yes. Do you?"

"Only what Schwerin told me. No sign of him then, is there?"

Voss turned away from his cape full of cards and pointed to me. "That boy is fucked, I can tell you. You know why? Because if you got out on that road and ran like hell for a couple of hours you'd be at the American lines. But Breder doesn't know that, so he may go that way. Oh, we're close all right. We're close to it all happening. What is it—December tenth already? We're closer than you'd like to know, Westland. Now if Breder runs into some Yank patrol, they'll want to know exactly what an SS man is doing there, because as far as the rest of the world's concerned, there's nothing in these woods. We're thin air, Westland. The Yanks think there's a couple of soldiers poking around. A couple. They're stopped at the Belgian border to wait out the winter, but if they find an SS man belonging to a division not supposed to exist anymore, they'll break all his bones to find out what's going on. And then he's killed all of us. This time the only thing we have is surprise."

Kaslaka reached over, looked at Voss's cards, then sat back again, and for the first time looked up and smiled at me.

"I kind of knew Breder would do it." Voss looked up as if he were checking something out with God. " 'Member Peitscher?" He swung his head around to Kaslaka, eyebrows raised so high they had disappeared under the rim of his cap.

"Who?" Kaslaka dug something out of his ear, looked at it, then shook his head.

"Peitscher. Deserted in Normandy. Ran off into a minefield by mistake." Now he was staring at me again. "He got what he deserved. What does Breder think? That he can hide in the woods until it's over?"

"Maybe." I reached over and took Kaslaka's brandy glass, drank what was in it. Kaslaka watched me and said nothing.

"What do you know about it?" Voss was pointing at everything. He had gone a little mad in the night.

"Less than you. I was out on the perimeter half the night."

"And what do you think you're doing drinking Kaslaka's brandy?"

"Oh, I don't mind." Kaslaka shrugged, looking down at his knees.

"Yes, you do. Go somewhere else, Westland. I'm sick of all you recruit bastards. Nothing's even happened and you're already running away. If the Yanks don't get you, then I sure as hell will, Westland. You bear that in mind." He sat still for a moment, then swallowed, coughed into his hand, and held out another gob of blood in his palm. He looked for a moment like he was going to cry, then told me again to get lost.

I SAT in the driver's seat of the truck and played with the radio screwed to the back wall between the two seats. Sometimes Voss picked up music stations on it.

It hissed at me, then talked, the speech fading away as I pushed my ear closer to the speaker. Then suddenly it exploded into songs, and I had to turn the volume down.

It wasn't any music I'd heard before. At the end of the song a man came on speaking English, his voice rising and falling unnaturally with the fading out of the tune. I ran and fetched Voss. We both listened to the voice for a while, neither of us understanding what he said. Then a song came on that made Voss smile and call for Kaslaka. They said it was "Chattanooga Choo-choo." They'd heard it before.

"We gave them 'Lilli Marlene' and they gave us 'Chattanooga Choo-choo.' It was a good trade. We used to hear this all the time."

Kaslaka reached over and turned down the volume. "That is, we listened to it until the officers said they'd shoot us if they caught us again on enemy channels."

The music sounded all the same to me, a lot of trumpets and

trombones. After I'd turned it off, I thought of the radio waves veering over woods and borders and rivers and burrowing down through the trees into the metal box of the radio, the enemy having found us out, the Thin-Air People, and they didn't even know it.

I heard the trucks of other companies driving up onto the road and leaving. There were three truckloads of us left. Waiting for Breder. Maybe I should have gone with him, I was thinking.

LATE IN the morning they dragged him into camp with ropes tied around his feet, and he was dead. Posner walked slowly behind, looking down at Breder's face.

He'd fallen into a drainage ditch and broken his ankle or something. When they found him he fired his rifle in the air and told them to leave him alone. So while the others backed off and tried to figure out what to do, he crawled into the drainage pipe, which went under the road and out to the other side. But the pipe went down before it went up again and he got stuck in the muddy water where the pipe bent to go up, and by the time they pulled him out, he had drowned.

Posner and I had already buried him when the others came back. The last I saw of him were his hands, crossed on his chest, and the watch on his wrist, the second hand going stubbornly around. Voss leaned against the truck, arms folded, looking the other way.

End of Picture. Darkness follows.

RAMKE WAS sitting at a fold-up wooden table on a fold-up wooden stool under the canvas flaps of his tent. The roof hung down around the center pole.

His driver, Bauer, was also sitting at the table, plinking at a typewriter, field cap backwards on his head and his tongue sticking out from the concentration of typing. I stood very still in front of the table, staring over the top of Ramke's head, arms straight at my sides, fingers tucked into my palms.

"Go ahead. Sit down." Ramke flipped his hand at me.

I looked around and there was nothing to sit on.

"Nothing to sit on, sir."

"Isn't there? Bauer, don't we have an extra chair?"

"Broken, sir." Bauer looked up, moving his mouth as if something were stuck between his teeth, then head down again.

"Just wanted to ask you, Westland, if you knew anything about this Breder boy running away. Deserting. You're the only one I didn't get a chance to see when we found him missing, because you were on perimeter duty."

I looked him in his eyes and said I knew nothing about it.

Ramke shrugged, chewed at his lower lip for a minute. The skin of his face was pulled tight over his cheekbones. "Did you know of any plans he had? Did he ever speak of deserting? Did he ever speak of being disillusioned?"

"Not that I know of, sir."

"So what did he use to talk about with you? Anything?"

"Usual stuff, sir. Nothing important."

Bauer whacked the typewriter bar back to the other side and started plinking again.

Ramke looked pissed off, but I was thinking no way could he know anything. Rule 1: Deny everything until you are blue in the face.

"No, sir. I don't know anything about anything."

"Don't overdo it, Westland."

"No, sir."

"Look, Westland." He pressed the palms of his hands to his face, then slid his fingers down his cheeks, leaving red lines in the skin. He loosened the Knight's Cross at his throat the way a man loosens his tie. "I realize he was a friend of yours and you wish to keep his record clean, as clean as it can be," and he flicked his chin with his finger as if to show what a small and pathetic wish that was, "but we can't just leave these things hanging in the air like rotten meat. We have to have some answers. Believe me, I know how hard it is for you now, all of you. It's harder than it was for us before." He reached back into the pocket of his greatcoat and took out a cigarette, the regular ration kind, but he lit it with a gold-and-silver lighter. "I don't mean the war's gotten any easier. Only to tell you the truth, in the beginning we didn't know what was happening. Westland, in '39 I served in a Panzer unit that was attacked by Polish cavalry. You know the story, Westland? I'm asking if you know the story."

"Yes, sir. Know the story." Everybody knew about that. It was in all the papers.

"Well, then you'll know they were on horseback. I saw hundreds of men ride down a ridge at us, Westland, all shouting, waving their lances, and I saw them all die. You couldn't have walked up that ridge in a straight line without treading on one of them. We ate horsemeat for days after that. We used Polish swords as spits to hold lumps of the stuff over the fire. We had javelin contests with their lances out in the fields in the break before it all started again. We bandaged our wounded with the silk from Polish battle flags. I ask myself almost daily what it was that made them come at us, because of all the things I have seen that made no sense to me that was the most senseless. I am not against sacrifice, Westland, but I also like to think I am not an advocate of pure stupidity. And the only reason, the only excuse I can reach for why those Poles rushed tanks with armor three inches thick, armed only with swords and spears, is that they didn't really know what was happening. Sure it seems ridiculous that it should have happened at all. *Now* it does. But then it was probably the only plan they had.

"And it was the same for us back then. We were brave because we didn't know what was going on. It was the same in Normandy. We just didn't know how much the Allies had put into it. We didn't know we didn't have a chance. So back then the cost and the aggression we put into holding little towns and riverbanks seemed worth the damage it did to us. What I am trying to say to you is that your people, your platoon, your company know more now than we did then about the way the war is going. I believe in the victory, Westland, but I am also aware of the cost.

"Your friend Breder seems to have decided for himself that the cost isn't worth the victory. Something has come along to change his mind. And I ask you now as a friend to tell me if he is the only one who thinks this way, because if he is not, I must ask myself not only whether I am fit to lead you, but whether you are fit to be led."

When I realized he had finished talking, I looked up from where I had been staring at my boots. The red lines were still on his face, as if the whole time he had been raking his fingers down his cheeks, while I studied the soaked leather of my toe caps and compared them to Ramke's boots, which stuck out from under the table, dripping water onto the pine-needle floor.

"It was only Breder who thought that way, sir. The rest of us are ready. I don't know what more to say, sir."

"Then say nothing. Just go." He offered me a cigarette, but I shook my head, bowing slightly forward to say thank you. Then he held the pack out to Bauer, who took one, put it in his mouth, leaned back from the typewriter, and sighed until his lungs were empty.

I CRIED without tears under the folds of my cape, smelling the mustiness of the waterproofing, pressing my thumbs to my burning eyes. It didn't last long.

WE STOPPED at a crossroads and waited for a column of tanks to pass. They were Panthers and Mark IVs, their sides rippled with Zimmeritt paste making them look as if they were made of concrete. Zimmeritt paste was to make the surface of a tank nonmagnetic so magnetic mines couldn't be used on it. The Russians hid in foxholes when the tanks rolled over them and stuck the mines to their undersides. We were taught how to use the German Teller mines, about twice the size of a dinner plate and painted green, which you could stick on anything metal and blow it up. But then you had to get close enough to whatever it was to stick the Teller on.

It was one of those moves called "Instant Iron Cross" because you got a medal if it worked, and if it was a tank you also got a white strip of cloth with a little tank on it to wear on your arm. Made you a better target for the next time you tried it. I saw a man in Bad Godesberg once, home on leave, wearing the gray wraparound tunic of a Panzerjäger; antitank crew. He had three of the tank strips: "Single-handed destruction of an enemy armored vehicle." He was standing at the end of a line of people waiting to buy bowls of soup from the station kitchen, and he was trying to scratch an itch on his back but couldn't reach. An old lady did it for him with her umbrella.

On the sides of each tank going past was a painted shield with a key on it. This was the first SS Division, the Leibstandarte Adolf Hitler, the LAH. Voss said they were going to spearhead the whole offensive. He said our casualty figures, compared to theirs, were so small it made ours seem like a joke.

"It's going to be an all-night party," said Voss.

"Nonstop Action Cabaret," whispered von Schwerin.

THE WORLD becomes very small. Isolated to a point of focus only a few inches from the eyes. Sound comes as if from under a pile of damp leaves. The tips of the fingers are numb. No protest from the mind. No attempt to clarify.

* * *

I LAY on my face in some tall grass covered with frost, holding up, like some offering, the brass link belt of Spandau bullets leading into the machine gun. Handschumacher lay beside me. I nudged away the brown metal box with the rest of the bullets in it: black tip, black tip, black tip, red tip for the tracer.

Lying the way I was, with the rim of my helmet jammed into the back of my neck, I couldn't see more than a few feet, and couldn't focus more than a few inches.

Handschumacher kept flipping the safety on and off, on and off until I told him to fucking stop it, please. Then he set the gun down, the bipod keeping the barrel in the air, and rested his forehead on his crossed arms. He told me to tell him if anything happened.

To the left and to the right, von Schwerin and Voss hid behind trees. Voss had smeared mud on his face.

I took off my helmet and set it on my bottom, thinking it might be of some use there. Then I could look up, and saw the road running out to the left, curve, and go out of sight in a crescent of gray asphalt. Trees, and behind us an open field, an empty farmhouse with the roof caved in and the windows thick with green fuzz.

I had begun to panic from trying to figure out whether someone was going to come around a bend in the road, or move through the trees, not come at all, or maybe one of them followed by hundreds. And there were to be no survivors. It was understood.

The order for no survivors had come on a piece of toilet-paper-looking stuff, which Voss read to us the day before. It was the directive from von Manteuffel, Leader of Armies and Untouchable, with much heel-clicking and leather greatcoats hiding gabardine gray trousers and riding boots. The piece of paper said it had orders direct from the Leader of All Things, for whom you could click your heels until your boots wore out and your ankles chafed down to the bone, and still it wouldn't be enough. The order said that in the upcoming offensive we were to show no human inhibitions. No enemy was to be kept alive except officers and then only for the purpose of interrogation. The offensive would be named Autumn Fog and would begin December sixteenth with a two-hour barrage along a seventy-mile front, at five thirty in the morning. The Division was to proceed along designated routes toward the towns of Rocherath and Krinkelt, past the customs house at Wahlerscheid, on to the towns of Büllingen and Bütgenbach by the morning of the seventeenth.

Holding Rocherath and Krinkelt were elements of the U.S. Second Division, identifiable by a large Indian head insignia on the upper left sleeve. They had been sent to the area for recuperation. The townspeople were believed to be friendly in those areas closest to the German border. Beyond that, in the Division's drive for the Meuse River bridgehead, any interference was to be judged as a capital offense.

As many as nine divisions were taking part in the offensive, and all of them were short of fuel. All enemy vehicles were to be requisitioned.

We were to trust in God and our Leader, and to understand that the balance of the war was in our hands.

About an hour later a patrol ran into the camp and said they had been seen by an American reconnaissance group. So everybody ran around in circles, and after a while we were lying by the side of the road hoping the Amis would show up. If I were an Ami, I would have run away home.

THE BASE of each bullet had an *S* on it and then a star and the number 42. It was the only thing in focus, except Handschumacher's fingertips, the nails rimmed black with gun oil and dirt, tiny sprigs of hair between the first and second joint.

* * *

HANDSCHUMACHER picked a bogey out of his nose and flicked it away. "So there's two nuns going through a town on bicycles, and the streets are cobbled, and it's dark, and they're lost. One nun says to the other: 'I've never come this way before.' The other nun says: 'It must be the cobblestones.' "

I looked up from the grass. "Did you make that up?"

"No. Kaslaka told it me."

VOSS GOT up from behind the tree, walked out into the road, and stood there with his hands on his hips. He coughed and spat, ground the spit into the road with the toe of his boot. Then he unbuttoned his trousers and took a pee, right where he stood.

I rolled up the bullet chain and put it back in the can.

Voss started walking back to the camp, so we followed him. The woods were empty. The world slowly expanded back to normal, unclogged my ears and twisted my eyes, like the lenses of binoculars, back into focus.

The cannons were being moved up—88s. They rolled on their half-inflated wheels behind the trucks. I never knew why they kept their tires half-inflated. They were old guns, with the marks of shrapnel in rusted streaks across their blast shields, white rings around the barrels to mark kills. And with them came men with red piping on their black shoulder straps, whom we saw fussing with their broken-down trucks. That was the only chance we got to look at them. Our camp was on ground like some African kingdom nobody could be bothered to explore, so they only passed through.

THE SOUND of dice rolling on the metal floors of the trucks became a permanent rattling through the camp. There was nothing to do with the money we had, so we bet it all away.

* * *

A PLANE flew overhead, a drone above the clouds.

A SPECIAL notice came in to be prepared for German troops wearing American uniforms attempting to come back through the lines. They were part of a special unit called the Skorzeny Kommando, Germans who could speak English, who were being sent over to the Americans to confuse the Amis. All Germans in enemy uniform identifying themselves as members of the Skorzeny Kommando were to be allowed to pass through.

Voss offered a pack of cigarettes for the head of each Skorzeny man.

A BOY walked past wearing Lise Hammacher's sweater, the one I had left on the barbed wire fence. He had worn a hole through the elbow.

WE GAVE our trench knives to Voss, who took them away to a farmer who had a grinding wheel. When he gave them back, we could cut sheets of paper in half by running the blade along them.

THE AUTUMN fog closed in on us, divided around tree trunks, and closed up again, dappled us wet and hung outside our cape tents, rose briefly into the branches of the trees, waiting for dark, then sank down again. If I had been in this place alone, I would have gone mad from the silence of it. The emptiness.

* * *

"JUMP UP and down."

We jumped up and down, and anything that rattled, Voss made us take off and leave behind.

We walked for a couple of hours along loggers' trails, past deserted huts used by the woodsmen in the summer. The trees were set in lines that seemed to cross and recross as we moved past. The branches were so thick in some places we could barely see the sky.

Another section came back along the same trail. They looked dirty and cold. Voss talked with the NCO, who gestured vaguely away to our left, cut a few precise slices in the air with his hand, and led his people away. At the end of their section was a small boy in uniform, only as high as my chest, who looked about fifteen years old, swinging two ammunition boxes the way children swing buckets of sand at the beach.

The trail gave way to a path, and the trees became thicker, less ordered. We came to a place where branches had been cut and woven into a fence, propped up with more branches and smeared with mud. It was half-sheltered by a strip of gray canvas, and in a neat pile outside were empty ration cans. Voss sat us down and worked the radio von Schwerin had been made to carry, piddling around with the stations until we could hear Kaslaka's voice at the other end. Voss said we were close now. No smoking, no cooking, no talking; see any Americans, then run away, no shooting, no using the radio unless there's an emergency.

He made the others stay behind, and I went with him down the path, the water dripping off the trees onto my shoulders until my cape soaked through and my knuckles were freezing. Often he held up his hand and stopped, and I went down on one knee waiting for the order to run.

The trees ended in white pasty sky. We crawled, side by side, almost to the edge, where holes like half-dug graves had been scraped into the dirt. Beyond the trees was a field thick with grass. A stream ran through the middle. Past the field was another stretch of woods. The open space was maybe a five-minute walk.

A clearing showed in the trees on the other side, and in the clearing was a pile of logs, behind which I could see the windshield of an American jeep, a machine gun mounted at the back, and a few people standing around. I looked across, and Voss was watching them with a pair of binoculars, his eyes crunched up, teeth bared from the concentration of trying to make them out.

When he handed the binoculars to me, I first had to wipe the steam off the tiny lenses at the front. Then I watched a man shaving, sitting on a tree stump, a little mirror nailed to the tree in front of him, using his helmet as a basin. He was wearing green trousers and a brown shirt. His dog tags hung on a chain around his neck. I couldn't see any other people.

Voss made me set the binoculars down, told me to stay put. He was going to go back and get von Schwerin. He and I would stay here about half the night and keep an eye on things. Then Handschumacher would come out and take over. If anything happened we should just run for it. We'd have to eat our food cold.

I watched the man shaving until he had finished, tipped the water out of his helmet, put a cap on his head and then the helmet. I was trying to remember if I had ever seen an American before.

Water dripped off the trees onto my legs. I covered myself with the cape and ate a cold can of stewed vegetables. The Amis were too far away to scare me. Besides, there was nothing to see. I had a wild daydream about a woman, all the bits and pieces I could remember of all the girls I could think of, and woke up when von Schwerin crawled into the hole next to me.

* * *

I n the dark we could see the light of a fire behind the American log pile. We crawled to the edge of the woods, listening for their voices but hearing only the sheets of wind come scrabbling through the tall grass into our faces.

We buttoned our capes together and sat back to back, knees pulled up under our chins.

I asked him if he'd thought about Breder.

"Some."

"I mean, do you think it was our fault?"

Von Schwerin lit a cigarette and said that would be okay as long as we kept it under the cape. The wind was too strong for them to smell anything.

"It wasn't our fault at all," he said. "There's a point after which you can't keep looking after someone. He's been through no more than we have."

I didn't know whether to tell von Schwerin that I'd known Breder was going to run. I shut up.

My ribs were shaking from the cold. We dug out the foxhole until it came up to our chests if we were sitting down. It started to snow around midnight, snowflakes rattling minutely on the ground. The American fire flared up in the wind. Through the binoculars I could see the fire reflected off the windshield, and a couple of faces, smoking cigarettes, walking back and forth.

I slept and woke with my ribs shaking again, a feeling like the blade of a jagged knife being dragged down my spine. I had nothing to say to von Schwerin. All I wanted was his warmth. I didn't care what he thought about Breder. I didn't care about Breder anymore. The most certain thing in the world was that someone was going to die in this. It didn't seem possible from what Voss said that all of us in the section would live. Somebody. Maybe all of us. In one bang. Then nothing. Darkness follows and the last anyone sees of me is my wristwatch still ticking. But it wasn't panic. I was too tired to panic. Too cold. And my supper coming back on me in stale vegetable burps. There would be time for panic.

Mother would be asleep. Walther asleep. Benjamin asleep or up reading all night. Stock would be comatose behind the bar. If I thought hard enough, maybe I could have woke them with their ribs frozen and their backs stiff, and they would have known it was from me. Somehow, maybe, I could kick my way into their dreams.

THREE O'CLOCK. Sky black and blue with banners of cloud. Handschumacher and Voss came with a water bottle full of chicken broth, said they had buggered the order not to cook and had also gone back for some blankets. They fixed up the hovel. A couple of tanks were rolling around, looking for their rendezvous points. Back on the trail the cannons were set up, ready for the barrage. Everything was going to happen tomorrow morning. We could expect to get no sleep for three days.

I walked into a couple of trees getting to the hovel, went past it and had to double back. Von Schwerin and I groped like blind men to get under the blankets. We used the radio as a pillow, and the static coming from its speaker sounded like waves in the distance.

ALL DAY there was the sound of squeaking tank tracks out of our sight. We stayed in our hovel. Handschumacher and Voss came back from the foxhole, brewing ersatz coffee and eating cans of meat run through with clots of white fat.

Other sections moved up and made their hovels.

By noon the whole company was there.

In the afternoon the officer named Heydt came by with a clipboard and told us it was our turn to collect supplies. We followed him to a truck, from the back of which two men were distributing boxes of bullets and grenades and ration packs.

We each got a box with sixty rounds, two grenades, and twenty-four-hour ration boxes. The men asked if anyone wanted to trade in their rifle for a Schmeisser. There was a black pile of the machine pistols behind the men in the truck. We didn't. They gave us a Panzerfaust, a tube of metal painted sandy yellow with a bomb at the front. The bomb had a firing range of maybe a hundred meters, and when it went off, you were left in a cloud of smoke and with busted eardrums. Von Schwerin got to carry it.

We filled our pockets with the rations and the bullets, stuck the wooden handles of the grenades in our belts, and went back to our hovel.

We passed the rows and rows of cannons, barrels pointed in the air, the crews sleeping in the trucks parked alongside them.

Someone had stolen our blankets.

SNOW CAME down and dusted the road.

VOSS GOT our blankets back.

I started to write a letter home, and Kaslaka stopped me. Said something about letters usually getting burned before an offensive. Tradition.

HEYDT CAME by again and said we were to report to tank number 411 by four in the morning. The tanks would be lined up on the road, which was a dirt alleyway bordered by trees.

SLEEP. Strange dreams. Waking up when someone shifts in our pig pile of tangled limbs underneath the blankets. More sleep. Food. Stagger off and take a piss. Worry. Acid in stomach. Headache. Bad taste in mouth. Snow. Blankets. Bright idea. Take socks and cut five holes in each one. Gloves. Sort of. No spare socks. Strange dreams. Late afternoon sun, vague brightness. Evening. Someone cooking. Sleep. Find an old piece of candy in pocket. Eat it. Wipe itchy nose on Handschumacher's leg. Welcome the end. We must learn to welcome the end. Run away from the end. Prevent the end. Sleep a little. Voss coughing up his lungs at the other end of the blanket. Learn to ignore it, like Voss. Remain aloof. Woman in a prison cell. Me running across the field in the night back in Pech only to watch her turn out the light and go to sleep. Foul wind and snow through the trees. Benjamin flipping the beer glass full of beer over on the table. Is this sleep? It has all happened ages in the past. I haven't seen Voss and von Schwerin for years. Sadness only an echo. Cold only a dream, echo of ice. Distant past comes crawling along the corridors of my memory. Handschumacher elbows me in the face in his sleep. If I was sleeping before, I'm not doing it now. Voices outside the hovel. Hiss of a match. Another match. Smell of phosphorus. The sound of the tanks moving up. Surely they know we are here. So much noise. Surely they know. Maybe they'll call the whole thing off. I'm going to wake them all up. Wake them up at home, wake them up cold so they'll know it's me. Do we pray now? Do we break open our box of sins and see what we've got?

I have been alive a thousand years. That's how it feels. Worry. Sleep. Strange dreams. Autumn Fog. Sleep.

X

MY KNEES hurt when I stood. Three forty-five in the morning. Someone put a cigarette in my mouth. I wanted to lie down, go back to sleep. I followed von Schwerin and his Panzerfaust Dragon Willy through the woods. The place was crawling with people, all moving in files through the woods.

THE TANKS were quiet on the road. NCOs moved back and forth, shining lights on the turrets to make sure of the numbers. On the other side the cannons were being checked by their crews.

The tank hatches were open. Orange light shone out of them. Boys sat inside smoking, talking into radios. Leather jackets. Boots stacked in a corner. The crew only had socks on their feet. We poked our heads in like people looking into goldfish bowls.

The road had already been stamped into mud. We found 411 far back at the end of the column. It was called "Lausbub," the name done in dull red paint on the rear armor. We were about five tanks from the end in a line of maybe twenty. A boy was sitting on the turret, his legs dangling down inside the machine, smoking a cigar. He looked up when Voss shone a flashlight in his face.

"We're your lot." The light went out. Voss rattled the torch and said, "Damn."

The boy shrugged and slipped inside the tank. Then the side hatch opened, a dust of the Zimmeritt paste falling down through the dull light. An older boy in an officer's cap stuck his leather-gloved hand out and waved at us to get on.

I found a place behind the turret where there was a bar to hold on to. The others sat on the back near the exhaust pipes, like the necks of two great, ugly swans arched over the rear of the machine. I knew I was going to fall off once the thing got moving. The tank smelled of iron and gasoline.

Across the road one of the artillerymen lit a storm lantern and hung it in the back of his truck. Boxes of shells were stacked on the ground next to the tailgate. Men moved in and out of the light. The helmets of passing soldiers shone like wet eggs.

Another section came up onto the tank because there was no room for them anywhere else. A boy I barely knew wedged himself half into my spot.

"Got a cigarette for me?"

I gave him a cigarette.

"What's your name?"

"Westland."

"I'm Neumann." He shook my hand without noticing the sock I had on it. "I'm freezing to death out here." He looked a little cross-eyed, and his front teeth were crooked. He had rolled up the sleeves of his tunic, and his arms, framed by heavy veins under the skin, were blocks of muscle.

There was some message being passed down the line of tanks, and the cannon people were moving faster now beside the guns.

"Cover your ears. Five minutes." That's what the boy on the next tank yelled across, but God knows what the message started as. Someone always got it a little bit wrong, then someone else, and by the end it didn't sound anything like the original.

I jammed my index fingers deep into my ears and heard myself swallow. I looked up and through the turret hatch into the tank and saw the commander unstrapping a water bottle from a place on the wall, drink some, then shake the bottle upside down because it was empty. He threw the bottle on the floor. In the front, in impossibly tiny seats, were the driver and the gunner. The gunner was on the right, hemmed in with belt after belt of bullets coiled around his legs and under the chair. The driver was crunched over the half-wheel, gear sticks between his legs. There was no room at all inside. The cannon filled up most of the space, sort of weighed down by a metal bucket underneath the breech, which was open. The cannon shells were in two racks on either side of the wall. Underneath their leather jackets the men wore tunics made of the tiny dot camouflage material issued to the SS.

The gunner turned around in his cubbyhole, looked up, smiled, and mimicked me with my fingers in my ears. Then he said something and I smiled back. He had green eyes, and his hat was on sideways so he looked like a big mouse. The commander's arm reached up, shut the hatch, and suddenly it was dark.

I turned to say something to Neumann, who was trying to test his knee reflexes by tapping the stem of a stick grenade onto his kneecap.

I opened my mouth, and from somewhere came fire and a noise that went through my head and my bones, left me hearing nothing but a far-off ringing. A blue sun splattered on my eyes. I put my head down next to where Neumann was, his face pressed to the metal.

All down the line the cannons were firing, first in an ordered line starting at the front of the column and sounding louder as the explosions moved back, but then firing again without pattern.

When I opened my eyes, I could see the flashes of other cannons firing though the trees, men, cannons, and trees frozen in white light, a man with his arm raised, others on their knees, leaning away, covering their ears. In the seconds when no guns were going off, I could hear the rattle of the empty shells hitting the ground, and shouts. Far away the impact explosions. Shocks in my elbows and my neck. Everything became a staggering of images made by the cannon flashes: the brass cases in a band of frozen smoke falling to the ground. A man in midstride to the truck. A man walking past with a clipboard. Trees. Branches of fire in the sky. Night over day over night. Snowflakes. Von Schwerin looking up, grimacing from the huddle of bodies on the tank, then in another picture, his head gone and back in the pile. Night over day over night. Voss climbing onto the tank, his mouth open with laughter at something and his teeth gleaming. Somewhere up ahead great pillars of light were shining up into the sky, bouncing off the low clouds and into the trees in the American lines. Skeleton fingers holding us in.

The engine of the tank started, and at first there was nothing but diesel fumes and shaking, then only the shaking. I could see the hatches being tightened shut.

It was five thirty.

For a long time I lay still, feeling the metal heat up underneath me, the shuddering of the engines, and my ears hurting from the constant rolling thunder.

Neumann tapped me on the shoulder, then put two fingers to his lips to show he wanted another cigarette. I turned away and looked down the barrel of the tank behind us. A small patch of light showed from the driver's vision slit. To the side of the machine, a man was pissing against a tree. I tapped my head over and over against the metal of the tank, chipping the paint on my helmet. Worry riding up behind my ribs.

The smell of cordite was everywhere, clouds of it around us, mixed with the diesel. I put a hand over my face and felt my temples pulsing.

Brass shell cases were all over the road and in piles next to the cannons, hundreds of them, shining. The cannon men built walls around themselves with the cases.

AT SIX THIRTY, over the space of a couple of minutes, the firing stopped. The whole place was thick with smoke. Fine rain falling. Blue-gray sky. Strange lights still broke off the clouds and shone down on the Americans. The ringing buzzed over all other noises. The road was a carpet of brass. My neck and stomach muscles were tight from flinching, and now the worry burst like bags of boiling water inside me. I heard the squeaking of tanks moving forward at the front of the column.

Our tank revved its engine, jolted, then stopped. Neumann yawned. I saw Voss put a magazine in a Schmeisser he had gotten from the truck. The tank in front moved forward and splattered mud over us. Then ours went; my helmet banged the turret. I held onto the metal bar, which I had claimed as mine.

The cannon men watched quietly as we went past. Some of them were drinking coffee, their faces smoked black. I was looking for a smile. Nothing.

We went fast along the alley of trees. I could hear Spandaus firing as we came to the edge of the field, bumped over some logs that the lead tanks had smashed, then suddenly down, the machine sliding, into the field, through the slush. Across the open space other tanks were going through the stream, leaving deep tracks, people hanging onto the sides like squirrels, and, beyond that, fires in the trees, caldrons of smoke in the sky. No sign of life.

When we came to the stream, the tank sank into it so deep that I could have leaned down and touched the water. Spray moved over the turret in a white arc, and we moaned as the cold soaked through our clothes.

The tank changed gear and began to move up the hill. It was searchlights set up at the edge of the woods that were making the lights which came down off the clouds.

The sound of the Spandaus, and of trees breaking as tanks drove through them. The field was covered with tracks.

We drove under the woods, as if under a canopy, back into the darkness. In the strange glare of the searchlights and the flashes of guns, I could see people running around. Smoke. The tank smashed into a tree, and two people fell off the back. They had to run to avoid being crushed by the tank behind.

I saw the first green uniforms running away into the thickness of the woods. Voss stood up and shot at them, bouncing the small bullet cases over the rest of us. I didn't see anyone fall.

Where the cannon shells had hit, there were black holes on fire and smoking.

The cracking noise over our heads was bullets, and the twang was when they struck the turret.

Neumann was still there, trying to load his rifle but losing most of the cartridges over the side.

My hips were aching from the jolts as the tank barged through trees, covering us with pine needles.

In the shadow of the searchlights, things flickered like an old movie, people seeming to move in slow motion, jerkily running to nowhere in particular.

I was sweating from the heat of the engine, the stream water clammy warm now on my skin.

Two men stood up out of a hole in the ground and aimed at us, their figures disappearing for a second behind the flicker of their guns. Voss shot off the rest of the magazine at them. They threw their arms in the air and fell over backwards.

There were holes in the ground covered with logs and moss. These must have been what they were living in.

The cannon fired, and close by in the trees there was an explosion and another explosion. In the gasp of fire I made out the framework of an American jeep.

I saw a man running at a German, waving a shovel, a big ditch-digging shovel. The boy was crouching on the ground over another SS who was wounded. It was an American, the one with the shovel, dressed in a greatcoat, a little olive wool hat on his head. The man raised the shovel over his shoulders and the boy jumped up so fast that they were together like dancers before I saw the boy had run him through with a bayonet. The boy stood back, fired the rifle. The American flew off his feet and down on his face.

An SS man ran past one of the log holes and threw a grenade in. Logs burped into the air and fell back into the hole. Then he ran on and did the same to another hole.

"Off! Off!" Voss yelled and started kicking people off the tank. *Ping, ping, ping, ping.* I slammed my face down to the floor again, and the air cracked over my head. The tank spun around. I fell off the other side of the tank from everybody else and crawled on my hands and knees to a hole, rolled in. The dirt was smoldering. I got out and crawled behind a log that was lying next to the hole, watched over the top of the chipped bark, feeling my knuckles burned.

I could see maybe twenty paces in front; tree trunks and more tree trunks and two bodies, both German, in heaps beside a hole. A tank went past, fired its cannon, rocked back, went forward again.

Neumann was still on the tank, and when it moved he started to slide off. His foot caught on the towing cable. It dragged him and then let him go. He didn't move from where he fell.

My insides were burning, and sweat dripped down from my

helmet liner, drops of salt stinging my eyes. Talking to myself: nothing words. Nonsense.

The rest of the section was running in the opposite direction, Voss yelling at everyone and the trees. The tanks were all up ahead, a wall of them, followed by people, crouched like apes, shuffling behind.

I ran over to Neumann and turned him over with one hand, looking around to see if anyone was coming. His eyes were closed. A piece of bark from the tree behind me flew off and left the tree with a pink hole in it. I saw the flash of another bullet coming, rolled away and ran after the others. Suddenly right in front, a man stood up out of a hole he had dug for himself, hidden in pine needles and dirt. He had his back to me and aimed a rifle at Voss. I almost fell over trying to stop and for a second clearly saw him: dirty green jacket, helmet covered with a string net. Then I put a bullet in his back. He dropped the gun, stood up out of the hole, and started to walk away. Voss and von Schwerin stood. The man tried to reach up to his back, his eyes open, then closed, fingers groping for the wound. He walked into a tree, then slid down the side of it, his chin pushed back, fell and tried to stand again.

Voss had come over, followed by von Schwerin and some of the others. Voss shot the man again, tugged at my arm, and we left.

SNOW CAME down in fat flakes over the fires.

WE KNELT in a bomb crater. Voss tried to tell us what was going on. I could hear only bits of it because I was breathing too hard.

"Rocherath . . . group . . . sector . . . shit . . . prisoners . . ."

Von Schwerin was looking at me, and I knew he was thinking about the shot man. I bowed my head and studied my boots, the laces tangled with mud and pine needles.

Voss told us to fix bayonets. So we did.

Kaslaka crawled out of the hole, came back with an American gun and a canvas belt with ammunition pouches on it. He put it on over his own. Then he took the bolt out of his old rifle and threw it away, dropped the rest of the gun to the bottom of the hole.

I followed von Schwerin, since I didn't know what was going on, except that I was burning up inside.

There wasn't much shooting now except up ahead, where Spandaus were firing until, from the sound, I could tell they had overheated and jammed.

Voss took out an empty magazine from the Schmeisser and threw it over his shoulder, hitting me in the face.

Kaslaka walked in front, swung his head from side to side like a large fish swimming.

Above the trees the sky was getting light.

I came level with von Schwerin, who looked away from me. It seemed as if he were embarrassed. Across from me a boy was wiping tears off his face.

A sound like a bell ringing, then a boom and more explosions. One of the tanks disappeared in a crack of dynamite. The hatches blew off and black smoke puffed out of them, streaked with orange flames.

There was a log hole up front. Kaslaka motioned for us to stop. We went down on the ground. He ran up and threw a bomb down the entrance, then between him and us the logs flew off. Two men like jack-in-the-boxes sprang out onto the dirt with their arms twisted and their legs bent under their backs.

We came up behind another section who were in a clearing full of dead Americans, stealing their boots and putting them on their own feet. We had only ankle boots. The Amis had ones that came up over the ankles with two buckles at the top. I saw Posner, lying on his back, trying to pull one over his foot.

"Hello, Sebastian." His face was squashed with the effort of getting the thing on. "Grab a pair. They're better than ours."

The Amis lay on top of each other in a heap. They had been shot after surrendering. It was pretty clear. I tried not to look at their faces.

My ears were still ringing.

"Hey, Sebastian, you need a watch?" Posner was holding up a dead man's hand with a watch on the wrist.

I shook my head.

One of the boys in Posner's section came running back from somewhere up front and said the tanks were at Wahlerscheid. A lot of prisoners. Trying to negotiate. Rocherath was about eight kilometers down the road from Wahlerscheid, but the woods were full of Amis. It didn't look as if we were going any-where. Voss asked about casualties. The boy shrugged, said maybe fifteen percent. (You line up all the Tölz boys, walk down the line. When you get to seventeen, you look at eighteen, nineteen, and twenty, and you say, "You're dead." The picture came into my head and wouldn't go away.)

THE AMERICANS called Wahlerscheid "Heartbreak Cross-roads." Everyone was going around saying that.

It was only one building, at a crossroads in the woods. Amer-ican machines were on fire all around, jeeps in ditches, half-tracks burning. Also bodies on the road, maybe fifty, most of them around the house.

Capes were being spread over the bodies of the German dead, which lay all through the woods before the crossroads. They had been shot by a half-track, in the middle of the road, burn-ing now, its side blown off by a Teller mine. The person who delivered it lay scattered in bits and pieces from the half-track to the ditch. They said it went off as soon as he stuck it to the machine. There was supposed to be a six-to-eight-second fuse.

The road ran straight for a long way, then either sank down or curved; I couldn't tell which.

The side of the house was full of holes, one of the windows blown out by a Panzerfaust. The dead were thrown out of windows and the front door. A body turned quietly in the air, down from the second story, and slapped on the ground.

A few officers were trying to reorganize sections whose NCOs had been killed. In two sections, only two out of six were left. In another, there was only one person. They said five sections were gone completely.

The American prisoners stood with their hands on their heads by the side of the road. Some of them didn't look much older than we. Handschumacher and I went up and stared.

Two Ami officers at the front were talking fast and quietly to each other. One of them was very tall and wore little round glasses. The other had a bandage on his face and a fat bottom.

"Give me your boots," Handschumacher yelled at the group in general. When nothing happened he pointed to one of the men and yelled the same thing, tapping the heel of his boot which he had raised off the ground.

The man started to walk forward when the officer motioned him to stop. He got back in line.

Heydt walked up and asked what was going on. Handschumacher told him. Heydt pulled out the biggest cigar I'd ever seen, bit the end off the way cowboys do, and stuck the thing in his mouth. Then he had to take it out again in order to speak. He talked to them all in English, then when they didn't move fast enough, he yelled. With only a little mumbling, they all took off their boots, threw them into a pile at the front.

I started to go through the pile, matching the soles against the soles of my boots, which had already soaked through. I was doing that when I heard the American officer yelling at Heydt and Heydt screaming back. I looked up and Heydt was holding up a boot knife and the officer with the little glasses was red in the face from anger. Heydt cut off the officer's shoulderboards with the silver double bar insignia on them. He cut the Indian Head insignia off his arm, leaving a hole in the man's shirt. Then he pushed him back among the other soldiers.

I found myself a pair of boots and threw my old ones to the Americans, who stood in the mud lifting their feet slowly up and down.

The snow was beginning to stick and the sun was up. Somewhere.

HANDSCHUMACHER and I went to show von Schwerin our boots. They were rubber-soled. It felt strange to walk on a road without the scraping sound of the hobnails.

Von Schwerin was standing in the road a long way from cover, looking at the burning machines and the bodies in the ditches. He said we should give the boots back. We said if he wanted dry feet he should go fetch a pair for himself.

"Besides, you heard the orders. No one kept alive except officers."

"They won't do that." There was some shooting back in the woods. We walked without hurrying over to a jeep and sat in it. The windshield was smashed out, the tires flat, and the radiator boiled over. White star and some numbers on the hood.

Everyone formed back into groups. Tanks lined up on the road. The wounded were being taken into the house. In a couple of minutes the order came to move again. I didn't know how long it had taken us to get this far or how long we had been standing in the road. My watch had steamed up with sweat and stopped.

"I'm not in the habit of stealing." Von Schwerin folded his arms.

"Look, they don't need them anymore. Not as much as we do, anyway."

"You could manage without them, Handschumacher. You too, Westland."

So we both said, "Fuck you, Schwerin," and went back to find Voss.

I heard a gun go off and turned around to see von Schwerin had shot one of the Americans on the road, who had been wounded and was trying to crawl into the woods.

Voss made us carry a boy into the house. His name was Mitzlar, and he had been shot in the leg. He kept asking us to tell him if he was all right, dragging his leg as we carried him over our arms through the front door where a man with a Red Cross armband was sorting out the wounded by rooms.

We took him up the stairs, which were chipped almost to nothing by gunfire, stepped over a body at the top and carried the boy to a place that used to be a study. A grenade had gone off and blown out the windows. The floor was layered with bullet cases and glass. Six people lay in the room, two of them unconscious and the other four staring into space as if they did not know we were there. I knew them. I knew all of them.

Handschumacher turned the body on the stairs over on its back. It was the NCO whom I had seen when the boy got shot at the stream back in training at Bad Tölz. The NCO had bled in a trickle halfway down the stairs, and no one had moved him.

Voss and Kaslaka both had American guns called Garands. Said they were better. Handschumacher, von Schwerin, and I bunched in a diesel cloud behind a tank and started down the road, the eight kilometers of it into Rocherath. Again, we were far back in the column. Only half of us got to follow the tanks. The rest had to move through the woods. Cannons were firing in the distance. The rest of the offensive. A rumor said we would be in Paris by New Year's Day. Fine with me.

I stayed close to the tracks, made dizzy by the bars of treads passing in front of me, mud flicking up in my face.

After five minutes, Handschumacher put his hand on my shoulder and pulled me down.

An explosion. Shooting. I ran for the ditch and jumped in, Handschumacher landing on top of me. The water in the ditch was rimmed with ice, and a temperature that would normally have sent me home to sit in front of the stove for the rest of the day.

An American tank called a Sherman was on fire in the woods just at the corner of the road, where it veered away to Rocherath. The soldiers who had been with it were dug in beside the ditches. We took potshots at them, then a section rushed the position with bayonets. We saw them fighting hand-to-hand and ran forward to help, but it was over before we got there. More boots, guns, and watches stolen. Someone found a bar of chocolate. Then there was nothing to stop us for ages. We had to jog to keep up with the tanks. I wasn't burning anymore. I felt sick and knew I would be sicker when I had a chance to sit down and think, but I wasn't on fire like before. My new boots were good. I could have done with some chocolate. Things couldn't be too bad if I still had my appetite.

We couldn't go any slower or the tank behind would run over us. I was sweating like a pig.

Maybe they had all cleared out of Rocherath and Krinkelt. Maybe I wouldn't see another American before Paris. They'd all turn around and run for it. I kept wondering if Neumann was alive. I had only seen his eyes closed. Someone would have gotten to him by now.

ANOTHER bell-ringing sound. I ran for the ditch and saw, as I was running, a piece of German tank track like a snake, whipping up into the air. The top hatch of the tank opened, and a man started to get out but fell over, shot, before he was off the machine. Then I saw fire coming out of the hatch and heard explosions of the shells hammering inside.

A different sound. A hollow metal cough. Dirt and bits of tree blew into the air and down on our heads, like a shower of small coins. Mortars. I followed Kaslaka forward into the woods, tanks crossing the ditches and spreading out into the trees until the only thing left on the road was the lead tank and a couple of people who had been following it.

I couldn't see anything up front, only Kaslaka's back. We passed a section gathered around its NCO, who was screaming and beating the earth with his fists, curled up in a ball on the ground.

My mess tin jerked off my belt, and I spun around. Fucking hell. I fell over and waited for some pain. Fucking hell. Everybody was down and shooting at some Americans falling back through the trees. There were about a dozen of them, six firing, the other six running, then vice versa. We advanced on them, doing the same thing, and one of the boys in the section that had joined us went over like a telegraph pole. I tried to run as short a distance as possible, then hide behind trees. Couldn't see anybody by the time I was ready to fire. Too much sweat. I was saying, "Jesus Christ," over and over. Then suddenly the ground shattered around the Americans, the trees nearby flew to pieces and dropped their branches to the ground. One of the tanks moved past, dodging tree trunks, firing its Spandau until, as I knew it would, it jammed. Before the Americans who were left could get up, we were running at them.

Most were already down. Another boy from the section fell quietly over dead. Voss caught up with the American who had fired, and bayoneted him, sticking the blade through the man's outstretched hand and pinning it to his chest with the force of the stab. Then he shot the Ami until the magazine was empty.

Kaslaka had a staring match with a man who stood in front

of him. They both pointed their guns at each other, but I could see the American's had lost its bolt. The Ami was retreating slowly, talking to Kaslaka, trying to calm him down. He bumped into a tree, Kaslaka lunged forward and swung the butt of his rifle into the man's face. The American lay on his back, coughing. Kaslaka took a pistol from the man's belt and shot him with it. When the American was dead, Kaslaka looked at the gun for a couple of seconds, then threw it away.

I was running after a figure disappearing into the trees. He had dropped his rifle and was running hard with his head back, gasping for breath. I dropped him on the second shot.

Von Schwerin brought me my mess tin. What was left of it. The side was gone, the leather strap flayed. We moved to go back for the two who had fallen, but Voss said their lives were over now.

I fetched the pistol Kaslaka had thrown away. It was a Colt .45. The Legend. I didn't search the body for more shells.

The tanks were far ahead. We had to run to catch up. Dead. The dead. The woods were full of them. Helmets like birdbaths lying around, bits of equipment and guns, piles of empty shells from machine-gun nests. Snow still trickled down. This would all be over soon. Then these things could all rust and go down to hell and the dead could go too and it would all be fine with me.

WE LEFT our footprints in the snow along the roads.

NOTHING. Not even the dead now. Nobody. Quiet woods except for the tanks. I was trying to figure out how many kilometers we had covered. I took off my watch, threw it away because it still wasn't working, then remembered it was a present from Walther and ran back to fetch it, strapped the damp leather on my wrist again.

A Sherman had gotten stuck in the road with one of its tracks off. The German tanks stopped. Everything had come to a standstill. Kaslaka, Voss, von Schwerin, Handschumacher, and I and the three who were left from the other section sat down to watch what would happen. The Sherman's engine was still running, hatches closed.

Two people carrying Panzerfausts ran along the ditch between us and the tank. They ran in little spurts, stopping, then moving, sloshing through the ditchwater.

The turret of the Sherman spun around with a humming noise and shot bullets up and down the ditch. We weren't sitting around anymore. Instead we were on our faces, and I was saying, "Jesus Christ," again in various ways. The Sherman splashed up ditchwater, chopped one tree over and hid itself with sparkles and smoke. Then one of the Mark IVs came around the corner, fired and missed, jammed on the brakes, started backing up. The Sherman swung around, still firing its machine gun, chewing up the trees, fired its cannon at the Mark IV. The shell smacked the front canopy but didn't go through, blew up somewhere in the air, and I went deaf again. Bits of tank scattered through the tree branches and across the road.

Another Mark IV came around the corner, screeching against the side of the other tank with a noise like fingers on a giant blackboard, fired, rocking back. The turret of the Sherman blew open, the barrel suddenly flipping into the sky, smoke, first white, then black, then one of the people in the ditch crawled out of the water with the Panzerfaust, the *poom* noise of air shot through the sand-colored tube, and the Sherman exploded again. The blast knocked the man back into the ditch, and, when I looked up, one of the Sherman's wheels was wobbling over toward the broken Mark IV. The Sherman was all fire and smoke, filling the woods with its smell of iron, cordite, and burning rubber.

The Panzerfaust man got out of the ditch with his partner. They were black like Zulus from the mud. When the first of them wiped the slime off his face, I saw it was Posner, still holding the empty tube of the Panzerfaust. He walked over to me, dragging his feet in the pine needles.

"I think I wet my pants." He looked down at his boots.

I laughed and offered him a cigarette.

"No, really, I think I did. I was underwater trying to hide from that tank, and I damn well went and wet my god-damned pants." He nodded thank you when I had lit the cigarette for him.

The tanks moved down the road. The crew of the Mark IV that had been hit dragged their gunner out of the turret hatch, set him beside the road, got back in their machine, and drove on. People went over to the gunner and looked down at him, then walked away, shaking their heads, breaking into a run to catch up with the tanks.

"No one will know."

"About what?" He was smoking half the cigarette in one puff.

"Your pants."

"Mm." He held out his hand with the cigarette stuck between his first two fingers, and I saw how it was shaking. "I could feel the fucking ditch shuddering and this fucking *zzt, zzt* noise when the bullets hit the water. But he was aiming in the wrong place. Look how bad I'm fucking shaking. Half my fucking section gone." He was blinking hard. "Fucking Herder. He's running to come help me 'cause he thinks I'm shot, but I only tripped up. He bends down to help me, and the next thing I know he's way the hell over someplace else and killed, and a Yank I thought was dead shot him, right next to me. Now why the fuck didn't he go for me? Eh? What is there in all this?" He took off his helmet and smoothed back his hair. "And all in one god-damned morning. One day you haven't even ever taken a swing at someone, and the next you've gone and killed half a dozen. Sebastian, I beat that Yank so many times on the head I broke the butt off my rifle."

It was quite quiet now with the tanks gone; the half-sound of the snow coming down, NCOs calling people together. That's all there was.

"Let's go," Handschumacher said quietly to me from close by where he stood.

"I'll see you soon then, Pos. We'll meet up in Rocherath." I patted him on the shoulder and turned.

"Yeah. We'll see you, Sebastian." He was standing by himself. Everybody else had already left.

XI

THE END of the woods. From where I stood, it looked as if the trees just turned into sky and dropped off at the end of the world. People were digging in and the tanks were lining up. Whistles bleated, calling us away.

Voss went to find Heydt to figure out what to do, and we stood at the edge of the trees. The road into Rocherath passed between fields and meadows bordered by thick hedges. A couple of houses stood on the edge of the fields. I could see only gray blocks and a church spire. The ground was covered with snow.

"I bet they grow wheat here in the summer." Handschumacher nodded to himself. "Bet they do. This is a farm town."

"Just like yours?" Von Schwerin was looking at a hole with logs over it, the same as the ones we had seen before. He rolled a log over with his foot and peered into the dark.

Handschumacher didn't turn around. "Pretty much like mine, yes. And fuck you, by the way."

We could see the last of the Americans running back into the town, black dots with legs and arms, struggling through the shallow snow.

Voss came back, drinking from a can of beans. "They're trying to figure out whether to take the town now or wait."

"Now," said Kaslaka. "We should go now."

"Yes, well, it's not our decision."

"So go tell them Kaslaka says now."

"But they're thinking maybe the Amis will pull back. Apparently some of our paratroopers are trying to take the south side."

"Paratroopers?"

"Oh, they didn't come in planes or anything. They're riding tanks just like us."

"So they're dressed up like paratroopers. That's all." Kaslaka unwrapped the tin foil from a bar of chocolate called Hershey, and the whole thing disappeared into his gray jaws.

"They're coming back." Voss was looking over Kaslaka's shoulder. He bit his thumbnail and tore half of it off.

Beetle shapes moved out of the town in a long fan. The bottled thud of mortars.

I followed von Schwerin into a foxhole. He tried to kick me out but impacts were already shaking the ground. They sounded way off, far back in the woods. But they came closer, walking flashes toward us.

I put my hands over my ears and said, "Jesus Christ," again until dirt falling through the logs got in my mouth. Von Schwerin huddled next to me, moaning, but I wasn't going to see if he'd been hurt. With my ears plugged and the roar of my blood very loud, I could still hear the last screech of the shells coming in before they blew up. I knew it had to stop soon or the Amis would be mortaring their own people. My leg cramped. I yelled.

Von Schwerin yelled back. I spat the dirt out of my mouth. Cordite in my lungs rammed up my nose like some rotten fluid. I was going to be mad as hell when this was over. I counted fifteen explosions close, five near, ten distant. The sound was like the bellowing of giant cattle.

Is it over? I wondered to myself. Then I asked von Schwerin. "Is it over?" I wiggled my ears, then stood up out of the hole. The earth was smoking. Half the trees were gone, pink stubs of tree trunks everywhere, branches down, sap splattered on the dirt. Holes smoking. Black earth. Broken stones.

They were close. I could almost make out their faces. They were in a steady walk over the field, spread out before Rocherath. Handschumacher dropped the Spandau on the ground, and Kaslaka took a belt of ammunition off his back and fed it to the gun, clicked his fingers at me to be the belt feeder.

"Short bursts," was all Kaslaka said.

I held up the belt, the strange offering, and craned my neck back. Handschumacher chambered the first round, clicked the safety on and off. My mouth was too dry for me to tell him to stop.

We waited for the whistle. I heard their footsteps in the snow, saw the tails of their greatcoats peppered white and their boots plastered with it.

Now.

Now.

Now. Please now.

Now.

Don't wait anymore.

I heard the first peep of the whistle and the belt ripped out of my hands. No short bursts. Handschumacher went down the line and back up the line, and when the rest took cover, he chopped apart the earth, cartridges ripping the skin off my hands, tracers arcing out into the olive-drab clothes, guns twirling up into the air, some running away, others trying to dig in, but too close, Ami, you're too fucking close and the belt's gone—oh, Jesus. Handschumacher rolled on his back, trying to unclip the next belt. They got up and ran at us. I took a grenade out of my belt, realizing that was what had been crushing my balls since this business started; threw it, bounced it off the chest of a man, but forgot to pull the pin out. They went down for cover, rolling away from the bomb. Handschumacher fitted the belt in, pulled the trigger, and it jammed. Fucking Spandau. No-good Nazi piece of shit. I took the Colt .45, shot three shots, empty magazine, hit nothing. "Oh, God," I kept yelling. I couldn't stop yelling, took the other grenade, and by this time they were up again; unscrewed the cap at the base of the stick, found the porcelain ball attached to the cord, pulled it out, and threw the grenade. Something cracked into my helmet, and I saw sparks. Five-second fuse. Handschumacher screaming, "Hell! Murder! Fucker!" at the Spandau, and it went off in his hands, firing everywhere. One Ami walked backward from the blows, farther and farther, until he fell. The bomb went off. I saw one of them, close enough so I could see the lines on the webbing of his canvas belt, rise up off the ground and fall open-eyed onto the dirt in front of me. I took out the switchblade, sprung it, and stuck it in his back; suddenly he was up again, almost dancing, and behind me Handschumacher looked dead. I got up, kicked the man in the groin as hard as I could. When he went down, I kicked him in the face, took the knife out of his back, yelling animal nothings until my throat tore open, kicked him again in the head. He covered his face and cried out. I picked up my rifle and ran away. Stopped. Turned around, ran back, kicked him again, just to be sure. Took Handschumacher by the arm and tried to drag him back with me, but too heavy; dropped him and saw from the corners of my eyes people beating the life out of each other with shovels and knives. The screaming was louder than anything I had heard before, shaking the skin off my bones. My face was burned from the blast of the grenade. I ran toward where I had last seen von Schwerin, almost tripped over an American trying to reload his rifle. He looked up, and I punched him in the eye. Nothing. He turned back to the gun, frantically trying to load the thing, then gave up and jumped back with his hands in the air. A bit of a fatty, this man, with what looked like eight layers of clothing on and rubber snowboots. He was talking to me with his hands stretched high into the branches. Talking. Talking. I picked up his rifle, chambered a round, motioned for him to run, and shot him before he reached the edge of the woods. All this seemed to take only a second. One second. Where was von Schwerin? More whistles blowing. Hey, Fatty, I didn't mean to do it. It's only I was afraid. Oh, Fatty, get up and go home. Get up. Get up. And I ran out to the snow and lay down next to him, half thinking he was something to hide behind because I'd done my bit. An American appeared from nowhere, running at me. I stuffed my face in the snow, hoping he would think me dead, but when the picture replayed in my head so I could understand it, I remembered he didn't have a gun. He was just running, so I got up on my knees and he kicked me in the chest, fell over, because he hadn't seen me, crawled away, got up and kept running. I couldn't breathe from the kick. Kaslaka shuffled over to me through the snow, aimed, dropped the man. The Ami stood and kept running, fell, stood, finally fell and stayed. Kaslaka started to drag me back to the woods, and I tried to tell him I was all right, but he let go of me again before I could say anything. He ran over to Handschumacher, who was standing now with an awful nosebleed swinging the Spandau around like a club at nothing in particular. Kaslaka was telling him to calm down. It was over now, he said. And it was over, except for people gone mad like Handschumacher and trampling the dead. I crawled on my hands and knees over Fatty and into the woods. When the canopy of the trees was over me, I stood up and started walking back. Still holding the switchblade. Had to use one hand to pry it out of the other. My belt was gone, water bottle, cape, mess tin. I had to pat my head to see if my helmet was still there. Dead people all over the place. Fucking dead people. Try to stop breathing so hard. Sebastian. Sebastian. Sebastian.

XII

HANDSCHUMACHER knelt with his head back, pinching the bridge of his nose to stop the bleeding. I was trying to start a fire to make some hot food. Kaslaka and Voss sat back to back eating stew out of cans, water bottles propped up against their helmets lying on the ground. They were eating viciously, as if that were all there was left to do in the world. Von Schwerin was picking his nails. No one asked where he'd been. Looked to me like he'd run away.

There was a dent in my helmet. Voss said it was a ricochet, and I laughed.

I was too tired to get up, too tired to do anything more about the fire than hold lit matches against a pile of pine needles until the flame went out.

It was quiet. The tanks were gone. Someplace. No idea where.

The loudest noise was the sound of spoons scraping in ration cans.

Someone standing over me sprinkled matches onto my pile of pine needles, then dropped down and lit them. The matches hissed one after the other and the fire started. The person blew at the embers. Von Schwerin.

"Where were you?" I fetched a can of food from my satchel, stuck my boot knife in the top, then stuck it in again to make a cross, pried back the ends. Rice pudding.

"Over there." He waved his hand over his shoulder.

Handschumacher heaved the Spandau off his shoulder and sat down. "Nice fire you have going here." Then he lay on his back and put his helmet over his face. He had bled from the nose all over his mouth and chest and hadn't bothered to wipe any of it away.

Back on the road, the wounded were being loaded into trucks. The dead had been dragged to the sides of the ditches where they lay lined up, faces covered with helmets or field caps.

"We'll be going again soon," von Schwerin mumbled.

"Where? Back?" Handschumacher peeped out from under his helmet.

"No. You kidding? Straight at the town. That's our route. The Amis are probably leaving the place anyway. We're just waiting for orders."

"Trying to figure out who's still alive to give orders." I swallowed the pudding. The fire smoked without flames.

Von Schwerin stood slowly, like an old man, and walked over to a body lying on its back, head staring upside down at us, and arms bent, still in the air. He turned the body over with his boot, came back and sat down. "Face was bothering me."

Handschumacher sat up, tipped his helmet back on his head, and grinned at us.

* * *

THE FOOD truck broke down before it could get to us, so we had to walk back past the lines of dead and the prisoners, half of them barefoot, walking on the other side of the road. They were being moved along by military police who wore long trench coats and carried Schmeissers.

I had to unbuckle a mess tin from a dead German lying in the ditch. Inside was half a loaf of bread and some oatmeal cookies that looked homemade.

Handschumacher, von Schwerin, and I squatted in a clearing, sniffed at the stew before tasting it. Wasn't the usual stew. No carrots or potatoes. There was a caldron of ersatz coffee, and I filled my water bottle with it when no one was looking. We were allowed only one cup.

One of the cooks was replacing the right front wheel of the food truck. He was on his knees in the mud, swearing and whacking the axle with a crowbar.

It looked as if a lot of people hadn't bothered to come to get food. Others sat by themselves or in little groups as we did.

Rumor was we were going in after dark. At the food truck they were handing out corks for us to burn and smear on our faces.

Handschumacher carefully poured his soup onto the ground, shook out the last few greasy drops. With the familiar rattling mess tin noise, he put it back together, looked up and grinned at us again.

We waited for him to say something, but he didn't.

DARKNESS. The sky gone gray and then black. All day the 88s, firing from far behind us, raised pieces of Rocherath into the air and dropped them down again. Sometimes a smudge of burning oil would stay in the sky. When the firing paused we heard trucks moving in the town.

I was wondering where the townspeople had gone. Maybe

they were hiding in another part of the forest, sitting in rocking chairs and barricaded by beds and chests of drawers that they rescued from the advance. But they wouldn't have had time. They were probably in their wine cellars choking in the dust knocked down through the floorboards by the guns.

Vague dreams of Paris by Christmas. Postcard images of the Tuileries and bridges over the Seine in the morning fog.

Constipation. Oh, yes, now that I thought of it, I was pretty constipated. Bloody stew, and no one told me I wasn't supposed to eat snow. Gave me a hell of a stomachache.

Darkness and wind. Icicles. Gunfire in the distance in the night. The click of bullets being loaded into magazines. Bursts of strange laughter. Cigarettes glowing. Dead men frozen on the road. The sad faces of friends staring down at them.

THE FIELDS between us and the town were a vast, blue-glowing space. Rocherath was completely dark. No sound came from it. The guns had stopped.

We had formed into new squads. We used to be A squad, but now we were Number Two Group along with half a dozen members of other broken units.

Voss gave me a radio and Kaslaka gave me some bullets for the .45, which I then went and retrieved from the snow. Nobody had bothered to move Fatty. I sniffed at the breeze, standing away from the trees, feeling very naked in the open field. Looking back into the woods, I could see nothing. I might have been by myself. Could have dreamed the whole damn thing up and wandered out here like an escaped loony.

NO WHISTLES. A harsh whisper and we walked, all of us in extended line, out of the forest and down the slope, the night wind hard in our faces. Voss said it was a stupid move to have stopped shelling the town such a long time ago. It had been more than an hour. He said he didn't think we'd get halfway across, told us to run for the hedges if they started shooting. The radio I was made to carry sputtered and mumbled on my back. I had to eat the rest of my food and whoever-he-was's oatmeal cookies to make room for the spare radio batteries I also had to carry. Voss said orders would be radioed when to go forward, when to fall back. It felt like I was giving a piggy-back ride to an old man who complained quietly in my ear. On top of that I filled my pockets with bullets, fixed the boot knife to the inside of my Yankee boot, stuffed four stick grenades in my belt, and had the .45 in my bread bag. Voss had us scared that the Americans were Indians, because of their insignia, said they'd start pelting us with tomahawks and arrows, said that under their helmets they had Mohawk haircuts and tattoos on their skulls.

I set traps for Indians in the woods back home, once made a box out of wooden slats and tied it up in a tree in such a way that it would fall if someone pulled at an old lamb chop I set on a tree stump; that was, if they didn't notice the huge knot I'd tied around the lamb chop bone. The box fell on my brother when he went to investigate. Three stitches. Spankings, one for me for making a stupid trap my father said wouldn't have worked anyway, and one for my brother for sabotaging my invention. My father was very fair. This was so many years ago.

Someone was calling for Number Two Group, so I asked what they wanted into the greasy telephone receiver smelling of other people's tobacco breath.

"Who's this?"

"Westland."

"This is Beck."

I didn't know who Beck was.

"What's up, Beck?"

"You see anything?"

I looked around. The vast night-blue sky spreading over us, past the town and on to a turquoise blur at the horizon. Black hedges. Strange glowing snow. The shapes of us all going forward, and our footsteps in the snow. Coughs. Whispers. Wind.

"I don't see a damn thing, Beck."

"Nor me." Beck sighed into the radio.

"So is something the matter, Beck?"

"I can't stand the quiet, Westland."

I shifted the weight of the radio on my back. The antenna wobbled above my head. "What am I supposed to do about it?"

"Nothing. Talk. When you think they're going to start shooting? How close you think they'll let us get?"

"They probably evacuated. Would you sit around and let yourself get overrun by the SS?"

"Knowing who we are exactly, I'd say it wouldn't be a bad idea at all, assuming we make it to the town."

"Beck?"

"What?"

I shut off the radio without saying anything else and ate some candy, rummaged past the .45 in my bread bag for any scraps to eat.

HISS. SSIH. The arclights of flares scraping across the sky, and the acid jumped in my guts. I was almost on my face when the flares popped and the whole valley lit up with magnesium brightness. I put my head in my hands. Guns started up from the first row of hedges on the edge of the town. I turned the radio back on and heard Heydt or someone yelling at Number One Group to advance. Across the field Number One Group all stood up slowly, the radioman calling the order, NCOs screaming, and the pop of the bullets overhead swinging toward them. They ran a short way and dropped; a spattering of flashes as they shot back.

"Number Two Group forward." Heydt on the radio.

"Number Two Group forward!" Me on my hands and knees trying to stand up.

Then we were running at the hedges, snow puffing up in lines beside us. The radio bounced on my spine, and when I saw the first man go down, I let myself fall, heard Voss bellow at us to keep going.

"Jesus Christ. Jesus Christ." I couldn't see a damn thing now because of the sweat in my eyes, and the fucking helmet sliding down over my forehead. Still couldn't see any people up by the town. Screech of the mortars. They dropped right into us. The blast hit me in the head. Heydt was still rattling off his Group numbers.

I didn't know how I got to be standing. Every bit of sense I had told me to lie down again. I ran behind someone until the next bomb went off and I fell over numb from the shock. Someone was screaming for help on the radio. I didn't know if it was Beck. I lost count of the shells coming down. We were already close to the hedge, a great tangled mass of black, and I could see some shapes running up the hill into the town. All but one of the guns had stopped. The mortars were too far back to keep throwing me over. I felt them, barking in my face and squashing my lungs. Someone was still screaming on the radio. Help me. Get a doctor. Help me. Get a doctor. Somebody, get me a doctor. It had to be one of the radiomen. A figure jumped from behind the hedge and raised one arm in the air.

"Cover!" Voss yelled.

And I was on my knees when a sound like *pang* went off in the middle of us. Smoke rose from a patch of ground behind me. The pig smell of an explosion.

There was a gap for a gate in the hedge. I could see the crossed planks of wood. The shape who threw the grenade ran past the opening, and someone close on our side shot him to pieces with a Schmeisser. Bits of the gate collapsed. I heard someone shouting in English. Darkness. Shapes running around. Radio hissing, then screaming for help. The whole hedge going up in flames.

Suddenly I was on my back looking up at the sky. Ears hurting. Something in them. Pulse of pain in my ears, like a hole drilled through each one. Blood in them. Another grenade or something. Standing again, moving over the fence. My fucking head coming apart. In the light of a new flare: Handschumacher climbing over the gate with the Spandau in his arms, strange armor of the bullet chains around him. "God, help, for Christ's sake!" the radio is still talking. "Number Two Group forward." Amis too slow getting back into cover with their machine guns. They are dragging their .30s up by the tripods and moving too slowly. Eventually our people catch up with them, and I see one of ours, swathed in a greatcoat, powdered with snow at every wrinkle, jam a fixed bayonet into one of the Amis and yell what the NCOs made us yell at bayonet practice. "In! Twist! Out!" Handschumacher running forward, firing the Spandau from the hip and howling. Oh, my fucking ears. Must have bust the drums or something. I can taste blood at the back of my mouth. Still haven't got out of the shadow of the hedge. Can't go very fast with the radio. Beck, or whoever, has quieted down a bit. Shapes move up the short slope to the level ground where it looks like there's a graveyard and some houses, the spire of a small church. "Number Two Group forward," says the radio. I take it off and throw it on the ground, then, thinking of the trouble I'll get if they see I've dumped good equipment, I take the .45 and let go about four bullets into the machine, the gun tearing the muscles in my wrist. I kick the radio around a bit, make sure it's not talking anymore. Start running up the slope.

V o s s a n d Kaslaka set up an American .30 on the stone wall surrounding the graveyard, and we waited behind the wall while they shot at everything in sight: stone, glass, wood, everything.

Cartridges bounced through the air like a mass of locusts. They used up three ammunition cans. I lay on the ground with my head resting against the wall, breathing hard from the short run and watching the field we had crossed, dapples of bodies left in the snow, the coal-colored woods beyond that.

A man ran out from behind the church. Kaslaka blew him off his feet.

"That was a German!" screamed Voss, and shoved Kaslaka away from the gun.

Another man dodged past gravestones, trying to get to us, waving his arms and shouting. He was carrying a box that was paying out wire as he ran. Someone started shooting at him from a skylight window in the town. I could see the muzzle flashes. He stopped at one of the gravestones, crouched behind it, panting. Then he threw the box over the wall to us and followed it, swan-diving past us into the snow. He slid halfway down the slope before he stopped.

"The Yanks have filled the church with their ammunition. That's where they've been keeping it." He was out of breath and choking, talking fast as he climbed the slope. He said he was a member of Number One Group and they'd rigged charges around the church, but the Amis had shot everyone before they had a chance to set the charges off. He said he was the only one left.

Voss set the plunger box on his lap and started to attach the wires from the spool on the side of the box. "You sure the wire's not been cut?"

"I don't think so. Listen, though, there's one more thing." He put his hand on Voss's shoulder. "The civilians are in there, too. That's where the townspeople are hiding. I got a look in through the window, and they're all taking cover under the pews. And there's crates and crates of mortar shells, landmines all stacked up by the main door. The Yanks have a gunpost right outside."

"You'll have to bypass the church." Von Schwerin, poking his head out of the shadows.

"Can't do it." The man squatted down on the wet ground. "There's soldiers in the church, too. None of us would get past that first gunpost anyway. This town's too small."

"You can't just blow up civilians."

"I don't think they're in the mood for negotiating."

Voss set the plunger box down in front of von Schwerin. "Hit the plunger, Schwerin."

"What!"

"I said hit the plunger. I'm ordering you."

"You can't just massacre a bunch of civilians!" Von Schwerin was wailing and shaking his head.

"Are you disobeying an order?" Voss sounded very calm.

Suddenly Handschumacher lunged out of the dark and slammed his fist down on the plunger.

At the first explosion we went down on our faces. I counted about five more, shaking the ground and spitting pieces of stone over the wall where we hid. Didn't look up. Dirt rattled down on my back. Cordite and blasted stone. Put my hands over my ears and shook. When it had finished, it seemed for a second as if everything had stopped. Complete silence.

Then Kaslaka started firing the machine gun again.

The roof of the church was gone. The spire had been peeled apart like a dead tree trunk. Smoke in angry waves heaved into the sky, covering the stars.

Not much to the town. Gray houses with slate roofs. Telegraph poles made of concrete.

Kaslaka fired the .30 until it jammed. Then he just pushed it in front of him, off the wall, grabbed a rifle, and began running through the graveyard.

Voss followed. We followed.

Dodged past stones and smashed crucifixes toward the narrow streets and houses. The cemetery was paved with gravel, and we were out of it before anyone shot at us.

Voss rocked back on his heels, firing the Schmeisser, knocked out the front window of a house. On his order, I ran at it from the side, threw in a grenade, and slid on my stomach, skinning my hands and tearing my trousers, past the front door. One. Two. Three. Four. The remains of the window and the frame blew out. The door flew open and we ran in, Voss firing half a magazine off at chest level and the other half at ankle level, the rest of us pouring in after him. Too much smoke. Couldn't see a damn thing except shapes running past to the houses outside. The coughs of bombs detonating. Eyes hurt from the smoke. Hung over the banisters was a body that Voss, running up the stairs, swung by the legs out into space and onto the floor.

I kicked open the door to the kitchen and saw the place was covered with smashed crockery. Didn't go in. I turned around and bumped into von Schwerin, who almost stuck me with his bayonet.

"I thought you had a radio."

I pushed past him back out into the street. Above me there was a crash and something fell into the street. It was a man. Wasn't a soldier. Just an old man. Voss had thrown him out a window, said something about partisans as he ran down the street, which by now was burning with ignited gasoline. An American jeep boiled in fire in the alley nearby.

I kept to the sides of the buildings. A boy in front of me fell back into the street, curled up in a ball and moaning. The line of us stopped as we came up to the door he had gone past, threw in grenades, and set the house on fire. Then we moved on.

I crouched in a garden, swayed back and forth with the pain in my ears, while von Schwerin and Voss shot at a sniper on the roof. The man slid down the slates and onto the road, where someone shot him again, then ran up and stole his rifle.

The light from the fires was bright, almost like day in some places, the crash of burning timbers falling back into the houses, loose slates all over the street.

I stepped over a dead woman, her dress up over her chest and face, legs pale and sickly in the firelight.

Another .30 started up from somewhere, and we ran into houses, gardens, behind corpses, or jumped back dead from the strike of the bullets. I hid in someone's living room, flinching uncontrollably, knees tucked into my chest as glass from the windows fell down on me, the .30 hacking the place to bits. Pictures dropped. A light bulb blew. The whole room flew to pieces in the sweep of the .30. And when it had gone, I stayed where I was, waiting for another sweep, but it never came. I blinked at the smoke and kicked-up dust. My lungs felt like two balloons filled with sand.

Out in the street Voss and another NCO whose name I didn't know had the American .30 crew, three of them, up against a wall. They must have given in, I figured. They got shoved into a small garden, jostling with their hands in the air. Their helmets were off and short hair stuck up dirty from their heads.

Voss pushed the Luger into the chest of the one in the middle and asked him how many Americans were still left in the town. He replied in bad German that he didn't know. Voss said it again, not clearer, only louder, and the man said he didn't know. I saw the sharp lines of Voss's face under his helmet, silhouetted against fire and an iron railing fence, bent back in places where it had been struck by bullets, the ends curled up like the fingers of a witch. He asked the American one more time, then suddenly swung the Luger into the head of the man on his right and pulled the trigger. The man's eyes jerked around to white. He tipped backwards and slid down the rough stone wall, shaking. After that, the American in the middle started talking, fast and gladly, about anything, his hands raised to Voss in permanent begging. They had orders to hold the town as long as they could, then to counterattack later on that night. They had heavy losses. Only a little ammunition, a lot of sick people. He had a wife, two little girls. Did we want to see their picture? He spoke German very well for an Ami. Voss turned and left, ran across the road to where someone was talking on a field radio, the radio carrier dead on his face in the gutter. Kaslaka put the rest to death in the frozen garden before we moved on through the town.

I didn't know how long this lasted. The blood in my ears had clotted and dried and I had to scrape it out with my fingers in order to hear anything. I drank the cold coffee from my water bottle, in one long messy feeding.

KASLAKA HAD disappeared. Voss snapped his head about in movements like a bird, peering into houses and gardens, calling his name. He ordered us to find him. He was frantic looking for Kaslaka. I started turning over bodies, expecting to see his face, and none of them was him. But I knew the others, knew them all from the camp, lifted the dead radio carrier up by the hair to see his face and fished around his chest to see from the dog tag if it was Beck. And it was. A. O. Beck. Waffen SS 12. Blood type O. Someone came and tried to get the radio off his back, and I left him to it.

An American crawled across the road, holding his leg with one hand and moving himself along with the other. Handschumacher and I watched with vague interest, catching sight of an SS man, sitting like a goblin on a chimney pot, line the Yank up in the sights of his rifle. There was a crack and in the middle of the street the American stopped crawling, open-mouthed and eyes jammed shut, slowly turning over on his back and lying still. The SS man came down off the roof and out into the road, grabbed the man's gun, and dashed back into the dark.

Kaslaka crawled up out of a basement, draped with cobwebs and holding a violin. He held it up, smiling. Voss took it out of his hand, smashed it, and then hit him on the head with whatever was left.

Voss ordered Handschumacher and me up into an attic, told us to fire on the trucks leaving the town. We had to move some trunks out of the way, filled with I didn't know what, before we could get to the window, which we opened with rifle butts. Where the town ended, we could see how it dropped away into fields and hedges on the road out to the town called Büllingen. We could hear the trucks driving out, changing gears as they moved over the hill on the horizon.

We aimed the Spandau in the general direction of the hill and shot off a belt, tracers spiraling into the dark and somewhere striking metal. A few seconds later we heard shouting and screaming, saw a truck in flames. The Spandau bolt got stuck. Handschumacher said, "Fucking lousy Nazi shit," and set the gun down.

I put the belt slowly down on the windowsill and poked my head out into the air. We were quite high up, with a good view. There were stars in the windy sky, speckles and clusters and lonely ones. It looked as if they might all come unstuck with the force of the breeze and bunch at one end of the universe. The air was clean. It wouldn't snow for a while now. Instead it would freeze.

I opened a few of the trunks to see if there was anything I wanted. One of them was full of women's clothes, another of fishing tackle. I put my arm through a painting by mistake, crawling back to where Handschumacher stood, the Spandau in bits and pieces around him. He squinted at the pieces and held them up to the window before trying to put the gun together again. He clinked every time he moved, because he still had half a dozen bullet chains wrapped around him.

"Anything good in the trunks?"

"Nothing." I rested my chin on the windowsill. The sound of the fires was clear. Gobs of smoke spread out against the stars.

A few people stood in the road, talking quietly, pointing at the remains of the truck on the hill, which had burned itself almost to nothing. Then they filtered away back out of sight.

"You go see what's up, Westland. I'll hold the fort." Handschumacher worked the bolt in the Spandau, then took it out and tapped it on the end of his boot. I met Voss coming up the stairs.

"There's food in the basement here, Westland. Take what you need and then tell someone else about it. No good having a stampede."

We went into a bedroom and shared some cigarettes called Lucky Strike. Voss lay on the bed with his feet on the pillows and coughed lightly. Then he had a coughing fit, which ended with him spitting blood onto the floor.

"You all right?"

"Same old thing."

"So when the Amis coming back?" I sat down on a child's chair, slowly in case it collapsed underneath me.

"Couple of hours, maybe. We have fifty percent casualties after that last assault. That's every other man, Westland. Number One Group or whatever the fuck it's called doesn't exist anymore." He jerked his hands open. "Just doesn't exist is all. We can't hold this place. We got no backups, we took the town because they let us take it." Then he swung himself off the bed and stood. "Got a job for you. Have to show them the fear."

Voss's way to show them the fear was to drag as many of the dead Americans as we could find and line them up on the road at the end of the town. We made a pile of the bodies where they would be seen when the rest came back. Even some of the wounded were thrown on the pile. It seemed as important to Voss as anything else. The road was scattered with helmets, like birds' nests shaken out of trees. I took only one man to the pile, found him in a doorway, hit in the chest by a Schmeisser burst, dragged him by one leg to the place where the others were, and went back to Handschumacher.

He and I went down to the basement and found three cases full of canned food. One case was beans, another cherries, and another macaroni. I took one of each, mixed them together in the bowl of an American helmet I found on top of one of the cases, ate the mess with my fingers. We didn't speak, just ate in the dark. When Handschumacher had eaten what sounded like six cans of food, he lit himself a cigarette, and I saw him suddenly, clearly, his features exaggerated in the flame of the match, freckles like specks of copper.

"I been thinking, we don't want to be in this place when they come back. We won't have a chance. Got to find somewhere else to go."

I drank the syrup from a can of cherries. "So let's go." I stood up, slapped his knee, and we left after grabbing a few more cans.

We walked down the main street until we saw another couple of boys setting up their Spandau behind a burned-out jeep.

"Voss says you have to go set up in the attic of that house."

"Who's Voss?"

"NCO in command." I felt pregnant from the food and the lying.

"Why don't you go? You've got a Spandau." One of them stood with his hands on his hips. The other was already rolling up the bullet chains.

"Ours is busted." Handschumacher slapped the gun on his shoulder as if it were a bad baby.

"There's food in the basement. Lots of it. Good stuff." I lowered my voice. "But don't tell *everyone*. No good having a stampede."

"I want to talk to Voss." The boy's name was Kruger. I knew him now. A Leipzig boy.

"Well, he's around somewhere."

They walked off to the house, stopping to gape at the pile of American dead outside the front door.

"Now what do we do?" Handschumacher sat on the hood of the burned jeep, but jumped off because the metal was still smoldering.

"I got us this far. You get us the rest of the way." I took off my helmet and ran my fingers through my hair. Then I sat down on the ground and stared into space. "My eardrums are gone. Look." I twisted my head around so he could see.

"Looks like you're wearing red earrings."

"Hurts."

"I'm sure."

I spent a long time getting to my feet, then told him I was going to find von Schwerin.

He nodded and busied himself trying to clear his nose by pressing a finger against one nostril and sneezing.

Voss AND Kaslaka were rigging a mine on the Büllingen/ Rocherath road. It was a case of mortar shells set to go off when Voss touched together the skeleton hands of two splayed electric wires.

Heydt sat on the hood of a jeep he had found for himself. He had wrapped a swastika flag over the place where the white star was normally painted. On his clipboard he checked off wooden crates that the MP driver was unloading from the space at the back of the jeep. I knew the crates contained Panzerfausts. They looked around for someone to give them to, and I vanished because I didn't trust Panzerfausts. I didn't see any good reason why the bomb on the end shouldn't go off when you dropped it, or go off when you pulled the trigger. The whole thing looked much too simple. At the Bad Tölz range the instructor had pointed one at a junked Volkswagen that had been trucked in for the demonstration. He braced himself against a tree, and, in the middle of the boom when he set the thing off, he disappeared in the smoke and fire out of both ends. The Volkswagen jumped in the air, flipped on its side, all in flames, bits, and pieces, tires spinning away, and when it hit the ground it was junk.

Now I kept to the shadows and walked down an alley. All over the town men were hiding themselves away behind walls, talking quietly and smoking in twos and threes. Mausers and Spandaus were pointing at the sky, grenades set out along the ground.

The wounded were still being carried past on stretchers by other soldiers. There weren't any Red Cross men. A hand sticking out from a blanket on a stretcher brushed past me.

"Any of you people seen Schwerin? Have you seen Schwerin at all?"

Most people didn't even look up. There was firing in the far distance, big guns. The whole of the Ardennes in chaos.

I sat on a wall with some boys I barely knew and listened to what they had learned. The Americans had artillery up at a place called the Elsenborn ridge, but they didn't know where to set down the barrages because the lines kept changing. There had been breakthroughs all down the line except here. The town of Büllingen, four kilometers away, was already under attack from the Adolf Hitler Division, the First SS Division.

"Where'd you find out all this?" I said to the nearest boy. He turned around and looked at me from the corner of his eye. His face was swollen from a cut on his lip that went up to his nostrils. He pointed at a body spread-eagled on the doorstep of a burned house. The dead man's throat was cut back to his spine.

I FOUND von Schwerin dragging a body down a small cobblestoned alley between two houses. He was slipping on the stones, breathing heavily, and sweating. He had tucked the man's boots under his arms and was trying to drag the body out to the street. The man was still alive. Not very much, but still enough to be groaning and catching drainpipes with his arms to try to stop from being pulled. Von Schwerin didn't seem to notice, walked on the spot, his legs tramping the stone, while the man held onto a gutter pipe until one, then two, then all his fingers lost their grip and von Schwerin jolted forward.

"Westland." He nodded at me, still dragging. The man groaned.

"He's still alive, Schwerin."

"So? Have to show them the fear. Isn't that what Voss said? So I'm showing." He was sweating in the cold air.

"I think the pile's big enough now. Give it a rest." I handed him some cigarettes in one hand and a can of food in the other.

"Is that food?" He dropped the legs, and the man groaned again. The American's stomach was bare, black fur in a line up from his navel, clothes bunched around his shoulders and his face, which I couldn't see. He had two stripes sewn on the arm of his jacket, and I didn't remember if that meant he was an officer. His jacket was green with four pockets and a drawstring at the waist. Trousers looked like brown wool. Brown-green sweater. He had two rectangular dog tags on a bead chain around his neck. I wasn't able to see where he'd been hurt. Maybe he only had a bump on the head.

Von Schwerin crouched down, eating cherries from the can I gave him. The top was prised back in four triangles from opening it with two stabs of a knife, the way we all did it. He spat the pits out ineffectively. Sometimes they just fell off the end of his lower lip. He ate with a combination fork and spoon set, the spoon scraping against his teeth.

"Pile's big enough, you say?" He was eating so fast I thought he would choke.

"How big do you want it?" I leaned against the wall of one of the houses and slid down until I was in the same crouch as he.

"Show them the fear. *Ptuh.*" Cherry pit. "As big as it has to be." He rammed the fat, dark balls in his mouth and chewed.

The man rolled over slowly and tried to get up on his knees. Von Schwerin had his back to him. Eventually the man made it to his knees, but the rest of him was still lying on the ground. From the sound of his breathing I could tell his nose was squashed on a cobblestone.

"So you say the pile's big enough?" Von Schwerin looked across to me in the blue night light, and his eyes were huge. He was running with sweat.

I said, "Are you hurt?"

"Me?" he yelled, and I cringed at the sound. "God, no. Feel fine. Well, at least okay." He scraped around some more in the can, found nothing, so threw it viciously down the alley.

The man was on his elbows and knees, swinging his head slowly from side to side.

"It's all these fucking dead people, Sebastian." Von Schwerin laughed a laugh that turned into a cough. "I mean, good fucking Lord! I don't know how it was where you were, but me and this other boy—think his name's Karsten—we rigged up one of the .30s they'd left behind and shot up a whole truckload. You know, they'd jump out of the truck, and I'd aim the .30 at the tailgate, and they all just fell in a clump. And they kept *coming.*" He stretched out his hands as if he were holding two grapefruits. "Sons of bitches all died, and then there's one or two left still trying to get out—the belt finishes and I yell at Karsten to put a new one in. Look across and he's dead. Right next to me, Sebastian, and I didn't even know it. His whole head's gone, even. What the hell do you suppose happened? I didn't *hear* anything." He raised one hand. "I didn't *see* anything." He raised the other hand. "I couldn't even find where it went." He dropped both hands to the ground.

Then he peered over to where the man was on his hands and knees, crawling very slowly away from us down the alley. Von Schwerin jerked his head toward me, then back to the man again.

"Pile's big enough, you say?"

"For Christ's sake."

He looked around by his feet. "Do you know, I think I've lost my fucking Mauser."

"Nothing to worry about."

He put his hands together the way a fly puts its front legs together, and began rubbing them fast, smoothing them over each other. "Shall I let him go, then?"

I shrugged.

"Well, shall I?" He was shouting again.

"Sure."

"Good. Then that's settled." He stood up suddenly, walked to the end of the alley, and stood half in, half out of the sharp shadow line made by the night. He came back after a minute and crouched down, wiping the sweat from his face. "Any more food, have you?"

"No, Schwerin." I felt my last can in the bread bag.

"Shame." He picked up a cherry pit, sniffed it, then put it in his mouth. "Wonder if they're good for you, these." He bounced on his heels. "Well, I don't know what to say, Westland. All these fucking dead people."

"Let's go get Handschumacher." When I stood up, my knees cracked.

"He's still here? Well, good fucking news." He hadn't sworn this much in all the time I'd known him.

Something screamed over our heads and exploded a couple of houses away, then something else toward the end of the town, another, and the boom noise was followed by the squeaking of tanks. I was standing still, frozen in a half-crouch from the first explosion.

"Shelling!" Von Schwerin rolled into the corner next to the wall of the house.

"It's tanks. They're bringing tanks this time. I wonder where the hell ours are."

Spandaus started up from the end of town, and I knew it was the boys we'd sent to the attic, Handschumacher and I. The thud of a Panzerfaust. Three people ran past the alley with an American .30, one of them almost barechested, his SS camouflage was in such tatters.

Von Schwerin looked around hurriedly. "So what do we do?"

"Get behind a wall or something and wait for them to come."

We ran toward the cemetery and hid ourselves either side of the entranceway—two concrete pillars, each with a stone ball at the top. There was an iron gate between the pillars, heavy, painted, and smashed about by bullets. I found von Schwerin an American Garand rifle with a broken bayonet on the end. We waited.

Guns were firing until they jammed. Explosions were going up all over the town. A Panzerfaust went off, and a huge metal clanging was followed by a mass of detonations, the shells in the tank going up. Whistles. The single *pack-packing* of Mausers, and the faster firing of the Garands. Always the squeak of the tank tracks.

I sat cross-legged against the pillar and pressed new bullets into the rifle, holding the bolt back with my thumb. Across the graveyard the strange heads of crucifixes showed as silhouettes against dark blue. The graves were marked with photographs of the dead, printed on porcelain. The wreckage of the church still shuddered with smoke, the stained-glass windows bowed over by the heat and the blast.

Four people ran past the graveyard wall, and when I poked my head up, I saw they were Americans. Then my tongue swelled up in my throat so I could hardly breathe. I looked over at von Schwerin, and he was aiming the Garand through the bars of the gate, his lips curled back so I could see his pale teeth.

The Americans stopped and muttered to each other. They were breathing hard.

I took a grenade out of my belt, unscrewed the cap at the end of the stick, unraveled the wax cord with the porcelain ball at the end, and saw von Schwerin holding up three fingers. That meant he wanted me to throw it after three seconds, which meant it would explode in the air, or maybe in my face. "Only in extreme situations should this be attempted." I remembered it from the manual. I put the ball behind my clenched teeth, tasting armory grease, pulled the cord, and counted, one, two, three fast, lobbed the stick, cartwheeling in the air. The Americans shouted, the stick hit the ground, I said, "Fuck," and it exploded. I curled into a ball. Von Schwerin started firing the Garand, but it jammed after two shots. He rolled away into the dark.

My god-damned ears. They pounded inside my skull.

Without waiting to see what had happened, I took my last grenade, set it to go, and skimmed it over the wall. No shouts this time. The crack and the roll of the bomb. Then it detonated; I cried out from the pain in my ears and stood up with the Mauser pointing at the block of smoke in the road. Men were scattered on the cobblestones.

An American tank rounded the corner of the houses opposite the graveyard, and I ducked down. It drove out into the open space between the cemetery and the houses. I heard the whirring of the turret as it turned, searching. It backed up into a house, smashing bricks and glass and wood. Then it went forward again almost to the wall of the cemetery. My face was pressed to the marble of the gravestone I was hiding behind. A. Ziese. The dead person's name was A. Ziese, and he died in 1924. "Rests with God," it said. The turret whirred again. I licked the dew off the stone, tried to swallow and couldn't, let the spit run down my chin. My knees hurt from kneeling on the gravel. The tank's engine screamed, and it backed down one of the roads.

Another vehicle came fast out of an alley and smashed into a telegraph pole.

"You idiot! You blasted idiot!" German voice.

I looked up, and Heydt was beating the driver of his jeep over the head with his clipboard. The driver, who was an MP, held his hands over his head even though he was wearing a helmet. Another man from the jeep, standing by the telegraph pole, looked as if he expected to get shot.

"It stuck in reverse, sir. I can't do anything about it now!"

With a final slap, Heydt broke the board over the MP's head.

"Get out! We'll stop the tank on foot!" Then he saw von Schwerin and me blinking at him from over the cemetery wall. "You two! Here!" He pointed to a place about a meter in front of his boots.

When I was almost at the jeep, the MP by the telegraph pole lobbed a Panzerfaust across to me. I whimpered as it hit my chest.

Heydt was already running for the road down which the tank had disappeared.

The MP jogging alongside me talked through his swallows for breath. "We've been playing cat and mouse with this tank since the attack began. It almost blew us off the street when it saw us the first time, but its guns must have jammed. And now this man Heydt is going to get it even if he kills us all."

Halfway down the street was a barricade made of tables and chairs, a large path broken through the middle where the tank had gone. SS men were firing over the jumble of wood, filling the road beyond with the smoke of hand grenades.

A stretcher crew passed us on the other side of the street. The wounded boy they were carrying howled, and the stretcher man in front turned around and told him to shut up.

Heydt stopped and we piled into him. He bent down to do up his shoelaces, which had come undone. We were all wearing American boots. Even von Schwerin, noble nose. I had caught him earlier, springing up and down to test the soft rubber soles.

A green flare went up and popped emerald light off the roofs, stretching the angles of shadow.

At the barricade a boy on a table dropped his gun and slid onto the ground, shot. Another boy dragged him into the doorway of a house, telling him he was all right. Saying everything was fine. Over and over.

Half a dozen SS men ran through the hole in the barricade and hid behind it. Heydt still hadn't moved, pulling at his stubbled chin. From the shouting at the barricade, I guessed that the Americans were making another push to get through the town.

There was a crack like thunder, then another, then several more. Voss's mine. Must have been. I hugged the Panzerfaust. The pulse in my ears hadn't stopped.

"You! Westland! Up in that house and get the tank when it comes. Schwerin, stay with him. Blücher and you, Bad Driver, come with me to the barricade."

"I DIDN'T know he knew my name. Or yours." Von Schwerin heaved up the window and cold air pushed in.

I looked down at the mess of tables and chairs, lamps, coatracks. A boy lay on his face in front of the barricade, fallen in midstride. Fire. The windows flickered with the reflection of flames.

I felt sick. I walked to the corner of the room, a study or something—desk, bookshelves—and pissed on the floor. Von Schwerin had turned the other way. My hands were cramped so I couldn't do the buttons up on my fly.

Shooting coming closer. I snapped my fingers and pointed at the canteen on von Schwerin's hip. He unclipped it and handed it over. I took a mouthful of lukewarm water and swallowed, then handed the thing back.

Fuck the Panzerfaust.

"There's a kind of purity knowing there are no prisoners in

this. There is something absolute." Von Schwerin ran his finger along the titles of books on the shelves.

"Don't know what the hell you're talking about."

Down at the barricade they were starting to shoot. Someone advanced up the road out of view. I wasn't going to poke my head out and look. The waiting made me ill. Von Schwerin didn't have a gun. All I had was the .45 and the Faust. One of the MPs yanked the cord out of a grenade. I watched his body stretch back, then jolt forward as the bomb flew from his hand.

I heard the tank, the babble of guns at the barricade; stood back from the window with the Faust leveled at the road.

Then the barricade started getting chopped to pieces. I saw an MP bend over and fall, dropping his rifle. Heydt picked it up. The tank came into view, men in olive greatcoats crowded behind it, ducking down.

One of the Amis following the tank looked up at my window. I couldn't see his eyes under the rim of his helmet, which was covered with a string net. For a second I stared at him, and he paused, looking up at me. I closed my hand around the trigger piece. The Panzerfaust kicked and roared. The room filled with smoke. Outside, the noise of the explosion crashed about the street. Screaming and more explosions, all of it covered in smoke.

Turning to run, my lungs full of blast fumes, I saw von Schwerin standing close to me, his face almost blank, a little bit sad, the light of the fires on his cheeks, his hand raised so that the backs of his fingers were just touching his lips. The recoil which shot out of the back of the Panzerfaust tube had burned a trail across the ceiling, and the black was dappled with flames. I didn't dare go close to the window. Already bullets were chipping through the glass and knocking holes in the plaster.

I still didn't know what had happened to the tank. The town seemed to be collapsing in on itself.

We ran.

* * *

VON SCHWERIN swung himself on the wooden ball of the banister post. At the bottom of the stairs we saw through a window two Amis running for the front door of our house.

I hid to the side of the door and von Schwerin dodged into the kitchen. Sweat was dripping from the leather liner of my helmet. I reached down and pulled the trench knife out of my boot. In the other hand I had the .45.

The Amis on the outside kicked at the door twice, and it swung open. They ran in, the first straight past. The second plowed into me. I smelled his breath and saw a scar under his right eye. I put the gun to his chest and pulled the trigger. Von Schwerin stepped out of the kitchen, and the man ran onto the blade of von Schwerin's trench knife. The blade broke off in the man's stomach. Von Schwerin had the man by the throat, pressing in his Adam's apple with his thumbs. The man said nothing. His eyes were closed and blood came out of his mouth. Von Schwerin was banging the man's head against the floor.

I grabbed him by the collar, and we both ran down a short passageway to the back of the house. We came to a dining room, big stone fireplace and the fade marks of where pictures had hung on the walls, looking out a large window into a small back garden. But no door.

I stopped running and von Schwerin didn't. He dove through the window into the garden. For a second I saw the soles of his boots and his arse disappearing into the froth of smashed panes and wooden frame pieces. Then he hit the ground and I dove after him, a strangely pleasant feeling to be flying, took another chunk of the window with me on my way out.

The grass was hard with frost, and I rolled, trying not to get cut on the shards of glass.

Von Schwerin got up and ran past me, hurdled the picket fence and fell over in the street because there was ice on it.

I could see people fighting hand to hand in an alley, kicking the life out of each other, rolling in tangles.

Lying in the gutter was an SS man, dead on top of a machine gun, spent cases like a mosaic under him. My nose fizzed. I knew it was Handschumacher. I knew it was.

I rolled the body over and saw it wasn't him but a boy called Boehm. He always used to sit in the same place in the Mensa, at the end of a table. It got so that no one else would sit there even when he wasn't around. I rolled him back on his face.

American voices shouted in the alley. A German shouted "Please!" and then stopped. More American voices.

The sky was riddled with stars.

WE RAN to the other side of the church from the graveyard. There was no point in going back toward the center of the town. I could hear we were losing it. The sound of Garands far outweighed the Mausers. The street was covered with loose bricks and pieces of slate from the roofs. There was a chest of drawers in the middle of the way, with a mirror fixed on it, reflecting the sky. Someone must have dragged it out and then had to leave it because the fighting started.

There was a smell from the ruins of the church. A very clear smell. Better not to know what it was. Better not to think these things. But the smell hung in the air around the broken building, and you couldn't help breathing it.

I picked up a Schmeisser from a body lying on a woodpile next to a workman's shed. The damn corpse wouldn't let go. Had to put my foot on its chest and wrench the gun out of its hands. I took some spare magazines out of the tan canvas pouches attached to the dead man's belt.

A cat padded along the wall around the church and jumped down into the shadows.

We found a cattle trough behind the last house before the

fields. I pushed through the thin ice with the crown of my helmet and drank, water cutting cold bands down into my stomach.

SS men moved across the fields in twos and threes. Leaving the town. I didn't know what had happened to our tanks. Maybe we could have held them with the tanks. Fucking Panzer boys.

The firing came closer now. The streets were full of the sound of vehicles moving up. Flares popped over the houses, different colored suns glaring down and then vanishing.

I knew it had failed. Operation Autumn Fog just another bogus campaign at the end of a war. Soon forgotten. The dead put away in mass graves. Soon far in the past. The woods full of caved-in foxholes and rusted metal.

Von Schwerin and I jogged into the snow. My throat was raw from the cold. It was a long way to the woods, but I figured once we were there, no one would ask us to leave again.

Even my breath smelled of cordite.

THE HORIZON beyond the woods flashed yellow and blue. The flashes continued along the line of the horizon. Von Schwerin and I stopped, panting white air, and watched the barrage.

"I—" von Schwerin said after a while, peering around. There was a shriek and an explosion in the town. Then another. Still another in the cemetery. Shells started coming down over the town. The barrage got thicker, the horizon constantly blinking with gunfire.

"That's our own guns!"

"Run," I said quietly.

"It's our own guns coming down on us when we're still here!" Von Schwerin looked around as if to see whether anyone else was listening besides me.

"So let's not be here anymore."

A shell blew up on the road leading into town. I heard the hard crack as the road surface flew to pieces. The shells made a horrible whine as they came in. Voss said if you got shelled enough times, you could tell where one was going to land from the pitch of the noise.

We ran like hell for the woods. The shrieking came from all over. The town was getting blown to dust.

T H E E A R T H rose up crying in front of us, fire and darkness of spread soil, the noise breaking open my ears.

I lay on my side, and my face was stinging. Dirt dropped down. A house-sized pack of smoke moved over us. My lungs felt pancaked inside me.

Another shriek came down on the slope to the field. I stood up and said, "Run," again quietly, maybe to myself, maybe to von Schwerin. My legs wouldn't move properly. They were shaky and numb. I ran until I heard another shriek and dropped, the shock wave riding over my shoulders and slapping the soles of my feet.

We weren't even halfway across the field. No place to hide. I heard a house collapse in a rumble of bricks and snapped timbers. Down again on my face. Crumbs of cold earth on my neck and back, plinking off my helmet.

Another shriek. I went down but nothing happened. Nothing.

I ran past a crater, tripping on the chucked-up lumps of rock. The smell of broken stone.

Von Schwerin was calling to me. I turned and saw him walking in the wrong direction, fall to one knee, stand, fall again. Then he kicked his legs trying to get up again.

I ran to him. His helmet was gone and one of his shoulder straps. It looked as if half his buttons were missing. He was still trying to stand.

I took him under the armpits and dragged him to a shell hole. He was leaving a smear of blood, and when he raised his left arm, there was no hand left, only the remains of the sleeve. He bled a trail to the shell hole, and we slid down to the bottom of it.

"That was close, eh?" Von Schwerin was talking as bits of blood came out of his mouth.

A blast knocked the top of my head, and dirt peppered us. When I moved my jaw, I could feel a squelching in my ears.

I grabbed his forearm, and there was nothing to hold. I tore back his sleeve and his arm was gone from the elbow down. He raised his head to look, and I pushed it back down. He coughed and told me again, "That was close."

I held onto his elbow, clamped it with my fists. A couple of times he tried to get up. I held him down, pushing my forehead against his chest.

"Ah. I guess I'm hurt."

"Rest now."

"I'm hurt somewhere in my arm."

He bled through the cracks between my fingers. He bled over the strap of my stopped watch. The barrage hammered the town. Fewer shells fell near us now. Several times there were shrieks and no explosions.

My hands were fusing to his arm. Using my teeth, I looked for the bandage pack in his pockets, but it wasn't there. I had used mine for handkerchiefs weeks ago. I unstuck myself from his arm and took off my jacket, then my shirt, my back crawling with goose bumps. I tore the shirt in half, then in half again, the material warm and stale.

I wrapped it around his arm, and it soaked straight through. I dragged him out of the hole and heaved him up on my shoulders. My helmet fell off. I had the Schmeisser hanging by its strap around my neck. We walked toward the forest. Couldn't go very fast.

I began to tell him about the time I carried Benjamin across the Onion Field to get at the shot-down English plane, the same way I carried him now.

After a while we were both laughing at the thought of Benjamin and me staggering through the mud back to his wheelchair, and Müller's cows all shot up in the next field.

I told him of Eva Weiden. Her thighs. Her lips. Her eyes.

All these I confessed to him. And about the night I crept downstairs from her room and got caught by Mr. Weiden, who was sitting by the fire.

I asked von Schwerin how he'd rate her, and he said he'd really have to see before passing any judgment.

Told him about the night of his birthday, when I left him in his cattle-trough bath and went up the hill to the woman who fed me roast duck and sat by the fire in her husband's shirt, braiding her hair. I stumbled on a few paces in silence, trying to remember her name, trying to remember if I had ever known it.

I could feel his breath on my neck, and the pain in my arms from carrying.

I used to sleep with a woman who picked me up from school. She said she wanted to marry me. And that was only the tip of the iceberg.

I asked him what he thought of that, thinking I could tell him about Lise Hammacher and it would last at least until the end of the field.

"Can I have a drink, Westland? Westland? I can walk if you want."

"No, you can't. Rest now."

"Not very easy. You have bony shoulders."

"I do not."

I was trying to make out where the road to Wahlerscheid was. At least there I could get him to the hospital. He was dribbling on my neck. My eyes blurred.

"Get me a drink."

"Later."

"F-f-fucking hell." He spat and it landed on my arm. "Sorry. I think I'm going to be sick. My arm's gone, isn't it? I can't fucking tell."

The butt of the Schmeisser kept swinging into my balls. I had to go down on my knees to rest. He wasn't much lighter than I and wasn't holding on to me. It made him hard to carry.

The barrage was slowing down. It had been going for half an hour.

The snow was frozen and didn't give immediately; I had to put all my weight on it before my foot went through. I was freezing through my jacket. The dog tag felt like a hole in my chest. My eyes dripped tears.

"Westland." He was croaking.

"What?"

"Get me a cigarette."

"Later."

"What's this blood from my mouth? My shoulder hurts. Put me down, will you? This is embarrassing."

"Quiet. Rest."

It was strangely light out in the field. The moon shone a sickle blade. Sometimes it shifted behind the clouds but not now. Now it was bright blue as I walked up toward the woods. Von Schwerin shivered. I had to tread over bodies to get to the tree line.

I set him down in the snow just before the trees and gave him a drink of cold coffee, which made him cough at first. Then he drank some more. His bandage was loose, so I tried to retie it. Still bleeding. He wasn't making much noise. I could tell he was going into shock. He was sweating, but his face was cold. I wiped his forehead with the sleeve of my jacket. He closed his eyes and coughed. Then he raised his good arm and tried to hold on to me.

"Bony shoulders." His face was very pale.

I leaned down and kissed him on the mouth. Then I picked him up again and started walking through the trees toward Wahlerscheid.

Up ahead a truck and a Kubel were just pulling onto the road toward Wahlerscheid. I shouted, but they didn't stop. I called, but there was no one else around. They all must have taken a different route. I walked in the middle of the road, von Schwerin mumbling in my ear, then coughing.

After maybe twenty minutes, the woods quiet and leaning over the road, I heard a machine coming. It was a truck, lights off, and it almost ran over us. I shouted but it didn't stop.

Another Kubel went past, then a motorcycle. The man turned to look but didn't stop. I fell over and von Schwerin started crying.

The next time I heard the noise of a machine, I put a new magazine in the Schmeisser, unfolded the stock, set it against my shoulder. I knelt by the side of the road and saw a motor-cycle coming close. It was maybe twenty paces away when I fired and kept firing, trying to aim above the machine at the man's upper body, until his head and then the rest of him jerked back and fell away in a waft of trench coat onto the road. The mo-torcycle jackknifed and fell, skidded over toward the trees. The man slid across the iced road and into the ditch.

I wasn't sure how to ride a motorcycle. I think I went the whole way in first gear. Von Schwerin sat in front of me, and I tried to hold onto him.

The road was mostly straight with one or two bends. At each turn the ditches were jammed with wrecked equipment, pushed out of the way and layered with snow. I could hear nothing but the sound of the engine and the wind. Von Schwerin was quiet, his head resting back on my shoulder.

SOMETIME SOON. The end of night.

* * *

I ALMOST drove straight past the customs house. There were no lights on. No people moving about. No sound. I couldn't find the key to the motorcycle to turn it off, so I let it rev down, choke, and stop.

My footsteps seemed very loud, crossing the road. The bodies of the SS who had died coming through the woods were stacked next to the house. The door was open. The whole building quiet. Darkness seething from the windows. It seemed the place was about to explode from some energy cramped inside it.

"Where?" von Schwerin whispered.

"Wahlerscheid." I put him down, set another magazine in the Schmeisser, and walked toward the door.

For a while I listened, then ducked inside and listened some more. From somewhere the sound of water dripping. A breeze came out of the woods, blew through broken windows in the house and passed on. I crouched down and kept listening, the darkness moving back and forth in strange geometric shapes before my eyes, the static of a movie screen.

There were still people in the room to my left. I could see them dark against the pale walls, lying side by side on the floor.

"Hey! Hey!" I whispered to them. Then when there was no answer I walked into the room, took a match out of my pocket and struck it on the barrel of the Schmeisser.

Their dull faces stared at me and through me. All of them dead. The walls were full of bullet holes. Shell cases on the floor. Executed. The burn marks from the muzzle being close to their temples had singed their hair. I knew almost everyone. Gray flesh. I stopped breathing and backed over to the door, ran up the stairs and saw a Red Cross man sitting in the corner with his head at a strange angle, hands resting open on his lap. Dead too. All of them shot. Not a sound from anywhere. Their bleached faces looked toward the door, open-mouthed, teeth clenched, arms slumped back from being raised in surrender. In what was once the bathroom, on the table that had been turned into an operating room, there was a man half-naked, executed too. I kept treading on spent cases, striking matches to see some signs of life. But nothing. Even the Red Cross man, barged into a corner by the force of bullets striking. I turned the man over and his forehead struck the floor with a crack. I got some more matches from the pocket of his tunic and struck one. I held the flame down by the cases and saw they were 9 mm. German. The silence kept dragging itself over my back. My bowels were cramped, everything in me tightened until my stomach felt like coils of glass that would break if I moved too quickly. I struck match after match.

"IT'S OKAY. We'll just have to keep going." I took von Schwerin under the arms and started to drag him toward the motorcycle. "It's empty. Nobody home. Must have cleared out. Probably not too far away. How far can they get with a bunch of complainers like you?"

His head tipped sideways and a gob of something dark fell out of his mouth.

I undid the one button that was left on his jacket, then his shirt, and pressed my ear to his chest. I held onto his ribs and crushed his body against the side of my head to hear his heart beat. There were faraway noises in his stomach, little bubbling noises, but not the thud of the heart. I touched my lips along the line of his jawbone for the pulse, so as not to miss the even flowing of the artery. His eyes were half open.

Another breeze moved along the road and kept going toward the town.

I slapped him in the face to make him breathe. Then I punched him in the chest over and over until I thought his bones would break. His body jerked a little, and I sunk my head down again to hear him breathe, but he didn't.

When I was sure he was dead, I dragged him by his one good

arm over to the crossroads house and set him on the floor with the others in the first room. I took his watch, cigarette case, passbook, and wallet.

WALKING NOW. The echo of my footsteps pushing me faster. Now running, dead men streaming from the house and the woods, moving on stiff-veined feet over the ice. Now sprinting, head back, gasping, shadows of the dead flickering in the corners of my eyes. They rise up from the rotten leaves and the fog.

Heels jammed. Turning now. Anger in blocks of heat around my bones. Marble-eyed. Breath sucked in through clenched teeth.

COME FOR me now.

I STOOD choking in the middle of the road, staring hard into the night. After a while I put my hands on my knees and spat thick spit between my legs. I walked back toward the house, but carefully. A cautious pacing on sheets of mirror glass.

THE MOTORCYCLE wouldn't start at first. The thing kept lurching forward when I jumped on the pedal. Eventually I got it going, opened the throttle, set the Schmeisser on my lap, and rode back toward Rocherath.

AT THE edge of the woods before the fields, SS were gathered. As soon as I saw them, their silhouettes and the hard-angled outlines of their helmets, crossing and recrossing the horizon where it was not covered by trees, I stopped the motorcycle. Leaving it propped against a tree, I walked until I was in the middle of them. There were perhaps fifty people, one American jeep and a Mercedes truck. Heydt was there, looking at a map spread on the hood of the jeep, someone shining a flashlight down over his shoulder so he could see. That was the only light, except for cigarettes, the glow of cooking stoves, and shreds of dirty yellow in the sky.

I walked over to the jeep, reached through the mesh of bodies to get at a Camel cigarette sticking out of a packet on the hood. Heydt was talking so quietly I could barely hear him from this close. I had thought for sure he had died at the barricade. Hadn't given it a second thought.

A tank man was standing on the other side of the jeep, nodding at what Heydt was saying. He wore a black leather jacket, unbuttoned but held around him by an officer's belt. He had a cap like Heydt's, but with pink piping on the crown. He was tracing a line down the map with an unlit cigarette. Around him stood two more tank men, heavy people, also in leather jackets, black side caps with skulls on them.

I wandered away into the woods, out to the road, wondering if there was any place to keep warm. My Ami boots had soaked through, and I could no longer feel my toes.

Handschumacher came out to meet me with his arms open. But he didn't hug me. "You left me." His head was cocked back and he looked down his nose.

I laughed. "I got stuck in the graveyard with Schwerin. He was trying to drag a man to that pile of corpses at the end of town. Man was still alive."

He shrugged. "Didn't do me any good."

"But you're here."

"Yes."

"Don't give me a hard time."

"No. No." He shrugged again.

"You're here and I'm here. I got caught when the Amis came. You can't hold it against me."

"Let's go find Schwerin." He slapped me on the arm, walked a few paces back toward Heydt's jeep, stopped, waited. I didn't move. He understood. We didn't speak of it again.

XIII

COLD winter dawn.

PEOPLE WERE gathered around the ditch at the far side of the road, clicking their tongues in disgust. They turned away and spat, then looked again at whatever it was.

I found myself a sweater. A caldron had been set up, and soup was being served out by some American prisoners, most of them wounded or beaten up. I held out a mess tin, and a short man with a bandage on his face ladled me some food. I drank a bit out of the tin, watching him. It was only lukewarm, the soup. He watched back, then got nervous and looked to the next man in line. I leaned over and tugged at his sweater, told him to take it off. He put down the ladle and pulled it over his bandaged head after taking off his field jacket. He handed it to me, through the caldron's rising steam. He didn't seem to grudge it me. The thing was still warm from his body heat.

I crossed the road to the crowd, slurping the soup and chewing the shreds of meat that caught in my teeth. I leaned over someone's shoulder and peeked into the ditch.

There was someone frozen in the ice. He had died when the ditch was still full of slush and water, then in the night it encased him. His mouth and eyes were open and his hair spread like seaweed on his head. Fingers poked just above the surface like fat twigs, the rest of the hand palm up beneath the bubbled glass. People gaped. I bent down and saw it was Posner, his face with the expression of a very distant scream.

THE REMAINS of the Division were at a sawmill near a town called Hunningen. We had orders to bypass Rocherath and take Hunningen in the next few hours. Then on to Büllingen and Bütgenbach. On to Paris. Everybody knew about Wahlerscheid by now. Germans killing Germans. At first they tried to tell us it was partisans, but no one believed them, so they told the truth. No one had figured we would hold the town for very long. The Americans were expected to push us back a lot farther than Wahlerscheid. SS military police shot the wounded as soon as the second barrage began. There weren't enough trucks at the front line to evacuate them. The tanks had been diverted after the initial assault, to keep the Adolf Hitler Division closing in on Büllingen, which was their goal, five kilometers west of Rocherath. Kampfgruppe Peiper, headed by some Absolute Nazi called Joachim Peiper, had pushed all the way to Malmédy. There were rumors he had massacred more than a hundred American prisoners in a field above the town. They said it was even a man named Fleps who started the shooting.

All this was gossip passed on by the radioman who sat in the back of Heydt's Yankee jeep, picking up signals.

Some trucks came up some time in the morning, and we were ordered to get in.

Rocherath was still smoking. Through a pair of binoculars it looked like a burned animal on its back with its ribs exposed.

Handschumacher and I had made a tent from extra capes that we took from the dead. I didn't know how long we had slept when the sound of the trucks woke us up. My head unwound in madman's dreams, twitching, things rushing from the darkness of my closed eyes, trying to claw their way into my head.

HANDSCHUMACHER and I were the last people in our truck. There was no flap to tie down at the end, so we could see out. The Panzermen sat cramped inside with a couple of others.

"Where's your tank?" Handschumacher called to them over the sound of the engine.

The officer snapped his head around, scowling. Then when he saw Handschumacher meant no harm, he smiled and drew a finger across his throat. "Junk." Under their leather jackets, the tank men wore overalls made from SS dapple camouflage. I wanted to say something to let them know my father was a tank man. He had been dead more than a year. Handschumacher took off his boots and massaged his pasty white feet.

We drove in a column down woodsmen's trails, sometimes crossing over fields.

ONE RUMOR said we had already lost fifty percent in casualties, another said sixty. For all the talismans and absolutes, there is still no certainty. Either you die or you do not die. Nothing in my past to strengthen me. All the thinking and talking in the world could give me nothing in this place.

I was pissed off beyond words.

We rode out of a muddy trail onto a stretch of grass on which some old haystacks were rotting, spackled with ice. One of the boys in the truck was singing "Lilli Marlene." It was a song about a soldier who meets a girl outside a barracks, la-di-la, and maybe they'll meet back there someday.

I pressed my fingertips into my temples until I saw blue shadows in the dark of my closed eyes. I breathed in the streams of cigarette smoke and winter air. Not thinking. Possible now to be empty. I wiggled my ears, and pins and needles walked on my skull. I mouthed the words of "Lilli Marlene." Then I hummed along with the boy. Some other people sang. Somehow I'd had the impression before I'd joined the SS that we'd be singing all the time, but this was the first time I'd ever heard it. Mostly someone would sing, then get embarrassed and stop. I found Voss singing once. Breder, von Schwerin, and I caught up with him on the way back from town one night when we had leave. He didn't hear us until we practically bumped into him. He was singing to wake up the whole region, a song called "Erika," about a pretty flower on the heath called "Erika." Good to march to. He was his own parade, arms swinging, boots crashing down. When he saw us he stopped, put his hands in his pockets, and stared at the ground as he walked.

A SHUDDER in the air and an explosion against steel somewhere up ahead. Our truck slewed around, the tailgate came open, and from upside down as I went through the air, I saw two other trucks, one of them a shock of flames. I somersaulted, hit the ground on my knees, and slid backwards on my chest.

Then there was an explosion from the woods, and our truck flew apart in a crack of dynamite. I watched the frame of it dislocate, the canvas roof going up in a single breath of flames. Then I heard machine guns and the pop of Garands.

I didn't look to see if everyone was all right. I crawled toward the woods on the other side from where the firing was coming.

The last truck headed off for the road. People cried out in anger. Someone completely on fire walked a few paces from the cabin of our truck and fell over.

I breathed in gasps, acid all through my body, slithering as fast as I could for the trees. Someone was calling for help.

I stood up to run the last couple of meters into the permanent darkness of the forest, and something hit me in the back.

Get up. Keep moving. Nothing happened to you. Everything's fine. It didn't hit. Just the shock. Something in me, I can feel it. I can't feel where, but it's in me, I know. What the hell hit me? Nothing wrong. My body is humming the way a sewing machine does before the needle jabs. Nothing comes into focus. All things moving much too fast. I'm looking at the crystals of frost on blades of grass. Roll on my back and scream. Back all hot. Fucking heat from somewhere. No. It didn't happen. No. No. Not to me. My lips curl back over my teeth and a sound comes out of me I never heard before, ending in a scream. I can't get to the trees. Suddenly darkness. Suddenly light. On my hands and knees, moving slowly, trying to get away, things not working. No. No. Not me. Not in this place. My body humming and my breathing all fucked up. Hands knotted in the frozen grass. The earth rising and ramming itself in my face. This strange noise in me again. Dirt in my mouth. Is it me who's screaming? On my side now, the earth tipping me over, sky rolling in, dappled with smoke. Not happening to me. No. Darkness coming from all sides, waving through my sight, through everything.

LIGHT. Raindrops. Clouds. Darkness.

LIGHT. Great sadness. Raindrops. Fish belly pale space. Darkness.

*   *   *

I s a w American soldiers running from the woods, pausing, kneeling down, moving again. A couple of SS men stood with their hands raised, in the middle of bodies strewn around. The trucks were quiet pyres, giving out hard black smoke. Burning gasoline. I watched from the mesh of my eyelids, through my half-closed eyes. The Amis came to the first of the bodies, passed them, and searched among the dead. The ones who had given up were led away, made to keep their hands in the air. The ones who had American boots were made to go barefoot. I saw them hopping on one leg trying to tug the boots off.

It took a while for me to realize what they were doing among the bodies. I couldn't focus properly. I couldn't move. They were looting. I watched them going through the pockets of the dead. One man set an SS officer's hat on his head, put a finger under his nose to make like a Hitler moustache, and *Sieg Heil*ed the others.

One Ami took out a .45 on a lanyard attached to his belt, aimed carefully down at a body, and fired twice.

They were heavily laden with bedrolls and equipment. Most of them had greatcoats on, some of them rubber snow boots, big scarves wrapped around their throats.

One of them began walking toward me, and I shut my eyes, tried not to breathe.

He stopped a couple of paces away. I could hear him scratching his chin. His knees cracked as he bent down over me. I kept wanting to flinch, go for the switchblade in my breast pocket, pop the blade and stick it in him. My lungs and my face were burning from having no air. I could feel my heartbeat in my ears. My mouth was full of spit.

He undid the buttons on my pockets, took out von Schwerin's things, the cigarette case and his watch. He knelt on my chest, took out my passbook and dropped it. He took my watch.

There was nothing else to take. I wasn't worth his trouble. The man dug his hands under me and rolled me over, and while I was rolling, I breathed a little. I felt the ground cold on the side of my face. He emptied out my bread bag, stale crumbs rattling down onto my back. Then he took back the .45 I'd been carrying, stood up, and I breathed again. I felt something hard against the back of my head and then heard a click. He had tried to shoot me with the pistol, but it was empty. He left, boots squelching in the mud.

They didn't stay long. From the sound of it, someone German was wounded and trying to persuade them to take him along, or at least give him something to drink. I heard that part very clearly. I heard the cap of a water bottle being unscrewed. He said, "Thank you," sighing. The water-bottle cap clanked on its chain against the container. Then there was a shot and everything in me tensed up.

When I looked up, very slowly, still peering through the fuzziness of my eyelids, they were gone. I dragged my hand to my face and scratched my nose.

There was a coldness around my shoulder, but still no pain.

I raised myself on my elbows and looked around. The trucks were smoldering; the third one had stopped at the point where the woods closed around the road. The fourth and Heydt's jeep were gone. There were bodies scattered all over the field, and clumps of them by the trucks. In the one by the woods, I could see a man hanging down over the tailgate, his fingers dangling just above the ground and his face staring.

When I twisted around, trying to get up, pain went through me. Then I shivered and the pain got worse. I lay back down again, felt behind me on my back but couldn't reach the place where it was cold on my shoulder. From the feel of the sweater on my skin, I could tell there was a hole punched in me.

I heard whispering in German. One of the people in the field stood up and ran over to another, who tried to stand but couldn't.

The first lifted the second and carried him, hobbling, over to one of the burned-out trucks. I saw as they got closer that the wounded boy was Handschumacher. His jacket was open and his shirt splashed red.

I waited a bit to see if the Amis were around. There was the sound of a stream running somewhere in the forest. It was raining from clouds jammed down to the tree line. I started crawling on my hands and knees, not able to raise my head because it made the pain in my shoulder worse. "Hey!" Whispers. "Hey, you guys! Wait for me!"

The boy ran over and helped me slowly to my feet. It made me nauseous to be standing. His name was Metternich. I didn't know him very well. He let me lean on his shoulder and walked me over to Handschumacher.

"Can you tell what's happened to me?" I looked him in the face and turned away again.

"Is that a joke?" Metternich snorted.

"Do I look like a fucking comedian?" I pushed away from him and held onto what was left of the tailgate.

"What's happened to you? I'd say, old man, you've stopped a bullet in the shoulder blade. Probably one of the little Garand ones. Anything else the Amis use and you'd be dead. I'll see to it in a minute." Metternich had always been a wise ass. I would have smacked his face if I hadn't needed him.

Handschumacher was very pale. He held his hands loosely over his stomach. He opened one eye, saw it was me, swung his head away and coughed. Still looking in the other direction, he talked. "Westland, you have to get me out of here. Not him." He jerked his Roman nose toward Metternich, who had gone looking for more survivors. "Fucking Metternich. Of all the people to have to rely on." He doubled over and gagged. I touched his shoulder. He sat back. "Right in the guts, Westland. I swear I saw the fucker coming. But you too, eh?"

"A little bit." I wasn't going to complain when he was like that. He looked so pale.

Metternich came back swinging a Schmeisser, his other hand full of spare magazines. "Take these, Westland. Look after yourselves."

"And where the hell are you going?" I took the Schmeisser, and its weight pulled back the pain.

"For help, you stupid idiot, unless you'd rather I didn't come back." Metternich wanted us to know he was in control. Metternich the Boss.

Handschumacher was shaking his head and mumbling.

"I'll go to Hunningen for help, send someone back. I'll be as quick as I can." He raised his hand and showed his palm, a gesture of calming us with his Control. But I felt like putting a bullet in Metternich and then having us all crawl and stagger to Hunningen like the Musicians of Bremen; rather that than Reichsführer-fucking-Metternich showing us the way.

"HEY." Handschumacher's chalk face had turned a little green. His eyes were bloodshot.

"What?"

"How do I look?"

"Handschumacher, you look like shit."

"I know. You too."

"Great. Wonderful." I banged my head back against the tire of the truck. Every time I touched it, I came away with a black ash stain.

"How long's Metterfuck been gone?"

"An hour maybe."

"And what time is it?"

"Why all the bloody questions, Handschumacher?" The ache in my body was making me angry. I wanted whatever was in me out, and then I wanted to go home on a fast train with women conductors and a café car serving hot chocolate and croissants.

"I want to know the time is all. Why don't you indulge the fuck out of me for a change? The Yanks took my watch."

"Mine too."

"Well, what time would you *say* it was?"

I spat at my boots.

"Westland, I'm dying. What time it is has become very important to me."

"Don't be dramatic. Leave it."

"I suppose it's one o'clock."

"There must be other ones alive out there, Handschumacher." I gestured vaguely at the field.

"Amis shot anyone showed signs of life. One reason they didn't shoot me, I guess. This arrogant son of a bitch just rolled me over like a ball of dough and stole everything I had. Couldn't believe it."

"Me too. Took Schwerin's things as well."

"I tell you. Soon as I get better I'm coming back out and rob everybody I can get my claws on, dead or alive."

"Oh, so we're not dying now, are we?"

"Hell, no. I'm going to be a super-thief. I'll be like Santa Claus in reverse." He fished in his breast pocket and took out a small metal shaving mirror. He stared at himself for a while, then dropped the mirror on the ground. "You don't suppose I'll stay looking like this, do you?"

"You need a holiday in the sun."

"That's the trouble with the Third Reich the way it is now. Nowhere you can go in it and get a good suntan."

We passed a cigarette back and forth, sat there for a long time, often in silence, him getting worse, his hands bloody and pressed to his stomach.

"Do you suppose"—he raised his head suddenly—"the Russians are in Leipzig yet? I have cousins there."

"Probably." I had been thinking about Lise Hammacher and trying not to.

"I feel it." He doubled over. "I can feel the fucker in me, Westland. Keeps moving around, like it's going in deeper.

Jesus! Jesus!" He rocked back and forth. I pressed him against the truck to stop him moving. He was sweating, and his skin was yellow-green. He spoke but no sound came out. Talking. Talking. A bright drop of blood ran out of his nose over his lips and splashed on his shirt, then another. The ones after that he wiped away with his hand.

"Hear that stream, Westland?"

"Yes."

He unclipped the canteen from his belt and tossed it onto my lap. "Get me a drink and I'll never ask you for another favor as long as I live."

"Handschumacher, you've got a gut wound. You know you can't drink."

"I know that. And fuck it. I only want to wash my mouth out."

"I don't believe you." I shook the canteen to see if there was anything in it.

"You want to see me beg? I'll beg if you want me to. Just a little mouthful. I'll bug the hell out of you unless you get me a drink. Please, Sebastian."

Sigh. "See what I can do. You aren't going to get much, mind. And when we get back to Bad Tölz you get me drunk at the Namenloser."

"Done. You're a prince." Pause. "You want me to keep laying on the praise, or are you going to go?"

IT WAS easier walking now. There was a little bit of sun from the mottled clouds. I had to stop to hear the stream since my own breathing covered the noise.

I stopped a couple of times, resting against trees, the nausea flicking bile into my throat.

The stream was maybe two hundred meters into the woods, lined with moss-covered rocks and trees with their thick roots nude against the water.

It was hard getting down on my knees, harder still leaning over and sticking my hand into the freezing water, waiting until the bubbles stopped coming up from the mouth of the canteen. Then I drank half the water in the thing and filled it up again.

I wished I had found a stream like this when I was eight years old. Then I would have built a bridge and a fort, kept it a secret. I said it out loud. Great sadness suddenly. One day I'll take my son back here. Show him the place. One day I'll have a son. I said it out loud.

Going back to the truck, I heard the sound of a small machine on the road leading into the field. I didn't start running. If they were German, Handschumacher would make them wait for me, and if they were Amis, I didn't want to see them anyway.

It was easier for me to walk if I stooped over a bit like a hunchback. They'd be sending me home with a wound like this. That's the thing with the SS. Either they want you perfect, or they don't want you at all.

I sang a bit of "Lilli Marlene," very quietly, barely forming the words in my mouth.

A gun went off. Echo. Echo.

I stopped and listened. Nothing. Then I crawled to the edge of the trees, burning and afraid, the dryness in my mouth again.

I saw two men walking to an American jeep parked by the first truck. They were Germans. I saw the bald head of Kaslaka before he stuffed his helmet on and swung into the driver's seat. And I saw the hard face of Voss. He was sniffing the wind. The ancient gesture of the beast. They spun the tires on the jeep and left.

His head was all broken apart, the bright cartridge of a Luger bullet on his lap.

* * *

I FILLED my bread bag with spare magazines, picked up the Schmeisser and started walking.

At the edge of the field I found Heydt's cap. Folded neatly and tucked behind the dirty leather sweat band were half a dozen letters to his wife.

METTERNICH'S BODY was lying in the mud at the side of the road. A sniper had got him in the chest, made a small hole above his left breast pocket, and blown his heart out at the back. It couldn't have been Voss. The mud of the speeding jeep had splashed him both coming and going. They hadn't stopped to look. I backed away into the trees, knelt down, hugging my chest to keep my own heart safe. I came out onto the road farther up, having walked for a while in the shadow of the forest.

THE SAWMILL was in the hollow of a valley, with a stream running next to it. In the yard was a King Tiger. It was the biggest tank I'd ever seen. Biggest in the world, I'd heard. I thought they were only used against the Russians. The King Tiger was a hotel with a cannon sticking out of it that ran around on treads. Parked beside it was a Mark IV, a couple of American jeeps, and two trucks. People walked in and out of the building. I watched them from up on the hill before walking down.

An SS man rose out of dead leaves and pine branches under which he had been hiding. "Identify yourself." He had a Mauser aimed at me.

"Westland. 28 Panzer Grenadier Regiment, 12 SS Panzer Division. Hitler Jugend."

"Good enough."

"Who are you?"

"Adolf Hitler Division. Reconnaissance Battalion." He brushed pine needles off his shoulders. "Where are you coming from?"

I jerked a thumb over my shoulder. "I was in a column that got shot up down the road."

He scratched his nose. "We just had some people go over there and check things out. Said there were no survivors."

I stood there and stared.

"You all right?" He stepped up onto the road.

"Who's down there? Down at the mill."

"What's left of your people, what's left of ours." He didn't have an unkind face. It looked a lot more professional than mine.

IN THE sawmill people were sleeping on the floor next to stacks of cut pine. Inside the building some were trying to cook food at the fireplace. Everyone seemed cheerful. Most of them weren't Hitler Youth. They looked too old and, like the sentry, too professional.

In one corner some men in American uniforms were talking perfect German, laughing with some SS men, passing around a bottle of brandy. I stared at them. One of the men in American clothes caught my eye, frowned at my staring, then laughed and pointed at me. The rest of them laughed with him.

"Skorzeny Kommando." A Hitler Youth boy whose name I didn't know was lying on a workbench, his arm in a sling. "There's a doctor in the next room if you need it." He tapped the toes of his boots together. "Better go see him."

The place smelled of sawdust. The stuff was all over the floor, in spider webs on the windowpanes, on everybody's clothes, powdering my wet boots.

THE DOCTOR was sitting on a table smoking a cigarette and yawning. He slid onto his feet when I came in. He wasn't wearing a jacket, and his suspenders were tight on his shoulders. Couldn't tell if he was an officer or not. I tried to salute. He

went straight over to a sink in the corner of the room and washed
his hands. Then he pinched his cigarette dead and nodded for
me to get on the table.

I took off my jacket. He had to help me with the sweater.

"Why didn't you come to me earlier?" He dabbed my back
with a piece of cloth soaked in alcohol.

"I just got here."

"Aha." He injected something into my skin and then rubbed
the spot with more alcohol. "Give that a minute."

"Are you with the Hitler Youth, sir?"

"No. I don't know where the HJ doctors are. I'm part of the
Reconnaissance Battalion. Are you with that dreadful man
Heydt?" He rattled some metal things behind my back. I looked
at the once-waxed floor, scuffed to garbage by hobnails. There
were some new bandages piled on a chair. The wallpaper was
the color of a manila envelope. My back went numb from the
injection.

"Now, can you feel that?"

"What?"

"Good." He dug around.

I gripped the sides of the table. I heard him muttering and
the blood storming in my ears.

"You're lucky we still have anesthetic. Some people don't get
any. This isn't too bad. It didn't go through the bone."

I felt him tapping at something. Then he tugged, and jolted
my shoulder blade.

"Here." He held down a Garand bullet between a set of for-
ceps. Then he dropped it in my open hand. "It just got stuck in
the bone. It's really not too bad. I'll stitch it up now."

I felt the thread sliding through my skin and the pinch when
he tied the stitches.

He dabbed the place again with cold stuff. It ached but there
was no real pain. He wrapped a bandage around my chest and
fastened it with a safety pin. "This will hurt when the anes-

thetic wears off." He raised his eyebrows to ask if I understood. He needed a shave. Before I left he gave me a drink of clear cherry brandy. He said there was a case of the stuff in the cellar, told me again I was lucky.

I put the bullet in my pocket. It was the length of the nail on my little finger, rounded at the end, copper covered with lead inside, scrape marks at the base where it had been stuck in the cartridge.

I FOUND Voss in a room by himself down the hall. He was sitting at a desk with a field radio on it, drinking a bottle of the cherry brandy. He had headphones on but didn't look very busy. He had the volume on the radio down very low, so the voices that came from it sounded more like the buzzing of flies.

"Well, well." He was very quiet; set the bottle down clumsily. "Back from the dead, Mr. Westland? Come to give me a haunting? Ha ha." He took off the headphones and dropped them. "Were you in that truck that made it out of the ambush?" He pressed his hands together so that only the tips of his fingers were touching. "Or have you been mixing with the Adolf Hitler boys?" One of his eyes was blacked. "Say something, Westland." He took another slug of the brandy. "You're boring me."

"No survivors, were there?" I found I couldn't raise my voice. I was comfortably numb from the injection, the bandage in a permanent hug around my chest.

"What? Back there? None at all. Kaslaka and I went past and saw no one alive. You can ask him."

"When did you leave Rocherath?"

"As soon as I could." The radio babbled. He grabbed for the headphones and pressed the receiver to his ear, then dropped it again. "I made sure I got out before the rest of your pathetic army messed things up. You know, Westland, my disgust for you and your people comes up to here." He slapped the underside of his chin. "I saw them running away. I saw panic. I'll tell you something, Westland." He drank again from the brandy bottle, the heavy liquid circling the clear walls of the glass before it settled again. "I *knew* that barrage was coming. I heard it on the radio. There *was* a signal, but I was damned if I was going to go around like a fucking nursemaid telling you children where to go. You had radios. You should have heard it for yourselves. You were so fucking *weak*, the whole pack of you. I saw you all come, and now I've seen most of you go, and I'm not One Tit surprised, Westland. In a place like this, the way you've run yourselves, you deserved what you got." He finished the bottle, a good three fingers' worth, and slammed it down again. "And I knew it'd be like this. Kaslaka and I knew. The other NCOs knew. Shall I tell you how we knew, Westland?" He reached behind the chair where his equipment was hanging from his belt. He fumbled in his bread bag, back to me, then spun around fast and smacked an SS ceremonial dagger into the wood.

"Why isn't yours in the well with everybody else's?" My shoulder ached more now.

"Because everybody else's *isn't* in the fucking well. The daggers your lot got are in the well. No one else's. We spread that rumor after we decided what a bunch of flimflam shitheads you all were. People like Breder, my God. You didn't fool us one minute. It's all I could do not to hate you every minute of the day. And now I'm drunk, and by Christ I'll tell you what I want. We spread the rumor and you ate it up, you little pigs. I can still hear the daggers going in, *plip, plip.* I don't think the officers even knew. It's an honor, the dagger, Westland. It's just one you didn't deserve." The radio talked again, and he stuck his ear back to the receiver.

Someone stopped in the doorway and I turned to see who it was. I was sweating and my knees were shaking. The man at the door was an ugly bastard from the Adolf Hitler Battalion.

He was holding about ten canteens looped onto a belt. The better part of a beard had grown on his face.

"You Voss?"

"Yes, who needs me?"

"Your man Heydt says you're to fetch water from the stream back in the woods. Not to use the main stream down here 'cause the water's not pure. The one in the woods. Got that?"

"Why me?"

The man chucked the canteens in a heap on the floor. "Now how the bloody fuck am I supposed to know?" He turned around and left.

"Those people, Westland. They'll eat you for breakfast."

"You said too much already, Voss."

"Too much for you, perhaps." He handed me the water bottles. "Come along. Have a drink." He stuck the empty bottle in my hand. I waited until I heard his boots on the stairs, then pulled the dagger out of the table and put it in my bread bag.

I watched his blond head going down the stairs, the blond suddenly disappearing as he jammed on his cap.

I followed him slowly, dragging my feet, letting the water bottles rattle down the stairs behind me.

It was snowing again outside, angry little flakes pecking at the ground.

My knees were still trembling. I stared at the back of Voss's head as he strode through the yard, following him a couple of paces behind.

He walked fast into the woods, without looking to see if I was following, without talking to me.

A path had been marked with strips of white cloth tied at shoulder height to the trunks of the trees.

I kept close behind, drops of sweat squeezing through my clenched fists, the pain in my shoulder getting worse.

We climbed up a short, steep bank and down a gully studded with rocks between the mud. I heard the stream, then saw it, moving fast in its shallow bed.

He stopped at the edge and only then turned to make sure I was following. He squatted down and raised some water to his face, grunted at the cold, splashed the water on his neck. Then, still looking at the stream, he held out his arm for the first canteen.

Not once did he take his gaze from the stream, handing the canteens back, dripping, when they were full. Five canteens. He reached out for the sixth and got nothing. He snapped his fingers.

I had dropped the canteens and taken out the dagger, twisting the chromium blade, the engraving: "My Honor Is Loyalty," appearing and disappearing as I turned the knife over and over.

He stood up and gaped at me. "What you doing with my dagger, you little shit? Give it here."

I stared at his eyes and did nothing.

He put his hands on his hips and frowned.

"You sure fooled us, Voss."

"What?"

"You sure put one over on us about the daggers. I can see them all now at the bottom of the well."

He laughed very loud. "No one's going to see those ever again. They say that well goes down for miles."

I laughed, and he laughed again. Then I stepped forward and stuck the knife in his stomach up to the hilt. I jerked it upward under his ribs. His mouth opened but no sound came out.

He stepped back with what seemed like great care and tripped into the stream. He went under and came up again, holding himself off the bottom with one hand, raising the other one up to me, as if to ask for help. He tried to stand but fell back down, and the current carried him a little downstream, while he grabbed at the far bank until he caught a root and held on to it. He opened and closed his mouth like a fish but said nothing, all the time looking at me, the stream water bubbling up around him and the knife still sticking from his tunic. He held on to the root for a long time, but then his face clouded over and he lost his grip. He didn't fight the current anymore. It carried him slowly downstream, bumping him into rocks and catching him in the shallows, but always moving, and I watched until he was out of sight.

A MAN I had never seen before held out his arm to me from the deck of the King Tiger as it was pulling out of the yard. I took his hand, and he swung me up next to him. The sound of the engine was deafening. I breathed diesel.

We were getting ready to take Hunningen, but some Amis still held the woods on the approach, so we had to take care of them first. It was late in the afternoon when we left.

No one had asked me about Voss. I'd taken the back way around so no one would see me come in.

The ride lasted perhaps half an hour, mostly on the road, but sometimes going through fences and grinding trails across the fields.

The Mark IV followed, and behind it were the trucks.

It was already getting dark when the tank stopped and everyone began to pile off.

We were at the foot of a small hill and hadn't gone twenty paces up it before someone started shooting from the tree line on the top.

I dropped down on the muddy grass and heard the Tiger's Spandaus firing over our heads. Then its cannon went off, and a piece of the hill splattered brown and black, falling away in smoke. The Tiger moved forward and we filed in behind it, crouching, bunched up together. The Mark IV moved alongside it, and I saw Kaslaka walking behind. He was smoking a cigar.

Another piece of the hill blew into the air, and another, as the tanks' cannons fired. Then suddenly everything stopped,

people muttering, "Cease fire, pass it back." I poked my head
around from behind the armor plate of the Tiger and saw men
on the horizon with their hands in the air, one of them waving
a shovel on which a Red Cross flag was tied.

We straggled behind the machines as they moved on toward
the top of the hill. Kaslaka skipped over to me, spitting the cigar
out of his mouth. "Have you seen Voss? Is he around somewhere?" I noticed then, for the first time, that his teeth were
bad. "He was back at the sawmill. Did you see him or not?"
He walked beside me.

"Not me, Kaslaka." I shrugged.

THERE WERE maybe a dozen men who had given up. They
said they had been ordered to hold the woods in front of Hunningen, but the first cannon shell killed their officer. One of them
spoke German.

They had dug holes for themselves in the wooded slope on
the other side of the hill. In the near distance I could see Hunningen, maybe half a kilometer away. There must have been
only a platoon to begin with, and one of the blasts had killed
almost half of them. There was clothing hanging from the
branches of the trees.

I ended up in a group of three Adolf Hitler men who were
taken aside to guard the prisoners. An SS man jogged over from
the main group, which was moving into the area of the Amis'
foxholes. He was swathed in camouflage, and only by his gestures could I tell he was an officer. He pulled me aside.

"You know what must be done, do you? The others already
know." He took hold of my elbow the way my schoolteachers
used to do, as if I were going to run away or something. "Take
them down the field. Finish the job before you get to the
bottom."

I waved at the American sergeant, showing he was to lead

his people down the hill. He nodded at me and yelled to the
other Amis, who still had their hands up. Most had dropped
their helmets and were wearing woolen caps. It was twilight,
and their olive-drab clothes made them only blurs against the
dead grass as they moved unsteadily downhill. We followed
behind. They kept looking back at us as they walked.

I saw the SS man next to me quietly drawing the bolt on his
Schmeisser. The one in the middle looked at us and, following
the movements of the others, I stopped.

One of the Americans turned and, when he saw us standing
in a line, he cried out.

I pulled the trigger and walked the gun through the mass of
men, seeing them spin around and down, crawling and stopping, all of it like a slow passing of slides in front of me. A man
raised off the ground, his hands stretched far in the air as if he
were trying to grab a piece of the clouds. A man running, suddenly arching his back, sliding on his knees, before rolling over
and away down the hill. The ground dissolving around their
feet. Men punted backwards, still crying out.

When the magazine ran out on the gun, I banged in a new
one, but the Adolf Hitler men were already moving down to the
bodies. I stood by myself while they searched for signs of life
and, finding none, walked back up the hill, past me, as if I
weren't there. I watched the lumps of corpses in the half-light,
then went quickly after the others.

I picked up another .45 from the gun belt of the dead officer,
who was upside down at the bottom of a crater.

WE DIDN'T wait long in the woods. A lot of SS men threw
away their German guns and picked up American ones. I found
a tube of cheese spread and ate it, also a Hershey chocolate bar.
The Adolf Hitler officer called us onto the flat ground leading
toward Hunningen, told us to spread out in open file and walk

when he told us to. He said a red flare would go up when the town was secure. At that time the tanks would follow us in.

Already I could see the sparkle of guns in the dark from the rooftops of Hunningen.

The officer blew a whistle and we started. I hung back a little, pretending there was something wrong with the Schmeisser.

MORTARS. They came down just in front of us. I could see the roofs of the town clearly against the last glimmer of light in the sky.

Suddenly the sound of the mortars doubled and grew louder. They started falling behind us. The officer blew his whistle and screamed for us to move faster. An explosion slapped me in the back of the neck. I ran forward to get out of the way. Great trunks of fire shot up ahead, and I saw the silhouette of a man spread-eagle against it. After a couple of paces I saw where the man and a few others had fallen, and slipped down to take cover behind them. The bombs dropped all around us. The pain in my shoulder was sharp from where the bandage moved.

By the light of explosions I saw Kaslaka lying next to me. I jammed my face in the dirt at the next detonation.

"Please." He was calling, barely an arm's length away. "Help me. Please."

I could see him clearly in the flashes, and then I could see nothing.

"Please. For God's sake. I'm hurt. Help." He started crawling toward me.

I took the .45 out of its holster and slapped it down flat on the ground in front of him. "You help yourself."

THE EARTH was coming apart beneath me. Dusty red columns punched up through the frozen ground. Then I was up, jumped over Kaslaka, and ran again, the sound of the whistle a continuous shriek in my ears.

I raced as fast as I could at the dark shapes and flicker of lights on the horizon.

I hope when this is over they don't find me.

I hope they say no prayers for me.

I hope they never remember my name.

A NOTE ABOUT THE AUTHOR

Paul Watkins, the son of English parents, was born in the United States in 1964 and educated at Eton College (where he won the Fleming Award for Journalism) and Yale University (where he won the Wallace Fiction Prize twice and the Willets Prize). At the age of fifteen, he walked alone across the famous battlefields of World War I, comparing the contemporary image of the landscape with that depicted by the great war poets. He has worked for the Providence *Journal* and the New Haven *Register*; his stories have appeared in a number of literary magazines. He is a graduate fellow at Syracuse University.

A NOTE ON THE TYPE

The text of this book was set in Walbaum, a type face
designed by Justus Erich Walbaum in 1810. Walbaum was
active as a type founder in Goslar and Weimar from 1799
to 1836. Though letterforms in this face are patterned
closely on the "modern" cuts then being made by Giam-
battista Bodoni and the Didot family, they are far less rigid.
Indeed, it is the slight but pleasing irregularities in the cut
that give this face its human quality and account for its wide
appeal. Even in appearance, Walbaum jumps boundaries,
having a more French than German look.

Night Over Day Over Night was composed by PennSet,
Inc., Bloomsburg, Pennsylvania. Printing and binding was
by The Haddon Craftsmen, Inc., Scranton, Pennsylvania.
It was designed by Peter A. Andersen.